Rhea and Jack re_____ rail station without incident and went to the last car of the train; except for the two of them, it was empty.

"Now," Jack said, "can you tell me what the hell is going on?"

Rhea waved out the window. "This is Unchained home base on planet Earth—I think we were being followed by devils."

"Well, why in the world would they do that?" he said. "And if it's demons, why are we running? Devils can't hurt us any more than the gargoyle on my roof can."

"Usually," Rhea dropped the word like a bomb. "There are exceptions to everything. And that's *devils*, not demons."

"But—" he started to say when a blast of displaced air almost knocked him from his seat. Suddenly there were four *devils* in the car. Devils with switchblades.

One of the devils, a female, slowly, contemptuously shoved Jack aside as she advanced on Rhea.

"Well, Avy," she said, "there's someone who wants to talk to you." She motioned with the knife. "But aside from your being able to talk, they don't much care what shape you're in." They grabbed Rhea's arms and legs. She struggled, but couldn't shake them.

Jack grabbed the picnic bag, willing his hands not to shake; he had no time for clumsiness. He grabbed the Super-Soaker water gun inside. A child's toy. The female saw him and her lips drew back in a smirk as he pulled the trigger—and all Hell broke loose.

# HELL ON HIGH

# HOLLY LISLE
# TED NOLAN

HELL ON HIGH

A Baen Books Original

Baen Publishing Enterprises
P.O. Box 1403
Riverdale, NY 10471

ISBN: 0-671-87780-1

Cover art by Clyde Caldwell

First printing, May 1997

Distributed by Simon & Schuster
1230 Avenue of the Americas
New York, NY 10020

Printed in the United States of America

# DEDICATION

For my father, Dr. Edward F. Nolan,
the finest man I know,
who will tell me he likes the book even if
he doesn't,
and will love me even so.
—T.N.

To my readers both old and new,
with thanks.
Without you there would be no more
books.
—H.L.

# Chapter 1

"I'm going on vacation."

The angel Gabriel looked up from polishing his trumpet and almost dropped the instrument to the ground. God stood before him, dressed in orange Bermuda shorts, a Hawaiian shirt with red, blue and green macaws and palm leaves against a vivid fuchsia background, navy blue nylon dress socks, and penny loafers with the pennies in. He carried two cameras around his neck—an expensive Nikon 35mm and a cheap Kodak Instamatic—and he wore RayBans and a Panama hat with a red, white, and blue checked band. He had given his features a distinctly Japanese cast.

Gabriel cleared his throat. "Vacation?"

"Absolutely. Do you have any idea how long I've been working?"

"Well, you had a day off—"

"—Billions and billions of years ago," God said, and for a moment he sounded just like Carl Sagan, who was currently making himself known in the Celestial Special Events department of Eternity.

Gabriel swallowed. "Yes. It has been quite a while. So when are you planning on taking your vacation, Your Magnificence?"

Two battered suitcases appeared at God's side. "Now."

"You've got to be joking," Gabriel yelped, and looked around to see who else was listening in.

1

"No, I don't."

"Now? But I have so many things I'll have to do in order to get ready. How am I going to set up a communication link for you? How am I going to forward all your calls in a prompt and efficient manner? How am I going to establish a priority policy for contacting you with emergencies? How am I going to forward your mandates dealing with Heaven and the Summerland and Valhalla and . . ." His voice died away to silence.

God was smiling. He wore the silly grin of someone who has heard Heaven's celestial bells for the first time, and discovers they're playing Jimmy Buffet's "Cheeseburger in Paradise." People rarely suspected that God was a big Jimmy Buffet fan. Gabriel didn't like that smile at all, and he liked it even less when God said, "You aren't."

Gabriel thought he might faint. "Then what are we supposed to do while you're gone?"

"You're supposed to handle things."

"Handle things? *Handle* things! How are we supposed to do that?"

God kept right on grinning—a very toothy, Cheshire cat sort of a grin.

Gabriel cringed.

God patted him on the shoulder. "Think of this as a learning experience. All of you will do just fine."

He started to fade from view, and Gabriel shouted, "Wait! Where are you going? When will you be back? You can't just leave like this!"

"Don't worry," God said, his voice growing faint even as he began to shimmer like a desert mirage. "Be happy!"

And then he was gone.

Gabriel shivered and stared around Eternity. The words *don't worry—be happy* circled in his mind with the tenacity of bad lyrics tied to a catchy tune. Easy for God to say. The Almighty was on vacation, leaving the angels in charge.

Billie Holiday wrapped up "Billie's Blues" in the background, and started into a cover of Sara Hickman's "Time Will Tell" from the *Necessary Angels* album.

It will, won't it, Gabriel thought. Time will certainly tell.

He hoped, perversely, that God got a bad sunburn, wherever he was. Maybe poison ivy. Maybe even a traffic ticket. Glowering, he cut off Billie's voice in mid-note, and announced "All archangels to the Mother Teresa Center in one millisecond for a staff meeting. Repeat— all archangels to the Mother Teresa Center in one millisecond for a staff meeting."

Then he tried to figure out what exactly he was going to tell them.

# Chapter 2

"OCT. 8 IN NORTH CAROLINA, TWO YEARS LATER"
*Time* magazine Special Report

It has been two years since North Carolina nurse Dayne Kuttner changed the world. Two years since she prayed for a redemption so all-encompassing that it stirred the heights of Heaven and the depths of Hell—or so Dayne has said in her rare interviews. In the month of October two years ago, Dayne says she prayed, demanding that God give every damned soul a chance at redemption. All that is known for certain is that, whatever she did, when she did it, Someone—or Something—was listening.

What happened next is beyond dispute, though its meaning seems destined to be endlessly debated. On that night in October, roughly sixty thousand creatures materialized in North Carolina. They claimed to be denizens of Hell, bound to North Carolina by a contract with God, and offered second chance at the redemption of their souls. First in North Carolina and then around the world, people stopped what they were doing as the news got out. They tried to understand what had happened. Some believed the Hellraised; others said North Carolina's plague came from outer space, or from Mars; psychologists claimed mass psychosis—at least until they traveled to North Carolina and discovered they could either diagnose themselves as among the psychotic or they could find another hypothesis. Fully twelve percent of the population fled the state in the first year, temporarily devastating the economy. The end of the "Second Exodus" came when a Raleigh DJ proved that the Hellraised could be turned around; with the Great Devil Makeover campaign came a migration into the state that hasn't stopped yet. Now North Carolina's economy is booming, and life goes on. In this special report, *Time* presents October 8 in North Carolina, Two Years Later. Join our correspondents from the Blue Ridge Mountains to Kittyhawk as they look inside the greatest enigma in human history.

Lucifer, First of the Fallen, Architect of Damnation, Big Man in Hades, threw the scorched copy of *Time* aside, and blown-in subscription cards flew everywhere. Bad enough it took him seven months to get a copy of the article. Worse that the tone of the article was so self-congratulatory. Where was the respect Hell's denizens deserved? Where was the amazement at their presence in North Carolina—where, for that matter, were the interviews with Hell's denizens? The article skipped all of that, concentrating instead on the humans, and how they'd managed to work around what one of them had the balls to call "God's challenge to us."

Life goes on indeed, he thought. Smug little mortal bastards. They stood up there smiling, saying, See? Hell sends its worst and evilest, and we're still doing just fine, thanks.

He glowered at the magazine, and thought, We'll see how upbeat you are when you end up in my little corner of Eternity.

As if in response to his thoughts, all the subscription

cards and the magazine simultaneously burst into flame. And suddenly he realized what that niggling, impossible-to-pin-down annoyance was that had been irritating him all morning. Lucifer slammed a fist on the intercom and roared, "Pitchblende! Get in here! The damned air conditioning is on the fritz again!"

His secretary appeared immediately, already in boot-licking mode. Pitchblende had once been a human named Adolf Hitler. He'd arrived in Hell with a sufficiently high evilness index to guarantee him a place in management, and he'd risen to a spot at Lucifer's right hand, where he was damnably unhappy and perpetually terrified. If Lucifer had cared anything about the justice of the punishments meted out by Hell, he would have said that Hitler was getting what he deserved. Lucifer didn't give a damn about fairness, however. All he cared about were results.

The exec-sec groveled. "It's the demons, Your Excel—" he started to say.

Lucifer detested excuses, especially legitimate ones. Before Pitchblende could finish the syllable, the archfiend bared a claw and pressed it against the devil's throat. He felt the rise and fall of Pitchblende's Adam's apple when he swallowed—exquisite. "I made you responsible for the office," Lucifer said. "You're not about to tell me you can't handle the responsibility, are you?"

Pitchblende swallowed again, and a drop of ichor oozed from the puncture under Lucifer's claw. "No, Your Hellaciousness," he gasped. "I was merely going to offer an explanation."

"How lucky for you. I'm sure," Lucifer added gently, "it will be a good one." He eased pressure on the single talon infinitesimally.

Pitchblende said, "I've checked into the matter, hoping that it was within my realm of authority, so that I could simply attend to it. Unfortunately, the problem lies not within the office domain, but in Transportation." The devil was keeping his voice admirably steady, though the shifting of his eyes and a pronounced nervous tic at the outside of his left eyelid told Lucifer that Pitchblende was merely putting on a confident act. He was still scared shitless. "Heaven has tapped too many of Maxwell's Demons to go Topside, and they're the only ones who know anything about molecules and heat. Unfortunately for our air conditioning, Transportation hasn't been doing anything to block the assignments; and of course Transportation is under the direct command of the fallen angel Kathemius, who has stated in no uncertain terms that she doesn't answer to me."

Pitchblende could call that an explanation all he liked; to Lucifer, it still *felt* like an excuse. The Lord of the Pit balanced the pleasure of rending Pitchblende limb from limb and molecule from molecule before getting really creative with the torture against the bother of training a new secretary. It was a near thing, but he sheathed his claws. A more amusing idea occurred to him. "Let me solve this dilemma," he said softly. "You may tell Kathemius that you now have oversight over Transportation—though of course you must still stay on top of your regular duties here, as well. Deal with this problem immediately. I'll not accept any blame of Heaven for continued problems, and I will hold both of you responsible for any delays or failures. Understood?"

Pitchblende turned a delicious pale shade of gray-green and nodded. "Yes, Your Hideousness." He straightened his shoulders and tucked his wings back at parade rest, waiting to be dismissed. A little mannerism that remained from Pitchblende's human days, Lucifer supposed.

Well, let the whiner stew for a few minutes. Literally, in the frigging heat.

Lucifer returned to his previous train of thought. He wasn't at all satisfied with the state of Hell's affairs in North

Carolina. Soul collections had begun trending back up with the opening of the Devil's Point theme park, but they weren't hitting the levels he'd expected. There was no exponential leap, not as there should have been. Meanwhile, the Big Meddler had kept his own hand well hidden in dealing with the mortals, eschewing any visible sign of his realm's existence, and *still* souls were soaring Heavenward at an alarming rate. Lucifer needed to put someone on the problem who had a feel for both sides of the issue.

He frowned.

Both sides . . . both sides.

And then he knew. He needed to put the bitterest fallen angel in Hell on the job. Averial. His lawyer, back in the days of that first Misunderstanding.

Lucifer smiled. Averial hadn't believed he'd been right, but she'd stood up to God to defend him, insisting that in a fair Heaven, Lucifer would be able to try his theories on the mortals. God hadn't seen things her way, and when Lucifer Fell, Averial went crashing down with him.

And bitter, bitter she had been—bitter as wormwood; bitter as pain. Too proud to apologize or to give God the admission that he wanted—that she had been wrong to defend Lucifer's easing of mortal travails—she had suffered in Hell since the Fall, convinced that she was there unjustly. She'd twisted nicely in that time . . . but though she considered herself wronged by Heaven, she still retained her view of herself as an Angel of Light. She'd been a thorn in the side and a pain in the ass for millennia. Now, though, her weird point of view might come in useful.

"Pitchblende," he said, "before you go about your reworking of Transportation . . . do a little something for me. Fetch me Averial."

"Yes, Your Hideous Evilness," the devil said and vanished.

Pitchblende should have returned instantly, fallen angel in tow. He didn't, though. That he permitted actual time to pass before his return signaled to Lucifer that the problem he'd discovered was of frightening magnitude. When he did reappear, he was alone, and he was almost white, and his lips trembled and his eyes rolled. "Your . . . Malevolence . . . sir . . ." he whispered, "she's not here."

Lucifer stared at him. Pitchblende was talking nonsense. "Of course she's here. Where in Hell else could she be? She hasn't repented—I would have felt that."

"She's not in Hell at all," Pitchblende said. He paused. "I cannot find any record of her leaving, but I . . . I think, Evil One, that . . . that Transportation let her go Up. Only there's no sign of her on Earth, either."

The news stunned Lucifer—shook him to the marrow— but he didn't let Pitchblende see that. He surreptitiously brushed the dust away from the furrows his claws had just dug in his red lacquered desk and said mildly, "I'll have her hide for slippers. Transportation failed to make a record of her passage Topside, eh?"

"So . . . so . . . it, um, appears, O Magnificent Fiend."

"Bring me Kathemius. And my favorite peeler. And while I am solving our transportation problems, make a list for me of the Fallen who have demonstrated effectiveness in their dealings with North Carolina in the past two years. I'm going to put together a task team."

Pitchblende nodded so hard his head looked like it had detached from his body. He vanished, reappeared instantly with Kathemius in tow and the peeler in hand, and vanished again without a word.

Fear did so much to maintain office efficiency, Lucifer thought. He smiled at Kathemius. "Lovely creature," he said. "I've been told you have been remiss in your duties." He ran one talon along the curved tip of the peeler and sighed. "Unforgivably remiss."

# Chapter 3

The conference chamber where Kellubrae met with Venifar and Linufel was neutral ground. Kellubrae would have preferred to bring the other two into his territory; the Southern Baptist section of Hell, which he ran, had plenty of meeting rooms. But this meeting was as much about establishing dominance as it was about working out a plan for meeting the objectives set by Lucifer. And none of the three would concede power to the extent of meeting within the territory of one of the others.

So they met in the conference room of Communicable Disease Research, which was currently between directors and which had been offered as a plum appointment to whichever one of them Lucifer deemed most effective in this little task he'd set.

The other two fallen angels held the same memo as he, on official Mark of the Beast™ stationery with the holographic flame watermark in the left-hand corner.

"The fallen angel Averial," it read, "has through unknown means disappeared in North Carolina. Your job is to find her and return her to Hell. You may use whatever methods you deem appropriate. Your budget will be subject to direct approval from me, but if you stay within your time frame, it will be reasonable for the work you are expected to do. Your team will consist of fallen angels Kellubrae, Linufel and Venifar. You will choose your own team leader, who will report directly to me. Your current deadline for the successful completion of your goal is three months, subject to modification as events warrant and as I see fit."

There followed the lengthy list of titles so dear to the twisted heart of Hell's First Fallen, and Lucifer's grandiose signature, and in tiny little print at the bottom of the memo, a postscript: "Don't fail me. L"

"Averial?" Kellubrae said. "She hasn't been a player for a long, long time." Unlike the three of *them*—he'd been locked in a deadly power struggle with Linufel and Venifar for almost two hundred years now. The more hate-centered branches of Christianity bred Hellbound souls at a prodigious rate, and Kellubrae wasn't the only Fallen who wanted to corner that niche of the specialty Christian Torture market for himself.

"Averial is gone, all right," Linufel confirmed. "And more importantly, she didn't go up in one of the Heaven-listed shipments. She isn't on the log anywhere. I checked." She rocked her chair back from the massive black conference table and smiled slowly. "She found a way out of here, and she found a way to disappear when she got *there*. So you bet your wings and fangs Lucifer wants her back."

All three fallen angels had received the memo simultaneously, and less than twenty seconds before they'd arrived in the conference room. Kellubrae had spent that time negotiating for the Communicable Disease Research site. Venifar and Linufel had, too, he thought. Linufel's display of privately obtained information meant she had connections that he didn't, and she was letting him know it. She proved herself by that single action a more dangerous opponent than he'd even suspected.

Venifar waved the memo. "The deadline is—ambitious," he said. "We will have to work closely together."

An admission, Kellubrae thought, that he had no applicable resources, but was willing to steal from the other two.

He decided not to tip his hand either way. He had specific plans that he thought he might accomplish with this mission; the first of which was promotion to director of Communicable Disease Research. He had some neat ideas for a highly contagious particle-borne variant of leprosy that ought to increase crimes of hate and cruelty tremendously. And he felt that Lucifer had been in his post entirely too long. What one fallen angel could rule, another could rule as well (or better?), and he had ideas for the reorganization of Hell that were . . . well . . . demonic.

But first things first. He needed to avoid being made team leader. "Venifar makes a good point," he said to Linufel. "On the strength of his suggestion of teamwork, I nominate him as team leader."

Linufel's eyes gleamed. He could see he'd beat her to the punch, but this time she wasn't going to mind deferring. "You're so right. I second the motion."

Venifar swallowed, and his eyes went round. "I'm afraid I must decline . . ." he started to say, but Kellubrae cut him off.

"All in favor?"

"Aye," Linufel said.

"Aye," Kellubrae said.

"All opposed?"

"I'm opposed, damn you!" Venifar shouted.

Kellubrae ignored the shout. "Motion carries by a two-thirds majority. Congratulations, Venifar. You'll be working closely with the Big Guy."

# Chapter 4

NC CORRIDOR NIXED
By The Associated Press

Richmond, VA—Virginia Governor Douglas Wilder put the last nail in the coffin of the proposed North Carolina Corridor today. Speaking before the Virginia legislature, Wilder vigorously denied rumors that he supported the project.

The now defunct proposal called for the extension of a narrow strip of territory from the current North Carolina/Virginia border up the shoulder of Interstate 95 North, through Virginia and into the District of Columbia, where a throughway to Capitol Hill had already been negotiated with Congress and the District government. The whole corridor was to have been under the nominal sovereignty of North Carolina, with extraterritoriality rights granted to all encroached legal entities. The project was proposed by North Carolina Governor James Hunt to "provide equal access to the mechanisms of government to all our citizens, regardless of plane of origin."

Wilder's rejection of the plan appeared to rule out any hope of compromise. He told the gathered legislators, "The last time the sacred boundaries of our Commonwealth were altered, it took the

Grand Army of the Republic to make it stick,
and it'll be a cold day in Hell before I stand by
and let it happen again."

Informed of Wilder's remarks, Hunt responded,
"I'll see what I can do."


Rheabeth Samuels looked out over her domain and
thought furiously. She couldn't count on much more time
and there was still so much to do. She had enough work
for at least two of her—and now this. She crumpled
the fax and hurled it, sidearm, towards the trash. It
bounced off the edge of her desk, teetered on the rim
of the basket, and fell onto the carpet. Rhea wasn't
surprised—it had already been that kind of day.

In front of her, through the plate glass windows of
her corner office, the warm spring sun lit a perfect
Carolina morning. A gentle breeze was stalking cat's-
feet through the grass, and Burden Creek sparkled as
it rolled down into the pond. Rhea couldn't appreciate
it, anymore than she could appreciate the feel of the
lush carpet beneath her bare feet. Her world had
narrowed to debits and credits.

She strode over to her desk and thumbed the intercom.
"Jan, CCI's pulled out. The bastards didn't even have
balls enough to do it over the phone."

"I saw that fax, Rhea . . . and I'm not the only one."
Jan's worry came through clearly in her voice. "What
are you going to do?"

Rhea wished she knew. There wasn't time to line up
new investors. "When Roberts gets here, I'll take him
personally," she said finally. "Have someone haul ass down
to the conference room to flight-test the AV equipment
for a dog and pony show. I'm going to have to hit him
for twice what we had planned, and we can't afford any
screw-ups."

Rhea tapped the intercom off. Looking down, she

saw the offending fax again. She considered only a second before stomping it flat; then she picked it up with her toes and dropped it into the trash. She allowed herself a brief smile as it rustled down against the plastic lining—if only she could do the same to the craven who had sent it. Of course, she'd need a bigger basket. She smiled again, thinking of the greasy blimp from CCI that she'd had to wine and dine: make that a lot bigger basket. Well, if he couldn't understand that making an investment didn't give him the right to put his hands under her skirt, then screw him—or rather, let him screw himself *and* CCI. They were the ones who were going to come begging for her company's services. And she wasn't even going to have to wait that long to see it happen.

In her office closet sat several pairs of sensible, stylish shoes. Rhea considered carefully, then slipped her feet into a pair of dark blue Ferragamo pumps. She made a face at the constriction of her toes, but bore it because she had to. Executives expected other executives to wear shoes. She inspected her skirt and blouse critically in the closet mirror, and made minute adjustments to each. Her hair, of course, was perfect. She glanced at her watch. Ten A.M. Jan's voice came over the intercom. "Mr. Roberts has just signed in at the front desk, Rhea."

"I'm on my way." Deep breath, one practice smile, then it was time to go. Jan glanced up from her computer as Rhea walked past her towards the lobby and Rhea could see the computer screen reflected in Jan's glasses. The display looked a lot like a résumé, but Rhea decided she didn't really care to verify that.

Instead she asked, "How do I look?"

"Well," Jan said, "I'd invest."

"Careful. I may take you up on that." Rhea smiled— the confident we're-going-to-land-our-investor smile.

"Maggie is setting him up with a coffee and leading

him to the conference room. You've got about sixty seconds if you want to beat them there."

"No problem. Hold all my calls, and cross your fingers."

"I'll cross my legs if you think it'll help." Jan demonstrated. She smiled, but her own smile was nowhere near as confident as Rhea's. "Go get 'em."

"Count on it."

Jan nodded with enthusiasm, but just the same, Rhea heard her start typing again as she walked away. Rhea knew Jan's wasn't the only résumé that found itself in the process of revision and updating. Better land this one.

She took the service corridor and ran, and was in the conference room well before Roberts and his escort from Marketing. She'd had time to get seated, get her skirt and blouse smoothed, and present the appearance of someone who never needed to run to meetings. She rose gracefully when they entered.

Roberts didn't look bad at all; he was fortyish with graying hair and a straight no-nonsense posture. She'd studied his record. He'd put in twenty years active duty with Army Intelligence, all top-secret stuff—no details available— and he was still in the Reserves. He had taken a lot hush-hush engineering skills with him into industry and he'd worked his way up from shop floor to management. He knew his stuff.

Rhea held out her hand, giving him a hundred kilowatt smile. She knew it was good—persuasion had been her business for a long, long time. "Mr. Roberts," she said. "I'm delighted that you're here. Now let me tell you exactly why your company wants to invest in Celestial Technologies' manned spacelift program."

# Chapter 5

Jack Halloran was having a good day. It hadn't started out that way; there'd been a couple of little red imps, gremlins almost, following him around in the morning, waving their pitchforks and trying to get him to cut people off in traffic and speed through school zones. He'd finally gotten rid of them during breakfast at Hardee's by picking up a little litter in the parking lot and helping an old lady with her tray. It was the kind of thing you got used to quickly in North Carolina, and he didn't regret leaving Spartanburg for a minute. He'd been at Celestial almost two years now, and he'd never looked back.

He whistled a little of the Dominoes' "60 Minute Man" as he soldered the last trace onto the modulator board clamped to his workbench. Case in point: Where else could a thirty-four year old electrical engineer work on an honest-to-God space drive? He breathed the pungent fumes of the rosin flux and eyed the joint critically. It looked good, and he raised the iron, watching carefully as the solder cooled to a shiny silver jacket, ensuring a good connection. Perfect. He used the iron to conduct his imaginary band for a second, then flipped off the power and laid the soldering iron back in its stand.

"Okay," he told the board, "time to come to poppa." He loosened the clamp. His wrist grounding strap was barely long enough to reach the table where the trolley was set up, but he wasn't about to risk static blowing a chip after all the time he'd put into this board, so he left it on, working against the slight tension of the coiled cord. He oriented the pins and seated the board securely in its socket on the trolley, then worked the ribbon cable on over the edge connectors. When he was satisfied, he popped the strap free, and looked down at his handiwork. On the metal lab table a steel wire linked two solid blocks of bronze that were bolted to the frame at either end. Between them sat a little cart, just four wheels and a platform, with hooks rising at each end to curl around the wire for guidance. That was the trolley. The prototype drive sat on the trolley platform, with a long flexible lead connecting it to the power supply which hung from a stanchion under the table.

The power supply had a simple rocker switch; one side was OFF, the other ON. Jack put his hand on the switch, then hesitated. The design was his boss Rhea's (and there ought to be a law that all women that gorgeous be that smart), but the implementation was his. If this worked, then the name Jack Hannah Halloran was going to be in a lot of history books. Hell, if this worked, he was going to space. On the other hand, if it didn't work, he would probably wind up in a Leno monologue. "You knew the job was dangerous when you took it, Fred," he quoted to himself and threw the switch.

A pleasant hum filled the lab, but nothing else happened. Jack waited a second, then gingerly touched the trolley. It would roll freely in either direction, but showed no inclination to move on its own, and was certainly in no danger of running into the brass stops. The humming increased in frequency and suddenly a little puff of acrid smoke rose from the board he'd just finished. The humming stopped.

"Damn!" Well, he'd always preferred Letterman anyway.

# Chapter 6

Glibspet would never be handsome, even in his human manifestations. It didn't bother him—he wasn't one of the Fallen, and except for the leccubi, demons of the second rank weren't *supposed* to be attractive. So when he grinned across the table at his client, it wasn't a pretty sight.

"I've got your pictures," Glibspet told him.

The man squirmed uncomfortably in his chair. Glibspet had gone to a lot of trouble to find that chair. It was painted a deathly dull gray, sat unevenly and had a seat and back that didn't match human anatomy well at all. He'd gotten a great deal on it: The U.S. Army had five million of them, four million of which were always in transport between units as supply staff tried to fob them off on each other. His client gave up the battle and slouched back awkwardly. "Let me see them," he said.

"Sure," Glibspet said. "Right after you fork over my fee. I'm not picky, large bills or small ones, just so it's all there."

The man put his hands on the table and pulled himself forward, his fingers laying down trails of sweat. *What a loser*, Glibspet thought to himself. It was a wonder he hadn't destroyed his marriage before today. "How do I know you've got something worth it?" the man asked.

"You don't. You signed the contract; those were the

terms. I promised to come up with pictures showing
Donna being unfaithful, and you promised to pay, in
advance, for whatever I came up with. So, pay up, or
get a lawyer, a real good lawyer—we've got lots of
experience with contracts." Glibspet grinned again,
drawing his lips back over his incisors.

"Okay." The man took out his wallet and counted the
bills out one by one. His hands shook, and the crisp
teller machine notes rustled appetizingly. "There. Now
let's see them."

Glibspet shook his head. "Nope, I need two hundred
more. Expenses."

"What expenses?"

"I don't have to itemize. It's in the contract."

"But that's my last two hundred."

"You can eat peanut butter next week. Give!"

The man emptied his wallet, and Glibspet scooped
the cash off the table, rifling it back and forth, enjoying
the scent of fresh ink. He thrust his arm through the
solid metal of the five-foot doorless steel cube that served
as his safe and let the bills go. Then he felt around in
the cube until he felt a hefty clasp envelope; he drew it
out through the safe walls. "Here you go," he said, handing
it across the table. "Proof positive in Kodacolor."

His client's hands trembled as he opened the clasp
and drew out the stack of eight-by-tens. His face blanched
as the top photo came into view. "My God," he whispered.
"How could she? The slut!" He laid the photo face down
on the table, but the second one was worse. "*Shit!* She
never did that for me." He looked at the next one. "Or
*that*, either!"

"You never asked her, you putz," Glibspet said.

If the man heard him, he made no response. He put
down the third picture and picked up the fourth like a
shell-shocked vet. Unlike the other three, this one was
shot from far enough back that the pair's full figures

were visible, though exactly what they were doing was hard to describe. "And this one—hey! Wait a minute. That's *you*!"

"Yeah," Glibspet confirmed. "Do you think that's my best side?"

"What in Hell do you think you're doing, screwing my wife!" The man screamed, and Glibspet watched the veins on his forehead with interest.

"Well," he said, "first of all, I'm not in Hell, or I'd be doing worse than screwing her; and second, that's what you were paying me for, to get proof that your wife was unfaithful. Can you think of any better proof?"

"You weren't supposed to screw her!"

"I had to," Glibspet said reasonably. "She wasn't screwing anyone else, so I couldn't get proof any other way. It wasn't easy either. She loved you, and was pretty serious about that marriage thing. I got into the house by telling her you and I were friends. Then I told her you'd paid someone to spy on her, and that you'd told me all about it. I told her all the stuff you'd told me— naturally, I didn't tell her that I was the one watching her. When she'd heard the whole story, she wanted to get even with you. Of course, she realized this morning what she'd done, but I'm sure you were there for her when she woke up crying, right?"

"So she was never unfaithful, and you, you bastard—"

He lunged at Glibspet, and landed on the floor with a crash as Glibspet casually reappeared five feet to the left.

"That's right. She was never unfaithful. Too bad you didn't hire me to answer *that* question. Oh, by the way, how well ventilated is your garage?"

The man gave an inarticulate cry of rage and shame and ran for the doorway.

Glibspet called out after him, "The two hundred was for the handcuffs!" He heard the outer door slam, and the sound of burning rubber. He didn't see how the man could be in time. You never knew, though. Maybe traffic would be light. He picked up the stack of pictures and leaned back in his own, very comfortable chair, leafing through them appreciatively. This detective racket wasn't half bad.

# Chapter 7

Roberts knew his business. He had sat quietly through Rhea's presentation with a bland half-smile on his face, but his eyes didn't miss anything. Rhea could almost hear the wheels turning as she made her key points. When the final slick multimedia spot had come to an end and Rhea had laid down her pointer, he leaned forward and pulled a small penscreen from his jacket pocket. "Very impressive, Ms. Samuels. Now if you can tell me what I *really* want to know, we can make sure this time is productive for both of us."

"Gladly," Rhea said. "And I'm sure you'll want to have the details in hard copy. I can have printouts of any figures you need before you leave the building."

Roberts made a note on his pad. "You run a very efficient operation, then." It wasn't exactly a question, but it was more than a comment.

"I keep it that way," Rhea said. "Look," she keyed an organizational chart up onto the big screen, "we've got thirty people in our core group here in the Triangle, and two more at our Manteo office. We don't try to do everything—I can contract out the construction work easily, so I always know exactly what all our people are doing. We don't have to deal with a bloated middle management structure like NASA or the main-line aerospace firms."

"And you can design and field a manned spaceship with thirty people?"

"I can," Rhea stated, "and I have. The design is complete, and our spaceframe is under construction at Manteo. It should be done in forty-five days. We're not like NASA—we don't have to invent ten new things before breakfast each morning. Our ship uses off-the-shelf hardware and we build to shipyard tolerances, not picometers."

Roberts made another note on his penscreen. Rhea looked closely and saw that it said *not picometers*. The one above that read *bloatless*, and the first said *nice tits*, with the *nice* underlined twice. She relaxed just a little; he was obviously using the penscreen as a prop. The realization made him seem a little more human to her.

He put the pen down and looked up at her again. "If it's so easy, Ms. Samuels, why aren't McDonnell-Douglas and Boeing building spaceships?"

Rhea smiled. "I said we don't need to invent ten new things everyday. We did have to invent *one* new thing— our MULE drive. They don't have that because they don't have me."

"You know what our physicists tell me about your MULE? They say it's fundamentally impossible for it to work." Roberts reached into his pocket again. "I have a signed statement here from one of them, promising to pay me one million dollars if it ever lifts so much as a feather."

"Hold on to that," Rhea told him.

"Oh, I intend to," Roberts said, "but the fact remains that the keystone of your whole structure seems a little loose."

Rhea shrugged, "What can I tell you? The MULE is a trade secret and I'm not going to explain it. I will say that we've seen a lot of things here in North Carolina over the past two years that are 'fundamentally impossible,' and that once you know something *can* be done, duplicating it gets a lot easier. You can check my publication record. Anyone without an ax to grind will tell you I do brilliant physics."

"I have, and they did. That's the only reason I'm here today—the quality of you and your people." He put down his pen. "Okay, let's take success as a given. What's the business case? You aren't offering stock—how is TRITEL going to make money by flying around in a spaceship?"

Rhea sighed. He'd watched the presentation, and she knew full well he'd been paying attention. Now he wanted to hear her sell, to know that she could pull in other investors. She couldn't blame him, but that didn't make the thousandth sales pitch any more fun.

"Let's start with satellites," she said. "With the communications and Net explosions, there are whole continents severely underserved with comsats."

"You can cover the world with four birds in Clarke orbits," Roberts said.

Rhea sat forward. He was feeding her lines. Was he already sold? "And two plus two equals five, for large instances of two. Just being able to see the birds doesn't say anything about capacity. Clarke orbits are too damned high. It's absolutely critical for voice traffic and even for lots of data traffic to keep transit delay to a minimum. The phone company that can offer satellite shots where you don't talk on top of each other is going to clean up. We need little birds in low orbits, and we need lots of them."

"Well, why don't I just contract with NASA, the French, or the Russians to place them for me?"

"How much does a satellite cost?"

"Well—"

"Too much. Too much because you have to build in quadruple redundancy, and you know you can't fix anything. *We* will go up there with a screwdriver if that's what it takes. Invest in us and you get cheap satellites and free launches."

He held up a hand to stop her. "Okay. Satellites. What else?"

"Crystals, semiconductors, superconductors, drugs, raw materials from the asteroids, tourism . . ."

"Pretty blue-sky stuff," he said.

Rhea dropped her guard a fraction. She was *nearly* sure he wanted to be convinced. "We sell the facilities, the rest will follow. We *will* make money on it, and—" She paused.

"And?"

"And it will save the world," she said quietly.

He studied her, his expression, for just a fleeting instant, open and quizzical and startled. "Have you ever sold the moon, Ms. Samuels?"

"What?"

"Never mind."

He made one more note on his penscreen, *full of herself . . . justified?*, then closed it with a snap. "Why don't you show me around your facility."

# Chapter 8

Memo:
From: Lucifer, Lord of the Damned, Grand
Inquisitor, Father of Lies, Originator of Sin,
etc., etc.
To: Putrid Pustule—Division of Law and Disorder

Putrid,
I want LOOPHOLES, damn you, and I want them now!
Tear this document apart if you have to, but
find me every possible way that we can cheat
this.

Lucifer
encl.: Rules governing Operation Tarheel


From: honorial@data_proc.chrstn.hvn.aftrlif.net
(Honorial, Chief of Data Processing, HeavenNet)
Received: from hellex.hellwire.info.net by
x1.hellwire.info.net for
<lucifer.the.fallen@chrstn.hell.aftrlif.net>;
Fri, 8, Oct 15:14:10 -0400)
Received from HEAVEN.aftrlif.net by
x1.hellwire.info.net; Fri, 8, Oct 14:17:41 -0500
Return path: honorial@data.proc.chrstn.hvn.aftrlif.net
To: lucifer.the.fallen@chrstn.hell.aftrlif.net
Subject: Operation Tarheel
Message-ID: <9605181666.ZZ131313HEAVEN.aftrlif.net>
- - - - - - - - - - - - - - - - - - - - - - - -

  Command from On High
  By order of the God of Heaven and Earth, Creator

of All Things, Eternal Parent of the Infinities, Bringer of Joy and Hope, Master of all the Realms—

O fallen angel who is anathema to me, you whose name shall not pass my lips until you have humbled yourself before me—

By my order and on my express command and through the intercession of my daughter, Dayne Teresa Kuttner, you shall send forth out of Hell, under my parole, exactly fifty-eight thousand eight hundred fifty-one fallen angels, devils, demons, and assorted members of the lower orders of Hell's crawling vermin into the state of North Carolina — this number being exactly one one-hundredth of the human population in that state at the instant of my reckoning.

Unchained denizens of Hell must obey the following rules:

- They will neither inflict, nor pay to have inflicted, any physical harm on any human.
- They will not parent a child with a human, either with or without the human's consent.
- They will not steal by supernatural means.
- They will not cause any disease or plague, nor will they act as the agents through which any disease or plague is transmitted.
- They will not impersonate a minister, God, or angel of God, or any divine messenger of God.
- They will not cause any virgin births.
- They will not leave the State of North Carolina.

The Unchained denizens of Hell may:

- Lie, tempt, deceive, mislead, and otherwise carry out the usual agenda of Hell.
- Impersonate human beings if that is within their nature and capacity.
- Own property, become citizens, hold offices, own and operate legal businesses, marry humans — if the humans are apprised of their true nature beforehand and no

intimidation is used — and in all other legal ways approved by the State of North Carolina attempt to achieve a normal life on Earth.

— Enter into binding contracts with human beings — with one of the two following stipulations:

    1) The human must be fully apprised of the nature of the contract and the nature of all parties involved in the contract; or,

    2) The human must sign the contract with his own blood. (Percentage of blood to inert materials not specified; blood must be less than twenty-four hours old in Earth-sequential time *only*, as per previous agreements between Heaven and Hell; human must know that blood has been drawn; no blood from blood donorship or other merciful blood collection agencies, or from accidents and injuries may be used.)

— Repent.

Unchained denizens of Hell must:

— Eat and drink mortal food, or their Earthly bodies will wither and fail, and they will have to pay Heaven for new ones. Heaven will charge a cost-per-body fee plus punitive wastage tax for any Earthly bodies above and beyond the one that will be issued free from Heaven per Hell-soul at the time of exit from Hell — this will be collected by the usual revenue methods. These Heaven-issued Earth-bodies will be indistinguishable from the individual Hellspawn's normal form and will have all the Hellspawn's usual abilities excluding those which would run counter to the above decrees.

— Obtain their sustenance in the normal mortal way — that is, by growing food or paying for it with cash or barter.

❖    ❖    ❖

Jack was bent over the fried modulator board with a jeweler's loupe in his eye, oblivious to the world, when someone tapped him on the back. He jumped, almost falling off his lab stool. "Don't *do* that!" he said, and then, "Oh, hi, Rhea."

His boss was standing there with a man Jack had never seen before. He was wearing a suit, but he looked intelligent. Rhea was wearing shoes, so it must be important. Jack stood up and brushed himself off, bits of wire and insulation falling to the floor.

"Jack, this is Al Roberts from TRITEL," Rhea said. "Al, meet Jack Halloran."

Roberts held out his hand and Jack took it. "Pleased to meet you," he said.

"Likewise," said Roberts. His grip was firm. "So you're Jack Halloran."

"Um, yes."

"I've followed your career," Roberts continued. "That was some dynamite work you and your team did for NCR on the SART project. Too bad about what happened."

"Yeah," Jack said. "It was the worst management and marketing screw-up since Xerox PARC, but we all got published and some of the technology is finally catching on. I think your company even puts out some of the SART stuff in your high-end line."

"The Ultinea, yes. So how do you feel about management here at Celestial?"

He laughed. "What do you expect me to say? She's standing right behind you. I'll put it this way, I've been here almost two years, and I'm not planning to leave."

Roberts nodded. "And what are you working on now?" Jack looked at Rhea, who nodded. He pointed to the trolley, which was still hooked to its guidewire, although he had ripped most of the electronics from the platform. "That's our MULE prototype."

"And does it move?"

"Only when I give it a good shove." Oops, Rhea was shaking her head violently. "But, ah, I've nearly got that worked out."

# Chapter 9

Glibspet didn't have a secretary, and he didn't want one. Not again. The women up here got upset about the simplest little things, like his grabbing a handful when they were bent over the copier, or when they noticed that peephole in the john. Sometimes they reported him. He could deal with the law—that wasn't the problem. The problem was having all his mail misfiled, having his calls rerouted, and handing out business cards that read *Glibfink Infestations* for weeks before taking the time to read one. Truly, Hell's office had no fury like a secretary scorned. Still, if he'd had a secretary, he might have gotten some warning before stepping into his office and coming face to face with three of the Fallen.

One was seated at his desk, while the other two flanked him like bookends. That book would never be a bestseller. "Sit down, Glippet," the one behind the desk said, and Glibspet felt an invisible hand grip him and press down hard. His knees bent and he sank into that damned visitor's chair. He dropped the bag of Twinkies he'd been carrying and the Twinkies jumped from the torn top in a high-fat stampede. The invisible hand let him go then, but he knew better than to get up. A prudent devil didn't mess with the Fallen.

Glibspet studied the three, trying to place them in the Hierarchy. All of them were in human form, and radiantly beautiful. Two of them were manifesting as males; those he pegged after a moment as Venifar, who was standing, and Kellubrae, who had taken over his desk. The third had chosen a female persona, and looked like Grace Jones, but as far as he knew, Grace Jones was still alive—though maybe he'd been out of touch too long. He couldn't place her . . . but he could think of where he'd *like* to place her.

"What do you want?" Glibspet asked finally, when it became apparent that none of them were going to say anything.

"We've got a job for you, Glippet," Kellubrae said.

Glibspet squirmed on the chair. "That's *Glibspet*," he said.

"Whatever," Kellubrae shrugged. "You're supposed to be a detective—we need you to find somebody."

"Well, find him yourself," Glibspet snapped. "I've got all the work I need." Even as he said it, though, his mind started spinning furiously. Devils didn't mess with the Fallen . . . back in Hell, anyway. But they needed him for some reason. And if they needed him, that meant that in some way he didn't yet understand, he already held the upper hand. All he had to do was figure out why.

The Grace Jones lookalike spoke for the first time. "Glubsput, dear . . . Lucifer is personally interested in this matter." Her voice was honey golden, and her smile drew his eyes irresistibly to her form, which was ripe and suddenly seemed to promise so much. She sauntered towards him, and he smelled roses. "Trust me, little devil. You *want* to help us. The rewards for success will be—considerable."

Glibspet's trousers grew tight, and as quick as that, he was furious. He'd done enough manipulating to figure out when he was on the other end of a well-played line. He stood up and faced the Fallen. "I can get my own women now, thank you. I may have to pay most of the time, but it's not like at home where you and the leccubi get all the action and down in the trenches we don't even get the *smell* of a piece of ass for thousands of years. I work for money, and lots of it. If you've got it, I'll find this guy for you. If you think you're going to get a freebie, though, bugger off—I've got paying clients."

"Have a care, Glibspet," Venifar said. "The terms of the Unchaining may limit the Hierarchy's power here, but you *will* rotate back down someday."

"Yeah, and maybe the Hierarchy will have changed by then." Glibspet held his ground. "It's not like the upper levels are known for stability. Take my offer or leave it—you can pay me lots of money, or you can sniff your victim out alone." The invisible hand clutched Glibspet again, but it did not crush him, and he stared Venifar straight in the eyes.

There was some kind of communication between the Fallen then, and the invisible hand loosened. "All right," Kellubrae said. "Your terms—for now. What you have to do . . ."

"Wait a second," Glibspet said. "My terms are, I sit in *my* chair, with you on the other side of *my* desk. Move it." He walked over to his chair and shook it. Kellubrae gave him a look that promised many things, all of them unpleasant, but the fallen angel moved. Glibspet sat down and put his feet up on the desk. "Hey, sweet tits," he said, "toss me a Twinkie."

# Chapter 10

Rhea was starting to feel like the Parisian who had never been to the Eiffel Tower. She had never seen her company in quite the way she was seeing it today. She thought she had taken Roberts to every room in the Celestial building with the exception of the women's restrooms, and she wouldn't have been too surprised if he had asked to see those. She was aware of her toes now, too; ten individual little beacons of unhappiness, hemmed in by her shoes. Rhea was of the firm opinion that toes should stay incommunicado unless they were immersed in lush green grass, or were being sucked on by a thoughtful friend. This was definitely neither case, and she wondered briefly if she could come up with some logical reason to ban shoes from the building without seeming too strange to trust with other people's money.

To prevent static buildup maybe, or as a requirement from some Japanese investors.

No, probably not.

Roberts was still going strong. He insisted on sticking his head into every office, and asking questions of whomever he found there. Some of those questions were amazingly perceptive, and showed a detailed knowledge of the person's career or field. Others struck Rhea as asinine: he asked Jan how she felt about WordPerfect, and asked Marketing's opinion about the president's new budget. She soon realized, though, that he was learning an awful lot. Maybe more than she really wanted him to. As the afternoon wore on, she tried several times to guide him up to her office, but he always wanted to make just one more stop. The man was indefatigable—Rhea was too, but she wanted out of those shoes and she did have paperwork that had to be done. Of course, she reminded herself, if Roberts didn't like what he saw, there wouldn't be any need to finish the paperwork.

Finally he let her lead him back upstairs.

"Make yourself comfortable," Rhea said. "The couch isn't bad."

Roberts seated himself, and looked out over Burden Creek. "Nice view," he said.

It was, but Rhea was still in no mood to appreciate it. "So, Mr. Roberts," she asked, "what do you think about my company?"

"That's a fair question." Roberts crossed left ankle over right knee and leaned back. He laced his fingers together and tucked them behind his head. It was the classic male-spreading-out-and-claiming-territory gesture. He wanted to convince her that she needed to listen to him. Subconsciously, he was trying to establish dominance. She kept her smile to herself. She wondered if he even knew he was doing it. He said, "All right then. Here's my answer. You've got a company of top-notch, dedicated people, all of whom want very much for your enterprise to succeed. Most of them are very worried that it won't. I think, Ms. Samuels, that your company is worth investing in, and that you need that investment a lot more today than when you set up this appointment."

"That's true," Rhea admitted, "I won't pretend it isn't, but by the same token, the return to TRITEL goes up with your investment."

"If you succeed."

"*When* we succeed," Rhea said fiercely. She stood up and walked to the window.

"I think there's a good possibility," Roberts conceded. "Anything that can keep people like Halloran interested for two years is a good bet—or at least an intriguing bet. How much do you need?"

"Three hundred million," Rhea said immediately. Roberts got up and joined her. He stared out the window silently for several minutes, and Rhea thought she'd overplayed her hand. Maybe they could have scraped by on two hundred. But that would take longer, and time was the most precious thing in the world. Finally, she couldn't take it anymore. "Well, Mr. Roberts?" she said, "It'll be the best bargain your company ever got. Do we have a deal?"

Roberts turned and looked her in the eyes. "I like impatient people," he said. "They get things done."

# Chapter 11

His back was starting to ache a bit, but Jack stayed hunched over his workbench, carefully easing his continuity probes down on either side of the tiny resistor. He glanced at his multimeter. The needle stayed dead on zero, indicating an open circuit. Bingo! He straightened up and stretched. A whole afternoon shot because of a ten cent part. Maybe he should consider paying at least a quarter for the next one.

He got up and checked his component bins. It always reminded him a little of going to the candy counter at the drugstore when he was a kid. The capacitors with their bright and shiny colors were the chocolates and hard candies; the resistors with their color-coded bands were the stick candies and mints, and the clear crystal diodes were the rock candy. Snarls of red and black wire trailed everywhere like licorice whips gone feral. Jack rummaged in the resistor bin until he came up with a likely one—the right ohmage and twice the amperage of its dead cousin. He started to take it back to his bench when something else registered. That really *was* a peppermint in the resistor bin. He took it out, sniffed it suspiciously, then unwrapped it and popped it into his mouth.

Not bad.

He tossed the resistor onto his bench. "Well, I know

an omen," he told it, speaking around the peppermint, "and this one means to go home before anything bad spoils it. You can wait."

He whistled a few bars of "Georgy Girl" as he made a final survey of the lab, grabbing a sheaf of papers that caught his eye, then turned off the lights and closed the door. Most of the other doors were already dark, and he checked his watch in surprise. Six-thirty—and it was Friday. He wasn't really taking off early at all. He grinned. Well, it was earlier than if he hadn't had his omen.

Jack jogged down the stairs to the first floor, and out into the parking lot. The sun was still peeking up over the trees, and purple martins were out, darting to and fro, and picking bugs out of the evening air like kids picking pepperoni off a pizza. He glanced back at the Celestial building. It looked like the light was still on in Rhea's office. Maybe he could go back up and see if she wanted to go see a movie. She'd said once that she really liked Disney, and the new animated *Dante* was supposed to be a riot.

Nah, better not. It would be nice to see a movie with someone for a change, but that'd be like sucking up to the boss. She probably had someone she went out with, anyway. Maybe that Roberts guy. The Mercedes in the parking lot didn't look familiar, so he must still be up there with her. *Hope I didn't screw things up for Rhea's funding with that little encounter*, Jack thought.

He had to admit it would be nice to get out sometime. He hadn't had much luck since breaking up with Carol. If anyone could call *that* luck. He still couldn't believe how stupid he'd been.

He got into his car and turned the key. The ignition gave a slight click, but the engine didn't turn over. Jack loved his Camry, but he had to admit that after four hundred fifty thousand miles and fifteen years, maybe, just maybe, it was starting to lose a little zip. He took a small ballpeen hammer from the toolbox in the trunk, and opened the hood. He aimed carefully, and brought the hammer down in a small precise arc against the side of the starter, then closed the hood and put the hammer away confidently. This time, the car started immediately. Plenty of life in the old girl yet. As he rolled out onto Cornwallis Road, he mentally itemized a bill.

Hitting car with hammer: $1.00.

Knowing where to hit: $99.00.

With the tape player blaring out the Globetrotters' "Rainy Day Bells," Jack rode off into the sunset.

# Chapter 12

"This is the one," Kellubrae told Glibspet. He cupped his hands and drew them upward to meet again at the top. The air inside the ellipse he had limned shimmered, then congealed in the form of a woman.

She was unmistakably one of the Fallen. She had that combination of radiant beauty and dark aspect that characterized them, and yet there was an indefinable feeling of something subtly off-key about her too. And something familiar.

"Hey," Glibspet said, "I know that frail. She was the boss's mouthpiece, wasn't she?" Detective talk was fun.

"Averial," Venifar confirmed, "the original devil's advocate during the . . . Late Unpleasantness."

"Missing almost two years now," Grace said, "though, not actually *missed* until today. Lucifer wants her found."

Glibspet unwrapped another Twinkie and popped it into his mouth. Speaking through the filling (Damn, that stuff was good!), he asked, "Weh, whuy dosen' he wind her 'msef?" He swallowed and licked his lips appreciatively.

"Because she doesn't *want* to be found," Venifar said, "and there's only one place above or below where one of the Fallen could hide from him."

"North Carolina," Glibspet said.

"That's right," Kellubrae snapped his fingers and dismissed the image. "We've done what backtracking we can in Hell. We've ascertained that she came up right after the Unchaining, simply because she hasn't been anywhere in Hell since then. And that's the last the Fallen or any Hellborn saw her. She can't have left the state; we'd have felt her dissolution. She can't have repented; she would have shown up on the rosters. So she's still up here, shielded somehow and a priori working on something contrary to the interests of the Hierarchy."

Venifar said, "You're the only Hellborn who's shown a talent for finding out things within the constraints of the Unchaining. You will find her now, and quickly, or I guarantee your homecoming will be talked about around the Pit for millennia."

Glibspet raised an eyebrow. "You already played that song, remember?" he said. "Threaten me and I'm liable to go off and work for my other clients and put your little problem at the bottom of my priority list. Keep this in mind. This is my investigation, my terms, and my contract." It was also a fascinating situation. One of Hell's finest had slipped the noose and hidden on Earth for over two years before anyone realized she was gone. This little fact would wreak havoc within Hell's ordered legions if news of it got out . . . and news would almost certainly get out. Even more interesting would be the reaction if Fallen Averial escaped Lucifer's clutches entirely. She had, at one time, been big, big, big in the organization. Why, her continued absence would be almost as devastating for Lucifer as the defection of his second-in-command, Agonostis, had been two years earlier.

So the three Fallen in his office would be in serious shit if they failed to return Averial. *Serious* shit. A smart devil like him could make his fortune from an opportunity like this. Glibspet reached into his safe and pulled out one of his standard contracts. He added a few lines, crossed through a few others, wrote in a figure that in other circumstances would have been nothing short of highway robbery, and handed the contract to the unknown fallen angel he'd nicknamed Grace.

He waited while she read it. When he saw the fury in her eyes, he asked, "Well?"

The air around her darkened to match her skin. Glibspet smelled a hint of ozone and got a feeling like the calm right before a lightning strike. He didn't have any hair on his arms, but the hair in his nose stood on end. It was damned uncomfortable.

"What makes you think I would *ever* give myself to you?" Grace growled. "You're a second-level pustule on the ass of a canker, and you're not worthy to lick my instep!"

Glibspet crossed his arms. "I had in mind starting a little higher," he said. "You decided you would yank my chain with your not inconsiderable . . . assets. I decided I liked the assets I saw. I told you I see mostly working girls, and I figure if I pull this off, I ought to be able to afford the best. What's more, I'm betting you're in the market."

She dropped the contract on the floor and stalked towards him. "You're my meat, Globsnot. I am going to fry you in your own fat and—"

Suddenly her arms fell to her sides. She strained to take another step, but failed. Glibspet saw that both Venifar and Kellubrae were concentrating hard.

"Now, Linufel," Kellubrae said, "I'm sure it can't be that bad."

Linufel? That was her name. Glibspet grinned.

Venifar picked the contract up from the floor. He smoothed it out and looked it over. "Really," he said, "you're making an issue out of nothing. He just wants you for a month, and he's included a clause here saying he won't cause any damage sufficient to require repairing your manifestation. It seems quite reasonable, considering. The amount of money he wants up front strikes me as much more unreasonable." He smiled at Kellubrae.

"It's not *your* ass he wants," Linufel snarled. She glared from one Fallen to the other.

"No," Venifar agreed, "not in the immediate sense, but consider that in the long run it will be all our asses otherwise."

"Then why don't you agree to serve the little slime-sucker's every desire for a month?"

Venifar smiled. "There aren't many advantages to being the team leader, but this is certainly one of them. You'll accept this portion of the contract, Linufel. I say so, and by your own vote, I have control over the details of the mission."

"Then you'll accept the terms of the contract."

Venifar scanned it again. "It seems in order," he said. "You will find Averial, and in return we agree to not work against you for the duration of the contract; to pay you one hundred million dollars and grant you the use of Linufel for a month." He reached through Glibspet's desktop and pulled out a fountain pen. "Now, Linufel, my lovely, Kellubrae and I are going to release you and then we are all going to sign this contract. You do understand?"

Linufel spat. "Oh, I understand all right."

"I'll take that as a 'yes,'" Venifar said. "Kellubrae?" Linufel finished the step she'd been taking, gave Glibspet a hard look, and walked back to the other two Fallen. She snatched the pen from Venifar, and scratched her sigil on the bottom of the paper. "Satisfied?" she snapped.

"Almost," Venifar said. He picked up the pen and added his sigil next to hers, as did Kellubrae.

"Great," Glibspet took the contract, folded it carefully and stored it in his safe. "Now the first thing I'll need is a good picture of the broad."

"You saw my seeming, Glippet," Kellubrae said. "What more do you need?"

Glibspet sighed. The Fallen just didn't have any feel for work in the mortal world. "It isn't like I can run off a thousand copies of your seeming on my copier. I can't hand a seeming out to people. I can't even pull it out of my pocket and show it around the corner drugstore without tipping people off that I'm not just one of the guys. Now can I? Look, Kelly," Glibspet said, "I need photos. I like eight-by-tens. If you can get any nudes, so much the better."

"What good would that do? She's not likely to be parading around North Carolina nude."

"No, but it will give me some inspiration," Glibspet said. "And you can make the first deposit to my account while you're at it."

"You haven't done anything yet," Venifar said.

"No, but I feel some heavy expenses coming on."

"Expenses?"

"Check the contract." Glibspet stood up. "I'm sorry you have to be leaving so soon, but I've got a lot to do."

Linufel had been silent since signing the contract. She spoke now. "Globsnot, where's your tail?"

Glibspet shrugged. "I worked out a way to demanifest it a long time ago. It just gets in the way up here. The chairs don't work with a tail, if you eat the food up here then you have to crap and tails get in the way sitting on toilets, and if I have to go undercover as a human, that damn sure doesn't work." He grinned. "It took me two months to get rid of it all. And not every second level could do it. Don't worry, doll. When it comes time for that, I'll have handles enough for you."

"I think you need a tail," she said. "All second level demons need a tail."

"Linufel . . ." Kellubrae warned.

"It can't be working against him to give him his tail back," she said. "It's only proper."

Glibspet was starting to get a bad feeling about this. "No, really—" he said.

Linufel put her hands together and pointed. Her fingers glowed briefly and Glibspet felt a sharp pain in his rear and heard his trousers rip.

Venifar and Kellubrae grabbed Linufel, and suddenly all three were gone.

Glibspet sank down weakly into his chair. And stood right back up again. Damn.

# Chapter 13

CHECKS TRACED TO DEMONS' AGES
Washington, DC — Washington Post

The Social Security Administration confirmed Friday that the recent disbursement of millions of dollars in erroneous checks was caused by a programming error. The error was triggered by the Administration's recent attempt to add North Carolina's Hellraised citizens to the Social Security roster.

"It's their ages," said Assistant Director Jeffrey Hall. "Those fields were only designed to be three digits wide, and when we started adding people a thousand years old and older, the resulting glitch overwrote another part of the program. The checks were just a mild symptom. After they went out, we had a total system meltdown, and it may be weeks before we're back online. In the meantime, let me reiterate: Do not cash those checks!"

The Administration's addition of the Hellraised to Social Security databanks came after the recent Supreme Court decision in Hildecar vs. the United States established that immortals must still pay Social Security taxes, even though they will not benefit from the system. "We're going to proceed," said Hall, "but, quite frankly, we're just going to make up ages on these guys. It may not be strictly legal, but we can't afford to rewrite all our software."

Asked for comment, a spokesman for North Carolina's Demonic Citizens Against FICA (DECAF), a group fighting for legislation to overturn the Hildecar decision, said, "This just bolsters our position. Not only are the government's actions unfair, they are pulling money from the pockets of all taxpayers to implement this. Yet I'm sure we will still get the blame somehow. We're damned if we do, and damned if we don't. Of course, that's always been true."

There were times, Rhea thought, when closing a business deal was a lot like staring at your date over the last slice of pizza: both of you want it, but neither of you wants to make the first move, and in the meantime, the pizza is getting cold. She and Roberts were eyeing each other that way now and Rhea was a little surprised. Everything she'd seen of Roberts so far had been direct and to the point, even the leading questions. Now there was *something* he wasn't willing to say.

"Look," she said, "we can stay here all evening and watch the stars come out. You're good company and I'd probably enjoy it. On the other hand, we could decide we've got a basis to deal, and I'd enjoy that even more."

"I've always loved the stars," Roberts said. "I could pick out each constellation for you and point to all the planets, but you're right, that's not what I'm here for." He turned from the window, and walked back to the couch. "Okay," he said, "TRITEL gets up to fifty percent of your satellite launch capacity for your first five years."

Rhea considered. It sounded like a lot to ask, but if things worked as planned, they'd be making so many trips that it wouldn't matter. "Done," she said.

"Stock options when you go public."

Again not a critical point. Rhea didn't care who had Celestial stock, as long as she kept fifty-one percent. And going public wasn't on her short list. It could be a very long time before that happened. "Done."

"And TRITEL gets constant reports."

Now that was starting to get a little sticky. She didn't think it was what Roberts had been hedging around, but it was like the camel's nose under the tent. Reports implied some sort of ongoing evaluation, and reports on demand suggested the possibility of an instant negative evaluation—justify your life and give three examples. On the other hand, she could hardly take the kind of money she was asking for and not provide some sort of accounting. She hesitated a second, then, "Periodic reports," she said.

Roberts nodded, "That's acceptable, if we can have someone on site."

"No," Rhea said. "Absolutely not. I do my own hiring and firing, and I don't need any help from TRITEL."

Roberts shifted a little on the couch and looked away momentarily. I'm getting close, Rhea thought.

"You're talking a lot of money for us not to have input," he said.

"Look," Rhea said, "you work for a high-tech outfit. You know that on any particular day, the odds are any given project looks like it's in the dumper. I'm not going to have a bunch of outsiders trying to micromanage me. I'm not going to be managed at all. You'll have input and I'll be glad to address TRITEL's concerns, but I'm not opening my company up, and I won't answer to TRITEL except to the extent that you can cut off my funding whenever you feel like it—period."

Roberts frowned. "Okay, maybe I can split the issue," he said. "You don't want to open up the development process. I can understand that, maybe the board can too. But we've got to have someone here during the testing to see if the result is going to meet our needs." Roberts was staring very hard at his shoes. "Especially during the flight testing."

*That* was it. He wanted to go. Wanted it so bad he could taste it. That's what all the pussyfooting was about. And more importantly, that was why he was going to come through for her. She smiled. "I don't think that will be a problem, Mr. Roberts. When we reach flight-testing stage, I think Celestial would be glad to accommodate an observer of TRITEL's choice—no," she paused a minute to bait the hook, "I know your record, and I trust your judgment. Make that an observer of your choice, personally." That ought to get him. Still she would have to examine all new hires with a microscope from now on to weed out the TRITEL plants.

Roberts looked at her sharply, then grinned. "Ms. Samuels, I have to pitch it to the board, but I think we may be able to do business."

Rhea got up and walked over to her desk. She wrote briefly on a Post-It note and offered it to Roberts. "This is my private line, my home phone, and e-mail. If you need any information, call. In the meantime, I'll have my lawyers draw up a contract along the lines we discussed. If TRITEL decides to back us, we should be able to hammer out the fine points quickly."

Roberts stood and took the note. He folded it carefully and tucked it into his wallet. It looked lonely there among all the green. "I can't give you a commitment, Ms. Samuels. Not here and not now—" He paused and smiled. It was a good smile. "—but I don't think you'll be disappointed."

He offered his hand, and Rhea took it. "And you won't regret it," she said positively.

Roberts looked thoughtful. "No," he said, "I don't believe I will."

Rhea escorted Roberts out to the parking lot. The building was empty. Even Jack had gone home, and the first stars were starting to appear in the evening sky.

"There's Orion," Roberts said, pointing up, "and Venus over near the horizon. I used to think that if I could name them all, somehow that would, I don't know, bind them to me, and I would get to go." He started to walk towards his car, then turned and looked back at Rhea. "And maybe I was right," he added. "Your prototype ship," he said, "what's it called?"

"She's named *Morningstar Rising*," Rhea said.

"Not bad." He smiled. "Not bad at all. I think it will take someone with a bit of poetry in her soul to give us back space."

Rhea watched as he got in his late-model Mercedes and shut the door. It closed with the solid thunk that came from two hundred years of Germans being very good at whatever they decided to do. Sometimes too good, she reflected—she'd known a lot of Germans. The engine caught at the first touch of the starter, and Roberts left the lot without looking back.

Rhea waited until he made the turn onto Cornwallis Road. Then she kicked off her shoes and threw them back through the open front doors. She padded across the parking lot and stood in the grass overlooking the small pond. The creek chuckled and somewhere an owl let fly a tentative hoot. Rhea waggled her toes and finally took the time to look around. She smiled to herself and stared up at the rising moon. It had been a long day. But not a bad one.

# Chapter 14

Jack woke up Monday morning before his alarm rang. That had *never* happened to him on any of his old jobs— he loved his sleep, but since coming to Celestial he beat the alarm three times out of five. There was just so much to do, and most of it fun. He brushed his teeth quickly, and jumped in and out of the shower. Dressing never took long; it was just jeans, a clean shirt and loafers. He was out the door within fifteen minutes of his head leaving the pillow.

Gotta clean this place up someday, he thought as he stepped over a stack of printouts spread out down the hallway. Could be a fire hazard. He picked out the deadbolt key and opened the front door. His newspaper was on the stoop. He kicked it back through the doorway, where it sat expectantly beside ten other similar rubber-band-secured bundles. Jack only read the comics, and there hadn't even been time for that lately.

He closed the door, gave it a sharp jab with his knee to seat the striker and reached to set the deadbolt. The key went in slowly and painfully, almost as if the lock were regaining its virginity, and he decided that this evening, for sure, he would remember to give it a squirt of oil. "Sure, I still respect you," he told it as he struggled to get the key back, "I'll call. Trust me."

The key came free and he pocketed it triumphantly.

Suddenly, there was a sound from above. Jack would have been hard pressed to describe it. It was something like an elephant's trumpeting, but more liquid. At any rate, he didn't have long to think about it, for an instant after the sound, a warm, runny mass of the foulest substance he had ever come in contact with enveloped him. "Son of a bitch!" He swore and wiped frantically. His eyes were covered and burning, and he could barely breathe—and what little air he was getting had a stench that seemed to leach all the oxygen out of it. He panicked, groping blindly for his keys, and dropped them on the front concrete. No time! He jumped the low porch railing, feeling his way along the outside wall until he came to the spigot. He turned the handle frantically to no result, finally remembering to push down to seat the loose screw. He was starting to feel faint. Another second and he would have to breathe through his mouth . . . and *taste* it.

The hose stiffened and he traced it down to the nozzle at the end. With the last of his strength, he turned the spray full on himself.

The torrent struck him like an electric shock, but he'd had enough of those over the years, and he kept it up, gasping at the water up his nose until the smell receded and his vision started to clear. The first thing he noticed when he could see again was a pair of joggers standing at the end of his driveway and looking at him curiously. He turned off the nozzle and gave them his best *Well, what are you looking at?* stare, and they moved on reluctantly. The second thing he saw was the gargoyle sitting on the eaves of his house, just above the front door. It was hard to tell with a face like that, but Jack thought it had the satisfied expression of a senior citizen whose bran muffins had just kicked in exceptionally well.

Jack got up and gave himself a once-over. His clothes were shot, and would probably have to be burned. He might—just—avoid shaving his head if he got into the shower right now. He saw his keys at the edge of the stoop, and darted in, grabbing them quickly. "Hey, you!" he called. "Shoo! Get out of here!"

"Not gonna." The gargoyle's voice was curiously high pitched. Oddly feminine.

Jack swore under his breath. First the imps, now this. Fifty thousand Hellborn in North Carolina and he got them twice running. He was going to have to figure out some better way to get rid of the things. No time now though. He went around to the back door and let himself in, leaving his clothes in a pile on the carport. He ran naked down the hall, grabbed a new bottle of shampoo from the shelf and turned the shower full on.

After twenty minutes, all of his hot water, and half of the shampoo, Jack thought he might be fit for human company again. He toweled off a view port on his mirror and inspected his hair carefully. It looked like he had gotten it before it set. He dried off carefully and smelled the towel. Not too bad; his clothes had taken the brunt. He dressed again and gingerly retrieved his wallet and checkbook from the pockets of the pile of toxic waste that had been his favorite jeans. He got a yardstick and used it to push his old clothes into a plastic garbage bag. What he *really* needed was a ten-foot pole, but he got the job done somehow, and the bag into the garbage hamper.

It was nine forty-five by the time he poked his head out tentatively from under the carport. The gargoyle was still over the front door but Jack decided not to push the issue. Gargoyles weren't the brightest of the Hellborn, and likely something else would attract her attention before he got home again. He was probably going to have to sandblast that porch though. He got into his car, which started perfectly, and headed off for Research Triangle Park and the office. The gargoyle's head swiveled to follow him, "You come back?" she called plaintively.

Jack rolled down the window. "No," he shouted, "I'm moving! You might as well shove off." His retired next-door neighbor was out watering the lawn, very carefully not noticing anything. Jack waved, but the man suddenly found a very interesting piece of pinestraw which needed his full attention.

The mold for Jack's day had been pretty well set, and nothing he did seemed to break it. He had replaced the blown resistor, and got the drive prototype back to the humming stage (A-flat, he'd finally identified it) only to have the modulator blow again—this time it was a Zerner diode that went. He'd traced all the circuits once more, comparing each of them against his printed schematic, and all of them were perfect. What's more, though he didn't fully understand the design, all the rules of electronics said that there was no way those circuits could generate overloads. It was against the laws of physics. Of course, the whole thing was supposed to violate the laws of physics, but he was looking to commit a felony, and he was getting collared for jaywalking.

He was at his desk whistling tunelessly when Jan came in. "Not going so hot, huh?" she asked.

Jack started and looked up from his schematic. "Oh, hi, Jan. No, not especially. How'd you know?"

Jan came over and scooped an armful of old printouts and trade magazines off his visitor's chair, looking around briefly for a clear space before dropping them on the floor. "You never sit at your desk when things are going good," she told him.

Jack considered. "Yeah, I guess that's true," he said. "I'm having a bad hair day."

"Well, cheer up," Jan said, "I found Rhea's shoes at the front door this morning, and she's been smiling all day, so I think we might be out of our hole. She's even got the rent-a-suit coming in this afternoon and you know how much she loves lawyers."

"Maybe," Jack said glumly, "but if we get the funding, we'll actually have to deliver a product."

Jan smiled and poked him. "Ah," she said, "but that's not *my* problem."

Jack grinned in spite of himself. "Thanks, Jan. You're just a little ray of sunshine."

"I try not to let it go to my head." She got up to leave. "Oh, here's some faxes that came in for you." She handed him the slick sheets. "Hope that helps."

He rifled through them. They were the manufacturer's component spec sheets he'd asked for. Hmm, maybe it *would* help. When he looked up again ten minutes later, Jan was gone.

The hours passed slowly after that. Jack read through the details of every component on the modulator board and, except for a brief bit of excitement over what turned out to be a typo, it didn't help. It was starting to get to him a little—he was irritated and edgy and he kept seeing things moving out of the corners of his eyes. He hadn't whistled anything more lively than "Taps" in hours. He was starting to suspect that he should have waited for the alarm that morning, and then pulled the covers up over his head, he would have accomplished just as much—probably more. *Monday is not part of the productive work week*, the quote came to him from somewhere. But he was *not* going to let a relatively simple circuit get the better of him. He picked up his schematic and started working through it again.

# Chapter 15

Glibspet loved Mondays. In the old days, he could get more souls on a Monday than the rest of the week combined. That wasn't his main job anymore, but just being out among the crowds of traumatized, post-weekend humans never failed to put a spring in his step and a gleam in his eye. And the Monday traffic jams! They were the closest thing to being back home he'd ever found. That was one reason he usually drove to work rather than porting in; he wanted to savor the whole experience. He'd done a study once, actually checked the records, and found that he could win more souls for Hell with a few illegal lane changes and some really bad exhaust fumes than with a whole week of enticements to adultery. Not that that wasn't fun too.

All good things have to end sometime though, and his exit was coming up. Glibspet sighed, and doffed the old fedora he'd been wearing. He sat up to his normal height and gunned the Lincoln Town Car up from thirty-five to eighty, leaving the far left lane and cutting across four lanes of hostile traffic towards the Roxboro Road exit. He took the barrage of horns and squealing brakes in stride as an accolade for a job well done. As he left the interstate, he thought he heard the sweet sound of metal on metal.

He turned right onto Holloway, drove past the gas

company and pulled the Lincoln into the lot by his office. Before locking up, he grabbed the rubber doughnut hemorrhoid cushion off the driver's seat and squeezed it experimentally; it was a little flat. No wonder he was sore. He'd worked all weekend on getting rid of his tail again. He'd gotten it back down to a three-inch stub, but that was almost worse than having the whole thing.

His outer office door was nondescript, just a stenciled G.I. below a mesh glass window. There was no external keyhole—all the locks were on the other side. He'd have to get a locksmith in to fix that first thing. Otherwise he was going to blow the cover he needed for the next phase of his work. Glibspet reached through and turned the bolt, cursing as the hemorrhoid doughnut rode up his arm until it looked like a water wing.

He pushed it down and stepped inside. The office didn't look too bad; he had a janitorial service in on Wednesdays. It wasn't spotless, but it wouldn't scare anyone away, and he expected a lot of visitors today. He'd placed an ad in the *Durham Morning News* on Friday for a research assistant and gopher—the payoff on this Averial case was just going to be too sweet for him to plod along on it. He threw the cushion back into his office and walked into the bathroom.

Glibspet studied his face in the mirror. He liked it—it had lots of character. His grin bared lovely strong canines and the fine, almost invisible red scales gave him a dignified, glossy look. Unfortunately, it wasn't a face that could pass for human, and it was a lot easier to hire people if they thought you were human. Customers, now, that was different. Being a demon was a draw for customers, and his Yellow Pages ad made no bones about it, but for this case he already had his customers. And if he *were* going to get an assistant, he was going to have to pass for human for quite a while.

He stepped out of his clothes and joined his hands

over his head. He concentrated hard on his fingertips, and gradually they began to glow. It wasn't the steady radiance one of the Fallen could have managed—it was more like the fitful guttering of a fire banked down to embers than the glorious blaze created by the higher-ups—and it was painful for Glibspet to evoke this new manifestation, but his little powers did what he needed them to do. He drew his hands apart, and a fat red spark arced between them like a crimson Jacob's ladder. Very slowly, he traced a Glibspet-sized ellipse in the air before him, drawing the spark out thinner and thinner until it seemed that it must break up. When it was no more than a red filament, his hands met and touched on the floor. Blue fire traced back around the completed ellipse, and the faint smell of brimstone filled the room. Within the boundary he had drawn, the air shimmered and gradually took on the shape of a naked human male. When he was satisfied the image was complete, Glibspet stepped through the oval, and the image clung to him like a soap film drawn across a hoop. It bulged as he walked forward and it tightened, trying to push him back. He kept going, and suddenly it snapped free of the frame and wrapped around him like a bubble, then collapsed in on him. The ellipse flared white hot and vanished; the glow left Glibspet's fingers.

Glibspet swore and turned on the faucet, thrusting his hands underneath the water. There was a puff of steam, then cool relief. He'd learned that one the hard way—after one of his initial disguise attempts, the first thing he'd tried to do was use the bathroom. The experience had been . . . educational.

When the steam stopped, he turned back to the mirror again. Not bad. The idealized figure had stretched to fit over him. It wasn't handsome by a long shot, but the face that stared back at him from the silvered glass was unquestionably human—except for the eyes, of course—

and he felt confident he could hold the seeming as long as he needed to.

The seeming couldn't do anything about the three-inch stub of tail behind him. That he'd have to hide with baggy pants and jackets until he could finish demanifesting it. He'd decided not to do anything about the ten inches in front of him—there were some sacrifices he wasn't willing to make. The eyes weren't as much of a problem as they sometimes seemed—shades and cosmetic contact lenses effectively disguised the square pupils.

Glibspet picked some appropriate clothes from his wardrobe and dressed quickly. He went through several boxes of business cards, finally settling on DOMINIC GLIB. That one had a nice ring to it, and he hadn't used it for a while. He grabbed a couple dozen cards and stuffed them in his pocket.

It was still early; he had specified nine thirty in his ad, so he had a little time yet. Glibspet retired to his office to consider his strategy. He put the doughnut on his chair and started to think. Since Averial was trying to stay hidden (and he dearly wanted to know how she'd managed that), she would be drawing as few Hellawatts as possible. Hell could trace Hellawatt usage. Probably she had taken on a human manifestation pretty close to her natural shape so that she wouldn't have to do much in the way of maintenance. A picture of her as Averial, humanized (a more Hellish version of Ted Turner's colorization) should give him photos that would make useful identification tools.

As for how she'd hidden herself . . . well, without the use of Hellish power, she was going to have to rely on human methods of dropping out of sight. He'd gotten good at working his way around those.

The easiest way to hide was to take someone else's identity. It was a lot simpler to amend an existing set of papers than create them all from scratch. Unfortunately, taking the identity of someone who was still alive tended to get both parties in trouble, and except in Chicago during November, it was hard to get much use out of identities whose owner had been pronounced dead. There was, however, a gray area. People living in North Carolina for less than nine months weren't citizens, so if they died, the responsibility for canceling all their records went to their home states, which left all their North Carolina records without an official status and easy to appropriate. If Averial was in North Carolina, she had probably started as a dead out-of-stater.

He was going to have to pull lots of obituaries—or rather his gopher was.

The buzzer sounded as his outer door opened. Glibspet looked at the clock: nine twenty-five—right on time. He stepped into the reception room and looked at his first prospect. She was probably about seventy, well dressed, and a little plump with silver hair. She looked a lot like Barbara Bush—a perfect grandmother type. Glibspet hated grandmother types. They tended to be bad influences on people—keeping them out of Hell. And their bodies! Glibspet was convinced that after about the age of forty, gravity gained complete mastery over human women. He had absolutely no desire to see naked a woman whose navel was granted honorary nipple status because of the company it kept.

"May I help you?" Glibspet said pleasantly as he walked over to the woman. She had a black patent leather purse under one arm, and a copy of the Durham paper under the other.

"Yes, thank you," she said. "My name is Helen Norton, and when I saw your ad for a research assistant, I knew I was just the person you were looking for. I recently retired as a research associate at the Library of Congress, and before that I worked in the State Bureau of Records and in the investigation department library at State Farm.

I've been kind of at loose ends since I retired. All my friends want me to come down to Florida and play shuffleboard, but I'm still raring to go do something useful."

"Research assistant?" Glibspet asked.

"Ah, your ad in the *Durham Morning News*," Norton clarified, a little hesitation creeping into her voice. "Established, innovative detective agency seeks part-time research assistant."

"I'm afraid I haven't a clue what you're talking about, ma'am," Glibspet told her. He leaned close as she held the folded paper up to him. He took the opportunity to ease his hand through her purse and draw out her car keys. Working carefully, so they wouldn't click, he placed them on the shelf behind her. He stole a quick glance. The key fob was a plastic rectangle with a child's drawing laminated into it. The art was completely unclassifiable, but the signature read LOVE, TERESSA.

"Right here," Norton said, "I circled it."

"May I?" Glibspet asked. He took the paper. "Hmm," he said, running his finger over the words. He thought fast for a moment, then angled the paper out of her sight and traced the ad with his finger again. Had the lights been out, Norton might have noticed a slight glow around the digit. Glibspet handed the paper back to her. "I'm sorry, Miss Norton," he said gently. "This is an ad for the Decorator Arbor and they want a retail accountant, not a research assistant, and it's on Hollow Oak Drive, not Holloway Street."

"What?" She took the paper back and looked at it incredulously. Her face fell. "I'm so sorry," she said. "I've never made a mistake like that before. It's not like me at all. I certainly didn't mean to waste your time."

"No problem, ma'am," Glibspet said kindly. "You've given society so many useful years; it's the least we can do to help you out when—ah, that is . . ." He stopped as if realizing there was no polite way to finish the sentence.

Norton hung her head. "I won't take any more of your time," she said, and turned to go.

"Miss Norton," Glibspet said, "you look like you could use some cheering up. You've got the day off, why don't you go see your granddaughter Teressa; I know she'd be glad to see you."

She turned back. "How did you know I had a granddaughter Teressa?" she asked.

Glibspet feigned surprise. "Why, you just finished telling me all about her."

"Oh," she said in a small voice. She opened the door and walked out, slowly and hesitantly.

Glibspet waited expectantly. Several minutes later, the door opened again. "Have you seen my keys?" she whispered.

"I believe you left them on that shelf, ma'am."

Yes, he was definitely right about age and gravity, Glibspet reflected as she walked out the front door. He was pretty sure she had been about a foot taller when she came in.

It was nine thirty-five. More prospects were bound to start showing up and Glibspet didn't want to start anything complicated. Pork rinds, he decided. Not complicated at all. There was a pound bag in his desk drawer, beside the Twinkies and on top of the Little Debbie oatmeal cakes (which were a blatant case of false advertising. There wasn't any of Little Debbie in them at all, and he hadn't had one since finding that out). The *how* of pork rinds escaped Glibspet, he figured it was probably the same way they made rice into Rice Krispies—*Snap, Krackle, Oink!*— but he was enchanted with the idea of a food with no positive nutritive value whatsoever. They were almost as good as inflight meals. He'd finished the entire bag, except for one blackened, twisted, mutant rind, when the buzzer rang again. Damn! He'd been saving that one. He licked his fingers and went out to check the next prospect.

This one was quite a change. She was young, as young as Norton had been old, and gravity hadn't had its way with her at all. Her breasts sat high and firm and her nipples made we're-happy-to-be-here points against the thin fabric of her blouse. The blouse itself left most of her midriff bare, failing to meet by a good three inches the tight jeans that hugged her perfect ass and legs. And she was a blonde. False blonde. Glibspet loved fake blondes; they were easy to manipulate. Probably the peroxide damage to their brains. This applicant looked eminently qualified.

"Hello," she said, "I'm Muffy Springer, and I am so totally stoked on this job." She held out her hand, and Glibspet shook it.

"Stoked," he said.

"Totally. It's like I told my roommate, Cindy, when she tried to get me a work-study job in the cafeteria. I am *so* sure, Cindy, I mean, that's like my sole goal in life, that's why I transferred from Southern Cal, so I could pick trays up off of tables. She's such a bagger sometimes. So, it's like, when I saw your ad, I'm like 'well I can do that,' I've watched all the *Magnum P.I.*s, and I know all about detective stuff like that. It's so, you know, self-empowering."

She took a breath, and Glibspet held up his hand to forestall any more information. It didn't work. "So, I can, like be an *excellent* detective, and I can work afternoons and evenings, except like this Friday when there's this really bitchin' concert in Greensboro or I have to get my hair done, or maybe when my boyfriend wants to frob and we have like an *event* . . ."

Glibspet had been in pits of Hell with less effective torments. If it weren't for that body . . . He decided to probe one more time for traces of sentience. "Muffy," he said.

"And sometimes if maybe the Chi Alphas throw a kegger or—"

"Muffy."

"And I can drive, so I can do, like, car chases . . . Uh, huh?"

"I'm looking for someone to help with research, Muffy. Can you read?"

"Books are like, the tongues of Western Imperialism, you know? It's like if you see something in a book, and, like, that's not how you are, you don't actualize, and your self-esteem is like, *detached.* I think we should all be more holistic and like, in tune with each other. Why should we, you know, oppress each other with white male words when we can empower each other just by being an organic unit. Wouldn't that be bitchin'?"

"Absolutely," Glibspet said. "Thank you, Muffy, I'll be in touch."

"So like, when do I start?"

"I can't tell you, Muffy. I think the room may be bugged," Glibspet said.

"Gnarly! Who by?"

"It's the capitalists, Muffy—the European white male capitalists."

"So, I'll call, then."

"No," Glibspet said quickly. "My, uh, phone might be tapped. In fact, it's probably not a good idea for you to even drive too close by here again. You've seen *Mission Impossible*?"

"For sure."

"Well, I'll be in touch. Go now, hurry—they're probably watching the building."

She turned to go, and Glibspet watched the cheeks of that wondrous ass rise and fall. What a waste. "Muffy," he asked as she reached the door, "what's your major?"

"Multicultural gender neutral childhood education."

"Ah. I thought so. Hurry now!"

The door closed behind her, and Glibspet leaned against the wall. He felt so useless sometimes. How could Hell do any worse to these people than they did to themselves? Then he remembered Helen Norton and cheered back up.

Glibspet heard the door handle click this time before the buzzer sounded. The door swung open slowly and revealed a dark-haired young man in his late twenties. He was staring back over his shoulder at something. He stood that way a second, then shrugged and walked across the threshold. "Oh, hello," he said as he looked ahead and saw Glibspet. "Do you know what that was all about? I just ran into a girl in the parking lot and she seemed terrified of me. Called me an imperialist male pig, and drove off like someone was after her."

"I don't have any idea," Glibspet said. "We get a lot of strange types around here. And you are?"

"Oh, sorry. I'm Craig Mindenhall. I'm here about your research assistant position. I would have been here sooner, but there was some sort of terrible pile-up out on I-85, and I was stuck for forty-five minutes."

"It happens," Glibspet said. "I'm Dominic Glib."

"Pleased to meet you," said Mindenhall, shaking his hand. "I was reading your ad, and I think I might be a good match for you."

"Do you have any research experience?" Glibspet asked.

"Yes," Mindenhall said. "I know it's not exactly detective work, but I used to do trademark searches at an ad agency, to make sure we didn't name a product something that already existed, like calling a new car 'The Timex.' I also worked at a newspaper, and I had to verify all the facts in the consumer reports."

"Hmm, not bad," Glibspet said. "Can you give any references?"

"I can for those two jobs," Mindenhall said, "and for my time at Clemson, but I can't give you anything recent, because I've been working for myself as a freelance designer the last several years. I plan to keep doing that, but I need some more cash coming in to keep up the house payments because I just split up with my housemate. No, wait a minute—" Mindenhall stood up straighter and looked Glibspet in the eyes. "I told myself I wasn't going to weasel. Because I just broke up with my boyfriend. Is that a problem?"

Well, that put an interesting spin on things, Glibspet thought. He generally sought out women, but he wasn't averse to a little equal-opportunity work—and the guy *was* attractive. Setting him up might be a worthwhile project. Especially if he could help Glibspet find Averial during the process. "No," he said, "in fact, I'm gay myself."

"A gay P.I.?" Mindenhall said.

Glibspet shrugged, "Hey, we're everywhere. You know that."

"Yeah, somehow I just hadn't thought about P.I.s before."

"Believe it," Glibspet said. He crossed his arms over his chest and stared down at his shoes for a minute, trying hard to appear deep in thought. When he looked back up again, he sighed and smiled. "Okay. I've decided. I'm going to offer you the job."

Mindenhall blinked in surprise. "Just like that?" he asked.

"Just like that."

"But, my references, my school record . . ."

"Anyone can get references," Glibspet said, "And fake out a professor. I go on my instincts, and they say you're my guy."

Mindenhall frowned. "You're not offering me the position just because I'm gay, are you, Mr. Glib? I don't like quotas, even reverse ones."

"Not at all," Glibspet said. "I won't lie to you, Craig. Your being gay is a minor plus, but I run a business here, and I'm going to pick whoever can help me do it best. Come into my office and we'll talk about salaries and job descriptions, and you can decide whether you want the position." He opened the office door, glanced in, and turned back to his new hire. "By the way, you'd better wheel one of those chairs over there in—the one I've got in the office right now isn't very good. Oh, and call me Dom."

It didn't take very long to come to terms with Mindenhall on salary. Glibspet was determined to have him, and was willing to go to the far side of generous to get him. Job duties took a little longer.

"I understand all that, Dom," Mindenhall said, "but do we really have to lie about what we're doing?"

"Sometimes, yes, absolutely," Glibspet said. "There are a lot of people who will spill their guts to anyone—except a detective. Can you handle that?"

Mindenhall looked troubled. "I guess so," he said finally. "I try to be a good Catholic, and I think lying is wrong. But as long as we aren't working to hurt someone, I think I can do it."

A good Catholic—better and better. "I only take on the best causes, Craig," Glibspet assured him. "Finding runaway children for their parents, locating missing wives or husbands for spouses who need to know what has happened to the people they love. You're going to be doing public service work." He pressed his fingers together and gave Mindenhall his best sincere smile. "Sometimes it's a mission."

The young man took that in, mulled it around for a moment, and smiled at last. "Then we have a deal, Dom."

"Marvelous! I don't suppose you'd care to seal it over dinner this evening?"

Mindenhall looked surprised, then conflicted. "No. I'd . . . rather not," he said. "It's just too soon after Frank and I split. I need some time by myself."

Glibspet took Mindenhall's hands and held them between his. "It's all right, Craig," he said. "I understand about loss. I lost Mike several years ago, and there hasn't been anyone for me since then. If you ever need a shoulder to cry on, just let me know."

With a thoughtful expression, Mindenhall said, "It's . . . difficult to lose someone. I appreciate your concern." He stood up. "I've got some things I have to take care of. You'll call when you need me?"

"Count on it."

Mindenhall stopped halfway out the door. "The Yellow Pages' ad for Glibspet Investigations made it look like the boss was a demon."

"Devil," Glibspet corrected. "Is that a problem?"

Mindenhall frowned. "You tell me."

"Frankly, he rarely comes in. He's tired of the place and looking to sell. If he makes the right offer, I'm looking to buy. Otherwise—nah, he's no problem."

Mindenhall nodded thoughtfully. "Okay, then. I admit I still worry about those guys." He shrugged and walked out, closing the door behind him.

Glibspet waited until he heard the outer door close, too. Then he smiled. "You should," he whispered. He started humming "Time is on My Side." This was going to be *fun*.

# Chapter 16

Jack had been staring at the same trace for ten minutes when a pair of hands closed on his neck. Hot hands. He bolted from his seat, ducked and turned. Spec sheets flew everywhere as he closed with his assailant. It was Rhea. He crouched in confusion for a second, his body saying "fight or flight," his mind saying "friend."

"Um, you looked like you could really use a good neck rub," she offered. Her expression was all wide-eyed innocence, and her tone was serious, but there was a twitch at the corner of her mouth as her lips threatened to rise in a grin.

"Don't give me that," Jack said. "I know y'all just love to see me jump. What am I going to have to do—put a proximity alarm in my door?"

"Well . . . you are very, um, entertaining, to surprise," Rhea admitted. "But the offer for the neck rub *is* sincere."

Jack sighed. He *was* a little stiff, and a neck rub would be the best thing that had happened to him all day. "Yeah. Okay, sure. That sounds good, actually." He sat down again, leaned forward, and tried to relax his shoulders.

Rhea's hands *were* hot, wonderfully so. And she obviously knew what she was doing. Her thumbs pressed and released, pressed and released against neck muscles that hurt more than he'd ever realized, while her fingers worked in tiny, soothing circles across his shoulders. He didn't have to concentrate on relaxing; then suddenly his head sagged forward and he caught himself, realizing that he'd drifted into a tranced state, almost into sleep. "Whoa, stop." He shook his head and rubbed his eyes with his knuckles. "You're going to put me to sleep," he said.

Rhea moved back, and the air rustling the hairs on his neck was cold by comparison. "Do you know what time it is?" she asked.

"Eight?" Jack hazarded, then looked at his watch. It was two A.M. "Damn," he said. "What are *you* still doing here?"

"I had some paperwork to do. Things don't just run themselves. Unfortunately."

"I know," Jack said. He spun his chair around to face her and leaned his elbows against his desktop. "Suit stuff. I hate it. That's why I'd never want your job."

Rhea frowned. "I suspect you're one of the few people at Celestial who could do my job, Jack. You don't have to *be* a suit to work with them. You just have to remember you're a lot smarter than they are, and keep the rules of their silly little games straight."

"I know," Jack said. "Sorry. I didn't mean to imply you were one of them. I've worked for suits, I know suits, and you're no suit."

Rhea laughed. "Well, I'm no Jack Kennedy either," she said. "And what are *you* doing here at two in the morning?"

Jack launched into his tale of modulator board woe, and Rhea listened intently. "And I've run emulations on my workstation, and traced the schematic fifty times. There's no way I could be getting any overloads in there, yet I've blown the circuit time and again." He looked up at Rhea; her titian hair framed a face deep in thought, with eyes focused a million miles away. Somewhere out with the stars she wanted to reach. She looked as classically beautiful as any statue, but he knew she wasn't marble cold. Not by a long shot.

Then her eyes were focused on him again, and he felt heat rising to his face as he realized he'd been staring at her, and that she'd said something, and that he hadn't heard a word of it. "Uh, what was that?" he asked.

"A-flat, you said?" she repeated.

"Yeah. Think so. I don't have perfect pitch, but I'm not bad."

"Hmm. A-flat. That's interesting. I wonder if we're getting some kind of bleed-through or resonance. Let me see that schematic." She bent down beside him and he was aware suddenly that her right breast was nestled against his arm. It seemed happy there, but his better judgment advised a hasty strategic retreat. *Not so fast*, his hormones argued. *A frontal approach might be a better idea*. He compromised on gridlock, not moving at all except to look down instead of across at her. That gave him a good view of her long, sexy toes and bare legs, which didn't help at all. Neither did the smell of roses that surrounded her, more subtle than perfume. Jack began to sweat. He certainly wasn't sleepy anymore.

If Rhea knew what she was doing to him, she gave no sign. The corners of her mouth were turned up slightly, but that seemed to be her habitual expression. Certainly her eyes were intent on the printout. "No," she said, straightening up again—a move that filled him with regret. "You've done a good job on the layout—I never would have thought of half these optimizations. I don't see where the margins are tight enough anywhere to give you any bleed-through, and it looks like you've got enough damping to handle any resonance. Can you fire it up for a minute?"

"Sure. It's ready to go now; I fixed the last blowout a while back." He took the much-patched board back over to the trolley, and went through the hookup ritual. He flipped the switch and the familiar A-flat tone filled the room.

"Kind of pleasant, actually," Rhea observed.

"Maybe," Jack said, "but you can get a pitch pipe for pennies that would be just as good." The tone suddenly gargled to a stop as a little puff of smoke rose from the trolley. "Well, there it goes," he said, pointing. "I've seen a lot of that lately, and if we check, it'll be some part that couldn't possibly blow."

Rhea came to a decision. "Go home, Jack," she said. "You're not going to make any progress beating it to death tonight."

"But . . ."

"No buts." She hooked her arm under his and pulled him up with surprising strength. "I don't pay you to work twenty-four hours a day—I pay you to solve problems."

"I always assumed you were paying for my good looks."

"Angling for a salary reduction, hmm?" Rhea laughed. "Go home and get some sleep. I don't want to see you back here until after lunch tomorr—today."

That seemed like a good idea. The rush of adrenaline was subsiding, and Jack was suddenly dog-tired again. By the time they got to the parking lot, he was weaving on his feet, and the drive home was a real ordeal despite the lack of traffic. It was understandable then, perhaps, that by the time he dragged himself out of the car and up the front steps, Jack had completely forgotten about his morning and his gargoyle. She had not, of course, forgotten about him.

Some days, he concluded as he raced through his second emergency shower in twenty-four hours, life sucks.

# Chapter 17

THIRTY-SEVEN INJURED IN NORTH CAROLINA
CONCERT FRACAS
Raleigh, NC — UPI

Tragedy struck the Walnut Creek Amphitheater Thursday as a mob of three to four thousand stormed the stage during the first public performance of the band Precipitous Descent. Thirty-seven trampling injuries resulted, six of them serious.

The violence broke out during an unrequested encore featuring songs associated with Barry Manilow and concluding with "Having My Baby," originally recorded by Mac Davis.

The first signs of trouble came earlier as the band opened with a medley featuring the Eagles' "Desperado" and "Tequila Sunrise," America's "Horse With No Name," and Debbie Boone's "You Light Up My Life." The audience began to boo the band, and escalated to throwing things when they performed a trio of Olivia Newton-John songs beginning with "I Honestly Love You," and ending with "Please, Mister, Please, Don't Play B-17."

Eighteen thousand hard-core and death metal fans had waited in line for as long as forty-eight hours to get tickets for the first stop in Precipitous

Descent's much-hyped Tour from Hell. Expecta-
tions had been so high because all the band's
members are devils, and as the leather-clad band
first took the stage, the crowd roared approval
and hundreds of young women near the front
ripped blouses and bras to throw at the band.

When the riot broke out, the members of
Precipitous Descent teleported from the amphitheater; none were harmed during the incident.
Reached later for comment, band leader Slash
Malendel said, "Well, what kind of music did they
think we play in Hell?" Malendel could not
confirm any further concert dates for the band.


Rhea pulled her car into the driveway and parked under
the old oak tree. She shut the motor off and gave a sigh
of relief. Roberts was apparently fighting an epic guerrilla
action at TRITEL, but no money had come down the
pike yet. Jack was still blowing circuit boards, and starting
to get really tense, and she knew probably half of her
troops had résumés out. On top of that, she had a briefcase
full of papers she was supposed to care about. She sat
in the car a moment, letting it all slough off. She was
home now, and she wasn't going to let it get to her.

Rhea grabbed her briefcase and shoved open the
Triumph's door, stepping out into the mild April night.
She could see stars up through the delicate lace of the
oak's budding branches. The leaves would be all the way
out in another week, and by June she'd be glad for the
shade. She walked up the steps to the front door and
let herself in. The cozy den welcomed her and she
decided that the briefcase could wait. Some quality time
was decidedly in order. All she really wanted now was a
cup of hot tea and good music on the stereo. Laurie
Anderson's *Big Science* and *Horowitz in Moscow* should
take care of the latter, and she'd been saving some Ceylon
Select for the former.

She slipped off her shoes, popped the audio ROMs into the player, sequenced them, and clipped the tracker to her collar. The mechanical rhythms of "Oh, Superman" filled the room, and she tapped her toes in time for a few seconds, then headed for the kitchen to heat some water. As she moved, the music followed her, staying perfectly balanced. Instant relief.

Except it was too good to last.

As soon as she felt the supernal barrier laid across her kitchen threshold, Rhea knew she was not going to have a relaxing evening. It could have been worse. The barrier could have been composed of negative energy—that would have been bad. This was so blatantly benign and cheerfully upbeat it almost hurt . . . and that was bad enough.

"All right," she said, "I know you're here. Come on out and show yourselves." The air shimmered and suddenly there was a glowing angel sitting on her counter over the dishwasher. It had been a long time, but she still remembered the energy, and the face. Miramuel.

"Hello Aver—" Miramuel started when something inside the refrigerator crashed and the door flew open. A large angel stumbled out amidst a shower of cold cuts and vegetables. He got his balance and began frantically reshelving things. Finally he looked at her sheepishly. Remufel. Some things never changed. "Hello, Averial," he said.

"Long time, no see, Remmy," Rhea said. She was startled to discover that she'd missed both of them. She hadn't thought about either of them in millennia, but now that they were in her kitchen, her heart felt like a huge hole had been filled. They had been her dearest friends once, but where she had sided with the right of free expression, however mistaken that expression might be, they had taken the more conformist line. Maybe they'd been right. She found, however, that the fact that they didn't take her side during that first big disagreement still hurt. The smile that had started to cross her face at the sight of them died, stillborn. Instead of the joyous greetings she'd almost given, she said, "I didn't mean you had to show yourself right at that exact instant, you know. You could have come out of the refrigerator first."

He hung his head, "I'm sorry, Avy," he said, "I just get so deep in thought sometimes that I get flustered."

"Deep in salami, more like." Miramuel arched an eyebrow.

"Well, you know we don't eat up there," he said.

"You don't get hungry either," Rhea said dryly.

"I know, but sometimes I *miss* being hungry, you know?"

Rhea cocked her head and smiled. "Really? Could it be that everything's not perfect in Heaven?"

"No, no! It's fine," Remufel glanced over his shoulder and winced. "Couldn't be better."

"You don't have to suck up, Remmy," Miramuel said. To Rhea, she said, "Remmy's been bucking for an assignment as a mortal. Ever since we got the news that Agonostis got out of Hell and got to become mortal, he's been itching to . . . ah . . . spread his wings, as it were. But what with new soul placements and reincarnations and . . . er . . . folks from *your* side of the Chasm converting to mortal status . . . and the sudden interest in advancement to mortality among the Heavenly Host, there's quite a waiting list for new births. And God is insisting that the Heavensent who convert to mortal have to start as newborns. No obvious miracles, he says. No direct signs of Heaven's presence."

Remufel said, "Everyone on the waiting list has gotten a little touchy."

Rhea smiled. Heaven's waiting lists for plum assignments were notorious. Apparently, while the idea of what constituted a plum assignment had changed, the structure hadn't. "So . . . what brings you two here?" she asked.

Remufel closed the refrigerator door. "Old friends can't just drop in for a visit? We've missed you, and we couldn't visit you . . . before."

Rhea pulled a chair out from under the kitchen table and sat down. "That's bullshit, Remmy," she said. "I've been here two years now. He has to have known that. I imagine you knew it, too."

Miramuel tapped her heels on the dishwasher and studied a nonexistent spot on the wall just above Rhea's left shoulder. "Everyone has been so busy dealing with details of the Unchaining that we just haven't had the chance to get away."

"You're a lousy liar, Mir."

"Averial—"

"Call me Rhea," Rhea said, "Averial was another person, a long time ago. And dim the auras a bit, too, would you? My eyes don't tolerate that light the way they once did."

"Fine. *Rhea*, then." Miramuel dropped her nimbus to a faint luster. Remmy followed suit. "Anyway, I'm sure His Gloriousness knew the second you arrived, and I admit, we knew you were here not too long after, but . . . we really have been busy with the events related to the Unchaining. We couldn't get here any sooner."

Half an eternity in Hell had given Rhea a good ear for bad stories. She was hearing one right then, but she couldn't figure out which part of it was true, and which was false. She decided to play along. Sooner or later her old friends would get around to what they really wanted. She'd figure out why they were lying about it when they did.

Remufel said, "You're right, though. There's more to our visit than just talking about old times. We want you to come home, Av—Rhea."

"Please. Just come home now. Apologize and everything

will be forgiven. *Everything.*" Miramuel punctuated the statement with a particularly strong tap, and the dishwasher surged into action. Startled, she sprang from the counter top, catching her vestments on the dishwasher latch. The hinged door crashed open and hot sudsy water and silverware spewed everywhere.

Rhea rushed to help Miramuel. Together they disengaged her robe from the washer door; the look on Mir's face as she tried to wring soapy water out of her robes was priceless. As Rhea tugged the hem free from the catch, she saw Remufel ease open the refrigerator door and spirit out a Saran-wrapped bowl of chocolate pudding. He looked so ridiculous; his oversized wings half unfurled, his movements furtive, the expression on his face one a little boy would wear when sneaking cookies from a cookie jar.

She couldn't help herself. She sank to the floor by Miramuel, unable to keep from laughing.

Both Miramuel and Remufel looked hurt, though Remmy didn't put the pudding back. Mir said, "That's right. Just laugh. Your house attacks me and you think it's funny." She thought for a second, picked up a wet fork and shook the water off of it. "I guess it is, though, isn't it?"

Rhea stood up, and gave Miramuel a quick hug. "I'm sorry," she said, "I couldn't help it." She opened the cabinet under the sink, pulled a towel off the rack and started to mop the floor dry.

"Going native?" Miramuel asked.

"What do you mean?"

Miramuel pointed, "Manual labor?"

"Never hurt anyone," Rhea said. "Besides, I'm lying low." She figured they already knew that, but if they were pretending not to, she'd pretend she believed them.

"My treat then," Miramuel said, and suddenly the floor was bone dry.

Remufel put down the pudding bowl and ambled over

to the open dishwasher, poking curiously at the disarrayed assortment of dishes and utensils on the shelves.

"Remmy, don't fool with Avy's stuff," Mir said. She pulled out a chair by Rhea's and sat down. Rhea settled back into her own chair. "Now, as I was saying, before I was assaulted—"

"Hey, Av—Rhea, what's this?" Remufel asked, pulling a long, slightly tapered cylinder of pink silicone from the back of the top rack. It glistened wetly and wobbled in his grip.

Rhea felt the blood rush to her face. "That's, um, a . . . uh," she stammered. "Oh, Hell, you don't want to know. Just put it back, and come over here and sit down." She wondered at her reaction. She had become inured to Hell, and the events of her life prior to the Unchaining would have made a sailor faint, but in the company of her old friends, she was blushing like a nun teaching the rhythm method.

Miramuel looked at her sharply as Remufel came over. Rhea met her gaze and shrugged, her face still hot. Remufel's chair creaked as he sat down. He leaned forward and put his elbows on the table. "What Mir's trying to say is that we need you. There's a lot of good to be done on this world, Rhea, and you could be one of the doers again."

"That's right," Miramuel said. "Heaven needs you back. Now more than ever. God will forgive the past."

"Maybe He will, but will I?" Rhea turned to Remufel. "Are we shielded here?" she asked. He nodded. "Okay, then, look." Rhea closed her eyes and concentrated, dropping her human manifestation.

When she opened her eyes, Miramuel and Remufel had pulled away from her, twin expressions of horror on their faces. "This is what I am now," Rhea said. "This is what happened to me because I argued that Lucifer deserved a fair hearing. They have a name here for what

I did: devil's advocate. I didn't agree with Lucifer, didn't think his plan was any good, but if you're not going to listen to what the angels have to say, why give us free will? Lucifer may have fallen, but I was pushed."

"That's not true, Rhea," Miramuel said, leaning close again. "Nobody had to go, not even Lucifer. All of you could have . . . can recant at any time."

"How can I recant something I don't believe was wrong? Are you saying I should lie, *could* lie—to Him? I was a prisoner of conscience. I never agreed with what Lucifer did . . . but I still agree with what *I* did."

Remufel said. "You've had a long time to think about everything. Maybe it's time to reconsider. You've already made a partial break with Hell—we couldn't be here otherwise. Why not make it complete? Come back with us tonight."

Rhea stood up and started pacing. "Do you know what it's like to be denied Heaven, Remmy?" she asked. "Denied Heaven by my thoughts, and denied Earth by Lucifer's orders? I spent thousands of years in Hell. I did things there, awful things—and sometimes I enjoyed them. Hell does that to you. I *did* have a lot of time to think, and when the Unchaining came, I knew exactly what I was going to do.

"Earth is the glory of Creation, and here I stay." She stopped pacing and looked out the window over the sink. Was there any way to make them understand? She doubted it. "You say I should be a doer, come back to heaven to fight for right—I am going to give these people the stars and trust *them* to do right."

Miramuel frowned. "Lucifer was going to make things easy for them, too, and look where it got him. If they aren't ready . . ."

Rhea walked to the kitchen window and opened it. A mild green-scented breeze idled its way in. "They have so little, but they're clawing their way up," she said. "How many symphonies have been composed in Heaven during the last ten million years, Mir? How many rap songs? Name me an angel who's written a book."

"That's not the point, Rhea," Miramuel said.

"Well, it is the point, in a manner of speaking," Remufel interrupted, "or at least it's *a* point. But it isn't what we're driving at. We see their worth. We love them too. It's unleashing their potential for evil that worries me. Us. That space drive—" He flushed and cut off the sentence midway. "The forces of Hell are loose in this state and the people are making an *accommodation* to evil. To Hell."

Rhea filled the tea kettle at the sink and set it on the stove to heat. Mir and Remmy knew evil the way some people knew Latin. Perfectly, and without any firsthand experience. "It's not that simple, Mir," she said. "They've lived over fifty years now with the ability to destroy themselves completely. They haven't done it, and I don't think they will." She shook her head. "We sit inside the borders of a country that has dedicated itself for more than two hundred years to the proposition that tyranny is not the natural state of man. It doesn't always do a good job of meeting its ideals, but it has never stopped trying. Reaching. I have people working for me now who once would have been flogged for trying to read, lynched for demanding to vote—except that brave men and women worked, suffered and sometimes died to forge those ideals into reality. And the idealists are still out there. Still reaching." Rhea spread her arms to encompass the world. "I'm moving them past a minor technical block. Allowing them to reach beyond the well of the world, Mir. Here I am, and here I stay. I can do no other."

Miramuel looked at Remufel. "Told you so," she said to him. He shrugged.

"We kind of expected that, Rhea," he said, "and we're

sorry you feel that way. We'll shield you from Hell as much as we can without specific authority. And, well, we'll be here in your kitchen for the duration."

That didn't sound good. "The duration? The duration of what?"

"Can't tell you," Miramuel said. "But our orders are to set up a permanent angelic presence, and we can't do it in a place where we would have physical contact with mortals. That leaves you. Here we are, and this is our headquarters."

"My kitchen?"

"They were *very* specific orders. Oh, we'll be making sorties . . . and doing observation work—"

"—lots of observation work—"

"—but most of the time, we'll be here. Right here. We'll have lots of time to talk."

"I've got a life, Mir. I'm happy to see the two of you, but not as permanent residents. What if I have company?"

"Don't worry. We'll go immaterial if that happens."

"But what if I have *male* company?" Somewhat to her surprise, Rhea found herself thinking of Jack.

Miramuel considered. "Are you married? I mean, as a human."

"Of course I'm not married! I just happen to like men— a lot. If that shocks you, I'm sorry, but it *is* my house."

"Well, if you're not married, I imagine we'd have to keep a pretty close watch on you and any man." Miramuel grinned. "If he were really a temptation, we might have to bless him with a sound, invigorating sleep."

Rhea closed her eyes. That was all she needed: two friendly but prissy angels watching her every move. "You're kidding, aren't you, Mir?" she asked.

Mir smiled her angelic smile. "Remember, you can leave all this behind at any time."

"Leave what you're doing here. Come back. Help us," Remufel added.

"Become a force for good in the world. *Sanctioned, approved* good."

Remufel said, "As long as we're here, though, have you got any more of that chocolate pudding?"

In the living room, Laurie Anderson sang, "Put your head in your hands." Rhea thought it sounded like good advice.

# Chapter 18

Jack was up early again. He hadn't really planned it, and at this stage, it was more anxiety than anticipation that drove him from bed. Still, a nice leisurely breakfast at home would be a welcome change from Hardee's, and still give him time to beat the rush hour traffic.

He stepped into the shower and turned the hot water faucet until the pipes started to vibrate, then backed off a quarter turn, counted ten and ran the cold water up half a turn. It was a combination he'd painstakingly worked out. He could run the hot up gradually from there, but any other start and the pipes would start knocking plaster off the walls. He'd have to fix that one day.

He dried quickly afterwards, and pulled on his clothes. He almost tripped as the printout that spread down the hall slid under his feet. It was really time to do something about that. It had to be a fire hazard. He bent over and looked at it. It must have meant something to him once, but now he didn't have a clue.

Better leave it, then.

*Pancakes*, he thought, surveying the kitchen. There should be a box of Hungry Jack over the stove, and a bottle of Mrs. Butterworth. There was, but he wasn't the only one who knew it. The pancake mix was full of weevils. He threw the box towards the trash. Amazingly, it landed right on the corner of the trash can, teetered and stabilized.

*Great*, he thought. *Weevils wobble, but they don't fall down*. He walked over and gave the box a shove.

Now what? Bacon, eggs and grits would be great, except he didn't have any bacon or eggs, and the grits had all coagulated into one massive king grit that seemed to dare him to boil it. Jack was starting to remember why he usually ate at Hardee's.

Well, cereal and toast then. Jack opened the refrigerator, hit the side panel twice to unfreeze the light switch and looked for the milk. There it was, near the 1983 fruitcake. He poured a bowl of bite-size shredded wheat, spooned a little sugar onto it and upended the milk carton. He didn't think *schloooourp* was a good sound for pouring milk to make. He was right.

Jack poured the whole mess down the garbage disposal. He looked outside. The sun was just coming up. If he left now, he could still go by Hardee's.

Jack had gotten used to going out through the back door. He walked to the end of the carport and looked up at the little mirror he'd put in the oak tree. It showed the roof, and even in the early morning gloom, he could see that the coast was clear. So far, his gargoyle hadn't moved from over the front door.

He waved up at her as he walked to the car. Actually, he felt a lot less hostility after the incident with the Jehovah's Witnesses, but still, he was going to have to do *something*. He'd tried everything he could think of to get rid of her: conspicuous good deeds, pokes with a sharp stick, KC & The Sunshine Band—nothing worked. She would answer his questions sometimes, but nothing else got a rise out of her. Maybe he should try to *talk* her down somehow. Otherwise . . . well, perhaps it was time to consider de-gargoyling as an engineering problem.

Jack buckled his lap belt and turned the key. Nothing happened. He sighed and popped the trunk. He was going to have to do something about that starter someday too.

# Chapter 19

It was still early when he got to Research Triangle Park, and there were only a couple of cars in the lot. Jan's shiny '55 Chevy stood out like a greyhound among wiener dogs. Jack loved his Camry, but for Jan's car he felt pure lust. He put his nose to the driver's side window and looked at the odometer: still only twenty-five thousand miles— Jan's great-grandmother had not been a champion explorer. He shook his head in wonder and tore himself away.

Jan was already behind her terminal when Jack got to the third floor. "Good morning," he said.

She looked up from her screen. "Oh, hi, Jack. What brings you up here? Slumming?"

"Nah," he said. "Just thought I'd save you the trip downstairs with my mail . . . and figured maybe I'd see if you've shaken anything hot loose from the grapevine."

Jan laughed, "You mean, like will we still have jobs?"

Jack sat down on the edge of her desk. "Yeah, that's a good one," he said. " 'Enquiring' minds want to know."

"I don't know, Jack," she said seriously. "It looked real good for a while there, after that TRITEL guy was here, but it's been holding at ninety-nine percent done since then, and I'm starting to get a bad feeling about it." She tapped her screen, "See my résumé?"

"That serious, huh?" Jack leaned over and looked. "Special Executive Assistant to the President in charge of Administration," he read. "Sounds pretty impressive."

Jan shrugged. "A little title inflation never hurt anyone. Besides, this one's a fishing expedition. I've already got three solid offers." She sighed. "Be a damn shame if I have to take one, though. This job has been about the most fun I've ever had vertical." She nudged him and unleashed a wicked grin. "Be a worse shame, though, if you leave without jumping Rhea's bones."

Jack knew he shouldn't be surprised by anything Jan came out with. She always said exactly what was on her mind, and as she'd told him more than once, A filthy mind's a terrible thing to waste. Still, even taking that into account, all he could think of to say was, "*What?*"

Jan winked. "She's warm for you, Jack. A woman knows. I'm surprised she hasn't attacked you in the stairwell yet. Think about it—all the other engineers come to her with progress reports. She comes to you for yours."

Jack shifted uncomfortably. "Nobody else is holding up the whole project," he said, but his body was remembering their last late night session and the scent of roses. Could it be Jan was right? Couldn't be, he decided. A man didn't get luck like that twice in a lifetime. But still—those hands . . .

"Earth to Jack, Earth to Jack." A nasal voice broke into his thoughts. His eyes refocused, and Jan grinned at him and let go of her nose.

"No, I don't see it," he told her.

"Don't see it, can't imagine it?"

"Nooo," Jack said slowly.

"Okay, then, stand up."

"What?"

"Stand up, right now."

Jack was suddenly acutely aware that he'd better not. He blushed. "I'm not finished with our chat," he said. Jan's wicked grin flashed pure triumph. "Thought so," she said.

"Maybe your *mind* can't imagine it." She leaned back in her swivel chair and put her hands behind her neck. "Life's a lot more fun if you don't let your mind run it all the time, Jack."

"Last time I didn't was a big mess," Jack said, remembering Carol.

"Have it your way," Jan said. "Maybe it's just as well. If this all falls through, then you'll only be losing a job." She sat back up again. "So, would you like your mail?"

"Uh, sure," Jack said, off balance again.

"Here," she stood and handed him a scraggly pile of paper. "Three copies of *Circuit Week*, each with a different spelling of your name, five companies trying to sell you test equipment, two calls for papers, three faxes that came in for you last night, and—for reasons which I can't pretend to fathom, but which I'm sure make perfect sense, one copy for 'Jake Hanloran' of Frederick's of Hollywood's latest catalog. Do be sure to check page thirty-four."

Jack checked page thirty-four. "That's certainly, um, inspiring, Jan," he admitted.

"Look at the price though," she cautioned. "To get that much money for that little fabric, they must be charging by the molecule."

He winked at her. "Yes, but those are very *happy* molecules."

Jan laughed. "Off with you then, before you corrupt my virgin ears. And Jack—" she said as he turned to go, "think about what I said, hmm?"

Jack did think about it all the way back to his office. Certainly Rhea had never shown anything other than a friendly interest in him. Had she? He was certainly going to look a lot more sharply in the future.

# Chapter 20

Rhea was coming up the stairs as Jack went down. She looked great, just like the *after* segment of a coffee commercial, and Jack would have sworn she was a morning person, despite the fact that he knew she looked just as good at two A.M.

"Good morning," she said. "In a bit early today, aren't you?"

"Couldn't sleep," Jack admitted. "This thing is still driving me crazy."

Rhea leaned back against the stair railing. "Still the same symptoms?" she asked.

"Yeah, about. I've got to the point where I can blow the lights now, too, sometimes."

"Well, now, that *is* progress," she said. "If you can scale that up towards stopping the whole world around it, the drive ought to move by virtue of inertia."

"I won't rule it out," Jack said. He shifted his grip on his mail. "What about you? Any word on our funding?"

Rhea looked down, and explored the crack between two concrete blocks with her toes. *Not a good sign*, Jack thought.

"I'm working it," she said finally. "I'll make an announcement to the whole company when I have something definitive to say."

Meaning she wasn't going to say anything else about

it to him, now. Well, he shouldn't really expect her to. "Hang in there," he told her. "We're all pulling for you."

"Thanks," Rhea said. "That means more than you know."

She paused and glanced at his armload of paper. "Interesting technical manual there," she commented.

Jack had forgotten exactly what he was carrying. "Um, research," he said. "Definitely research material. In fact, I'd better get it down to my office and get started right away. See you!" He passed Rhea and headed down the stairs.

"Remember, I can't use you if you go blind," Rhea called down to him as he reached the second floor, and then, as the stairwell door closed behind him, he thought he heard something else that sounded a lot like, "But I do a great page thirty-four!"

# Chapter 21

Glibspet was smiling. He'd just paid for a box of Bugles with a two-party check drawn on a Venezuelan bank, and he'd held the line up for thirty-five minutes. He'd even gotten change. Now he was sitting at his desk eating the little cornucopias and planning his next move on several cases.

He'd found the runaway kid he'd been looking for and he'd like to close the books on that one, but if he waited a few more days before telling her parents, she would probably have turned her first trick. *Wait*, he decided. He didn't need the money yet. If it came to that, *he* could break her in and still make a profit.

The lost dog case? Well, he'd never collect on that one, and he'd carefully worded the contract so that he wouldn't have to. He closed out the file. For a poodle that juicy and tender, it had been worth it.

The Averial case, though, was definitely still open. The past few weeks had been unpleasant, with the Three Stooges popping into his office at odd times and making life miserable for him. So far, though, they'd been careful not to do anything that would blow his cover with Mindenhall—they were catching enough hell in Hell for Averial's continued absence that they weren't doing anything that might make him fail. He'd never seen three Fallen so scared.

Scared was the way he liked them.

He pulled a list of ideas he'd been considering from his drawer and called in Mindenhall. He handed him the list. "These are some directions I've been considering for the Avi Baker case," he said. He'd come up with the name Avi Baker for Averial because he didn't think good Catholic Craig would take much of a fancy to hunting Fallen angels for Fallen clients. "Run these down, will you? I'm going to chase a few maybe-leads of my own."

Craig studied the list for a moment, then nodded. "I'll get right on it."

Mindenhall headed for the door, and Glibspet watched his retreating ass. The longer he didn't have it, the more attractive it got. Still, it wouldn't do to hurry; Mindenhall was a long-term project, and in the meantime, he was doing good footwork on the search for Averial. No leads yet, but every negative result narrowed the possibilities. And he'd gotten information for Glibspet that *had* broken a few other cases.

Glibspet heard the outer door shut. Good. Now he could eliminate some more possibilities. He opened a desk drawer and took out a small, bright red modem, which he hooked to the serial port on the back of his PC. There was no place on the modem for a phone jack or power cord. That didn't matter. He was calling up Hell Online. It was one edge the Hellraised had over Heaven—Hell had all the best programmers. Heaven had who? Grace Hopper, and that was about it.

Glibspet entered his user ID and password, and cursed as the welcome screen slowly and painfully crawled across his display: The red modem was only three hundred baud. It was, after all, a product of Hell.

Finally the message of the day appeared:

/usr/local/hell filled up again last night. I deleted all home directories and expired all Usenet groups except alt.flame. If you had important data on that partition:

tough shit. I've got better things to do than keep backups, and don't bother coming to me with tapes. Restoring your pathetic little files isn't on my list of top ten million things to do—Cron.

Glibspet thought of all his favorite poodle recipe files and sighed. Hell's sysops got to wreak havoc out of all proportion to their rank. At least they had finally replaced the mainframe and thrown out JCL. Satan himself had decreed that some things even Hell couldn't tolerate.

When he got the main menu, he keyed for access to the damnedsouls database.

Hell had always kept good records on its human occupants. It had to. But in the old days, an exhaustive search through the damnedsouls files would have taken weeks, and would have required stroking a half dozen different bureaucrats and archivists just to get into the file room. Now Glibspet could formulate a very restrictive query and have it answered within minutes. Probably the longest part of the process would be downloading the query hits over the three hundred-baud link.

He thought carefully and typed in an SQL (Satan's Query Language) statement to pull all the female damnedsouls who had died in North Carolina within six months in either direction of the Unchaining who were residents but who had lived there for less than ninety days: two hundred and forty-seven hits. He punched DOWNLOAD and dug in for a wait. He'd have to spend more time after downloading, too, because he was going to have to go through every single hit. Most could probably be eliminated out of hand. He didn't think it was too likely that Averial would have taken the identity of a damnedsoul. Although the information would have been readily available to her, she would have known that all Hell had access to it, too. On the other hand, she might think that they might think she would never do it, and so do it anyway. So he had to check, and he couldn't just skim. He was going to have to do this right.

Glibspet paced while the slow process continued. His silk boxers rubbed against the tender spot at the base of his spine, which started to itch ferociously. The spot had been driving him crazy for days, ever since he got the last of his tail demanifested. He scratched gingerly and looked at his screen. The download was only forty percent complete—he had a little time. He walked into the bathroom, dropped his trousers and rubbed baby oil on the afflicted patch of skin. It didn't help much, but thinking about the baby-rendering factory cheered him up a bit, and when he got back to his office, his PC was flashing READY.

He set the list to printing and unplugged the red modem. It was hot to his touch, and the insulation on the serial cable was a bit singed. That was to be expected; he had yet to find a cable that was fully Hell-compatible. Glibspet let the cable cool for a minute while he put the modem away. The next step would require only his PC's standard internal modem. That, a bit of bribery, some blackmail and probably some plain old-fashioned hacking should get him logged into the databases at the regional insurance agencies. It wasn't hard, really. There had always been a lot of insurance salesmen pledged to Hell, and the agencies had eagerly hired the Hellborn after the Unchaining. Glibspet always had favors he could call in from both crowds. He popped the top off a can of Vienna sausages and started dialing.

Half an hour and two cans later, he had been in half a dozen systems and had about four hundred possibles. He sucked the gelatin off another Vienna appreciatively (one of the few foods whose ingredient list didn't disappoint) and considered his finds. He'd been digging through the companies' "nest prospecting" files. Many insurance agents kept files on paid-out claims so that they could go back later and hit up friends and relatives to buy insurance from them. "Remember your old pal, Joey Feinmeister? We paid out $200,000 smackeroos to the little missus . . . and I know you've seen her new Cadillac. Just think, you too can cash in big . . ."

Glibspet could hardly think of a tackier practice. He figured insurance sales was where used-car dealers went when they couldn't meet the ethical standards anymore. He loved it. More to the point, sometimes the follow-ups found anomalies, and he had a whole list of them now to investigate.

He couldn't afford to neglect the more straightforward approaches, either. Averial was passing as human. One day she was bound to slip and call on Hell for something. All he needed was a single Hellawatt expended to her account; he could backtrace that and discover, if not her exact location, then at least a place where she had been recently. Odds were, it would be someplace where she was known. Where someone, shown a picture of Averial, would recognize a face. Unlike Linufel, Kellubrae, and Venifar, Glibspet wasn't in a major hurry—due to a little point in the contract that the three Fallen had overlooked, he didn't have any deadline for producing his results.

He smiled at that thought.

The three of them were already nearing *their* deadline. The Unholy Head of State wasn't dealing directly with *him*, so he could make things as miserable as he chose for the Three Stooges, knowing that the only repercussions he would face would be from them—and knowing that they didn't dare do much to him, because if they did, he'd screw them worse than he already was.

He ought to tell them he needed more money for expenses, too. That would thrill them no end.

Meanwhile, Averial would wait. She had nowhere else to go.

# Chapter 22

POSTAL CLERK SLAYS SELF IN SHOOTING MELEE
Winston-Salem — The Associated Press

Violence erupted at the main post office in Winston-Salem Tuesday as long-time U.S. Postal Service employee Waddel Fuller pulled a semi-automatic rifle from beneath the customer service counter and fired point-blank at a waiting postal patron. Fuller was killed instantly when the bullet ricocheted off of a chain securing a ballpoint pen to a writing counter and hit him in the temple.

The patron, a devil, was killed but instantly reconstituted. Other patrons, and Postal Service employees, who dived behind sorting racks and postal scales, were unharmed.

Co-workers say that Fuller was distraught at repeated, unreasonable requests from the patron on whom he fired. These apparently included multiple daily hold-mail/start-mail orders and odd stamp requests. Said colleague Mark Snyder, "This time the guy wanted six hundred sixty-six one-cent stamps, and wanted to pay for them with pennies. Wade had just had it."

Postmaster Bob Stern said that Fuller "was a quiet man, and a darn good counter agent. I just can't believe it."

Asked for comment, the devil, who declined

to be identified would say only, "This unfortunate incident should not discourage anyone from stamp collecting as only fifteen stamp collectors have been killed by post office employees during the last year."

Following the incident, a bill materialized in the air over Fuller's body. The bill, for $24,371.35, demanded payment for the destruction of the Hellraised body, but was charged, not to Fuller, but to the Postal Service. Postal officials are forwarding the bill to Washington, DC.

"Dear Steve," Rhea typed. "Thanks for letting me look at your paper. It's brilliant as always, but I think you could derive that tensor sequence on page three a bit more cleanly." She pulled down the math editing menu and keyed in a bristly, frightening-looking equation. "That should eliminate steps five through twelve," she continued. "I look forward to reading the finished version! Take care of yourself."

She added her digitized signature, and hit SEND. The message disappeared from her screen, and Rhea sat back and smiled. It was good to keep her hand in—she didn't get much time nowadays, especially the way things were going.

It had been a long week today. Jan had been on another line every time Rhea had buzzed her, and Rhea strongly suspected she was lining up interviews. It would be easy to check, and she knew Jan would own up to it if asked, but there wouldn't be any point. What was Rhea going to do—ask her people not to look after their own futures? If she couldn't guarantee their jobs, they had every right to look elsewhere, and those who weren't already looking would be soon; she'd seen the black mood during her walk-through this morning. The worst thing was that several people had tried to cheer her up. They were a good bunch, and she was letting them down.

Things had been a lot simpler in Heaven, where money was never an issue and everything worked more or less the way it was supposed to, and a *whole* lot easier in Hell—there you were supposed to let people down if at all possible.

She was worried about Jack too. Not about his job; he would have people calling him if he ever hinted he was ready to leave, but about his well-being. She knew he wasn't getting enough sleep, and she could almost feel the waves of frustration rolling from his office every time she walked in. She wished she could tell him to work on something else for a while, but the MULE drive was the heart of her program. With it, she would have investors. Without it, she had speculators.

She had her own work to do too to keep the ball rolling. It was time she got back to it. She kept three baskets on her desk. One said IN, one said OUT, and one said TOO HARD. The IN basket was empty, so she had no excuse to keep her away from the TOO HARD basket. She sighed, and picked a random sheaf of papers from midway down in the stack. After the first couple of pages, she was seriously considering establishing a TOO BORING basket, but she made herself read through the memo to the end, then drafted a short e-mail note to Jan for action.

Outside the sky was black with low-hanging clouds, and in the distance Rhea could see flashes of lightning. It wasn't raining yet, but the stage was set for a lollapalooza of a spring thunderstorm, and she had a front row seat. Maybe the TOO HARD basket would take a direct hit, but Rhea doubted it. *He* wasn't going to do her any favors.

She pulled another sheaf. This one was a government form with thirteen attachments, all written in Old High Federalese. She started parsing the first paragraph, got sucked down into a dependent clause and didn't come up for air until half a page later—and she still wasn't sure what it said. Rhea frowned. The words were all clear enough, but they didn't seem to get along well together. She pulled a pencil from her desk drawer and diagrammed the sentence. It fell neatly into place, and confirmed her original impression; the second clause completely nullified the first clause for a net meaning of zero. Your tax dollars at work, she thought and took a guess at what the government probably meant for it to mean. She filled out the rest of the form, then tagged it with a Post-It for Jan to mail.

She was debating the merits of trying another TOO HARD versus going skunk wrestling when the phone rang. It was her private line, the one that didn't go through Jan's switchboard. She let it ring three times, then picked it up. "Hello," she said, "Rhea Samuels."

"Ms. Samuels," the voice on the other end said, "this is Al Roberts, TRITEL. Figured you might still be there. Have you eaten?"

"No," Rhea said cautiously, "I haven't."

"Well, can you meet me at the Angus Barn at eight? You can bring the contracts we discussed—I don't think you'll be disappointed."

Rhea looked at her TOO HARD box and laughed. "I'm filling out government forms. A disappointment would be a step up right now. Something good would be beyond belief. So I'll see you at eight."

"Great."

Rhea hung up, smiling. Outside, fat, heavy drops of rain were starting to fall. But maybe, just maybe, she could see a rainbow.

# Chapter 23

The evening roads were slippery when the worst of the rain hit, and Rhea came around a corner too fast and the Triumph started to hydroplane. She came perilously close to expending Hellawatts to stop it. Only quick reflexes and physical strength let her tap the brakes, steer into the spin, and straighten out before she went into the side of the house built right on the corner. From that point onward, she drove at a much slower pace.

Rhea pulled into the lot at the Angus Barn and pounced on an empty parking space. The Angus Barn was a good place, and it was always busy, even at eight P.M. during crappy, miserable weather. She ran the motor for a few minutes, waiting for a break in the rain. It didn't come, so she resigned herself to getting soaked and made a run for it. She wielded her small umbrella like a sword and let her briefcase fend for itself. A slightly damp young hostess got the door for her as Rhea stepped into the old building. It really had been a barn at one time.

"Nice car," the hostess told Rhea as she checked the seating chart.

"Thanks," Rhea said.

"Will it really do two hundred?"

"I don't know," Rhea admitted.

"Wish I could take it out on a day like today—I've never driven a fast car in a storm like this."

"Triumphs are too light to drive fast in bad weather," Rhea told her. Rhea thoroughly approved of the infant and child stages of the human life cycle. She would have loved to have had a childhood herself. Teenagers though, scared her, and she didn't scare easily. But she smiled and said, "Maybe the rain won't let up," in a voice that said she hoped the young woman got the chance to go out and speed through it. She didn't hope that, but she didn't want to be rude, either.

"You think so?" The girl brightened. "I hope you're right. That'd be great." She looked into the vast main room. "Your reservation?"

"Roberts, for eight o'clock."

"Here you are . . . I can seat you now if you'd like."

"Wonderful."

"We'll put you at one twenty."

"Good," Rhea said. "Mr. Roberts will be joining me shortly."

"Got it," the hostess said, and led Rhea across the floor.

Rhea sat and watched the table's hurricane lantern waltz shadows across the red and white squares of the table cloth. She wondered what was keeping Roberts. He'd probably run into the new construction on the interstate. On the best of days, that would slow him down ten minutes if he weren't expecting it, and today was not the best of days. Rhea considered the wine list as she waited. She settled on a glass of Chateau-Reep '85, and sipped thoughtfully, enjoying herself as her waiter pampered her. She had been in some so called "good" restaurants where the staff seemed to have forgotten just *who* was serving *whom*. Not here though. Her waiter was attentive without being smothering, and helpful without being obsequious.

She took a cracker and loaded it with cheese from one of the three crocks on the table. Not bad.

Roberts showed up about fifteen minutes late, looking a little pale. "Sorry," he said as they shook hands. "Some maniac in a Lincoln shot through the roadwork on I-40 doing eighty on the shoulder. An eighteen-wheeler jackknifed to miss him, and about a dozen cars piled into it. I was almost the thirteenth."

"Are you okay?" Rhea asked in concern. "This can wait."

He shook his head. "No, I'm fine. Actually, as far as I can tell, no one was hurt, which has got to be a minor miracle." He sat down across from her and hefted the menu, which probably had more text than *USA Today*, although it had fewer pictures.

"What looks good?" he asked. "It's been a year or three since I was here."

"Well," Rhea said, "I think I'm going to start with the short ribs, but everything sounds wonderful, except maybe the broccoli."

Roberts grinned. "Come on," he said, "how can you dislike such an essentially fractal vegetable?"

"Well," Rhea said, "I prefer chaos theory myself, but it's certainly no strange attractor."

Roberts settled on prime rib au jus, and after the waiter had taken their orders, he poured a glass of wine and sipped appreciatively. He did a good job of putting his traffic adventure behind him.

"Well," he said after a moment, "I won't keep you in suspense." He set the wine glass down and rocked it around on its base. "I've been fighting a pitched battle the last few weeks, but I sneaked around their lines, came up from behind and yelled 'boo!' I don't think they knew what hit them, and I'm hoping they don't find out. If we can come to final terms today, I've got your funding."

"That's good to hear," Rhea told him, trying to keep her voice calm and even. It was hard—what she really wanted to do was jump up and start singing like the frog in the old Warner's cartoon. *Hello, my honey! Hello my baby! Hello, my ragtime gal!* And wouldn't *that* have a salutatory effect on negotiations. She could still blow it, she reminded herself. She could be Michigan J. Frog on the way home if everything worked out. Rhea opened her briefcase, and pulled out a manila folder, which she offered to Roberts.

"This is what my lawyers came up with, based on our last talk," she said. "I've read it, and taken out some of the more weasely sections. I think it's a good deal for both of us. See what you think."

Roberts took the folder and skimmed the boilerplate with an expert eye. It didn't put him to sleep, though Rhea saw him suppress a yawn. When he hit the real meat of the contract, he pushed back from the table and read more slowly, absently whirling his half-full glass with his left hand. "Interesting," he said finally.

Rhea wasn't sure that sounded good. "But?" she prompted.

"Well," he said. "I don't see our little subagreement, the one where—"

*The Ride.* Rhea suppressed a grin. She'd left that out on purpose to catch his attention and mask any other quibbles he might have had. She had him now.

"I thought it might pay to be a little circumspect," she said. She held out a hand and took the folder back, flipping pages rapidly until she was about three-quarters of the way through. "Look here," she said and pointed to a short paragraph.

"Primary TRITEL liaison representative will audit all final operational tests, wherever conducted . . ." Roberts read. He glanced from the paper to her, back to the paper, then back again to her. His eyebrow rose and a little half-smile curled across his lips. "*Wherever* conducted?"

"*Wherever*," Rhea confirmed.

The smile spread slowly across Robert's face until he was lit up like a lighthouse. He put the folder down carefully. "Ms. Samuels," he said, "we have a deal."

It was all Rhea could do to stay in her seat, but she managed. "It just so happens that I have a pen with me," she told him. She smiled at her own excessive casualness—after all, he had to know what a boon this money was going to be for Celestial. "May I?" She took the contract and signed with a flourish, then passed the pen to him.

"Shall I sign in blood, or will ink do?"

Rhea winced. Even now, two years after the Unchaining, some people didn't take it seriously. "Not funny," she said. "Take my advice; don't ever joke about that. Not in North Carolina."

Roberts looked properly chastised. "Sorry," he said, and signed his name with a bold sweep of the pen. "It's just so much like what we used to laugh at the Holy Rollers about that even now sometimes I can't take it seriously." He checked all the carbons and handed the contract back to Rhea. "Are you religious?"

Rhea took the contract, separated the TRITEL carbon and put Celestial's copy in her briefcase. "No," she said. "Not religious at all. But I am . . . careful. Very, very careful." Which was true enough, she thought. She shut the case and spun the thumbwheels of the combination lock. "I don't believe in taking unnecessary risks." She set the case down and grinned. "I do have a pretty flexible definition of necessary though."

Roberts smiled back at her and raised his glass. "A toast then," he said. "*Ad astra per aspera*. Bring on the necessary risks!" They clinked glasses and sipped appreciatively until the waiter arrived with the first course.

The food was excellent, and they made amiable small talk as the Barn gradually emptied. Before Rhea knew it, she was using his first name, and he hers. Finally, over wedges of chocolate cheesecake so rich that Rhea could practically see the militant little calories overflowing her plate and mustering on the table cloth, Roberts got serious again.

"You're an unusual woman, Rhea," he said. "Even today, it's still rare to find women in the sciences. And a physicist who understands business? Forget it."

Rhea didn't like where this was heading. "And don't forget," she interrupted, "a physicist with 'great tits.' "

Roberts paused, but he wasn't deflected. "Yes, they are," he admitted, "and you must have extraordinary eyes, too, to have read my screen from that angle at that distance. You weren't intended to see that. In my own defense, I'll say that it was a sincere appreciation from someone who intensely admires the female form, but realizes that packaging isn't everything." He looked her straight in the eyes. "And in your case, the content is quite as fine as the wrapper. I would consider it a great honor if I could see you socially sometime."

Rhea had been afraid of that, and she didn't know why. Roberts was an attractive and interesting man, and she knew she could do worse. *Had* done worse, on several occasions. Somehow, though, the idea of the two of them just didn't feel right. She laid her hand on his and squeezed lightly. "Thanks, Al," she said. "That means a lot to me. And I want you to know that I think the same of you."

"But—?" Roberts said.

"But, I'm afraid I can't mix sin and business." She smiled a sincere, professional smile and met his eyes. She was lying through her teeth, but he couldn't know that. She'd mixed sin and business with relish before (and it had been an excellent sandwich, she thought. Best on whole wheat.).

Roberts nodded. "Well the sin could wait," he said slowly. "But I understand." He freed his hand and proffered it. "Friends?"

"Friends." Rhea took his hand again, and this time shook it. "Barbecues, movies, poker—you name it. Just no dancing."

Roberts managed a convincing grin. "I can live with that," he said.

# Chapter 24

"Jack!"

Jack jumped backwards. His lab stool hit the floor and bounced twice; his multimeter swung from the probe he was holding and rapped him smartly on the breastbone. "Darnit, Jan! Don't *do* that!" He prodded his chest gingerly. That was going to bruise for sure.

Jan didn't look very apologetic. In fact she looked pretty pleased with herself—or with him.

"Why, Jack," she said, "I don't think I've ever heard you swear. That was—" She paused and considered. "—Lame. Very lame. Pathetic, even."

Jack grinned. "Yeah. I guess it was, wasn't it?" He put down the multimeter and righted the stool. "So how do I merit a special yelling visit? I only paid for nonyelling."

"You were resting your eyes so assiduously the first two times I called you, that I decided to throw in the third time for free."

"I was sleeping? What time is it?"

"Not that bad," she assured him. "It's only ten o'clock. I was doing a little work on my own time on the company computer, and noticed your light still on. But you look awful, Jack—the circles under your eyes are starting to get circles under their eyes. Go home!"

Jack yawned. "You're right. It's just that I don't think I'll ever get a good night's sleep again until I crack this thing."

"Look at it this way—if it's going to be bad no matter what you do, would you rather have a *bad* night's sleep in bed, or a bad night's sleep bent over a lab bench?"

"Point taken." He stretched. The idea of bed seemed very welcoming right then. "Come on, I'll walk you to your car."

Jack killed his bench light and locked the screen on his workstation. Jan flipped the overheads off, and they were out the door. All the other offices on the corridor were already dark. They headed for the stairs.

"I got a call today," Jan said, "from an old friend at Rockwell. I've had my feelers out, and he says they're hiring. I told you I've got other offers. If I get this one, I think I'll have to take it. Shall I pass him your résumé, too? He's connected—it'll completely bypass Personnel."

Jack held the stairwell door open and they started down. "Thanks, Jan. I've got my own in at Rockwell, but I'm not ready to use it. For now I'll tough it out here." He listened to his steps echoing in the stairwell and thought about working somewhere else, doing some*thing* else. "Where else am I going to get a chance to work on spaceships? To ride one? NASA? Forget it. It's been more than twenty-five years since they put a man on the moon, and they'd wet their shorts if anyone asked them to do it again." He gave Jan a tired smile. "I'm going to stick here until the bank starts carting off the furniture."

They came out into the front lobby, and walked out into the parking lot. The night air was damp, but clean. The storm had moved off towards Raleigh. Jack waited while Jan rattled the doors behind them. The locks held.

"I hear what you're saying," she said. She arched an eyebrow. "But are you sure that's your real reason?"

"What do you mean?" he asked, but that was more a formality than anything; he figured he already knew what she was aiming at.

"You couldn't have some other type of launch on your mind, could you? You know . . . what we were talking about the other day."

He'd been right. "Yeah, I remember, but—"

Jan reached up and grabbed his shoulder, pulling him down to her eye level. "Jack, I'm serious," she said. "Rhea's interested in you. I'm sure of it."

"She tell you this?"

"No. But she didn't have to. I've seen the way she looks at you. I've seen the expression on her face when your name comes up. You can go for it, or you can screw it up."

"Or I can get fired for sexual harassment."

Jan let go of his shoulder and grinned once more. "No," she said, "you can't harass your boss. Shit doesn't flow uphill—but if you play your cards right, you can be the harassee."

He stood by her car as she opened the driver's door of the '55 and slid smoothly under the wheel. The dome light shone down on the trackless reaches of the back seat and Jack appreciated for the first time exactly what he had missed by being a teenager in the age of economy cars.

She caught him lusting at her vehicle again and said, "Beats the hell out of a Volkswagen Rabbit, doesn't it?" She keyed the ignition. Jack nodded agreement, and stepped back. She dropped the three-on-the-tree into first, popped the clutch, and roared off for Cornwallis Road.

Jack watched bemusedly for a second, then got into his own car, where he sat and thought. Maybe Jan was right. Should he make a serious play for Rhea? Jan was sure. Jan, however, was also sure that if Harrison Ford stopped into Celestial *just once*, he would fall head-over-heels in love with her and ask her to marry him. He needed to keep that little data point in mind before turning his life over because of something Jan said.

Right now, he was one out of two in the relationship arena. That wasn't a great record, but he'd hate to drop it to one out of three. He especially didn't want to go to one out of three by being pushy. He yawned and turned the key.

The Camry started smoothly and ran like silk. It might not have the flash and power of a '55 Chevy, but he'd love to see anyone get three hundred thousand miles on today's Detroit iron. Before he could take that thought any farther, a car turned off Cornwallis and headed across the lot straight at him. He was caught like a possum in the headlights. He gripped the wheel and spun it frantically with his left hand while his right slammed the stick shift at the elusive reverse, the bane of all Toyotas. The shift clicked home, and he threw out the clutch. The Camry bucked but didn't move. The brake! He released the hand brake and the car began to pivot, but there was no way he was going to make it. His heart was pounding and sweat rolled down his forehead. Jack braced for a crash.

Suddenly the oncoming lights swerved to the side, and he heard the screech of brakes as the other car came to a stop beside him. Gradually his dazzled eyes began to work again, and he could see Jan rolling down her driver's window.

"Hey," she called. "You were looking pretty ragged when I pulled out. Just wanted to make sure you didn't drive home asleep. I could just see you forgetting and going in the front door."

Jack pried his hand from the wheel. There were new indentations in the hard plastic. The front and back of his shirt were soaked with sweat and he was aware of each individual beat of his heart. "Thanks, Jan," he said finally. "I don't think sleep will be a problem now."

She threw him a cheerful wave, yelled, "Great," and peeled back out of the parking lot.

He watched her taillights as she left again, then turned his car off and got out as the engine rumbled to a stop. He thumbed around his key ring for his building key. He was suddenly wide awake. Might as well make some use of it.

# Chapter 25

Connie Franklin was a tiny girl, Glibspet thought. She might be flirting with her hundredth pound, but it hadn't slept over yet. What there was of her was nicely rounded, naturally blond and on public display—he could see how she had passed for the eighteen her big sister's ID claimed. Not that the penthouse suite of the downtown hotel was any place for big sis, either.

Trouble in school, trouble in church, boyfriend nixed by her folks, and every Full Mental Jackit CD ever made in her room, and band posters on the wall . . . it hadn't been too hard to find Connie. Not with the Fulmens coming to town for a two-night gig.

She'd been in the lobby with the rest of the wannabees when he'd found her that morning, but after he'd dropped a penthouse elevator key by her feet the rest was inevitable. Now it was time to reap the rewards of his careful planning.

Glibspet looked at his watch. He had six minutes left. It was funny; he'd never synchronized watches before, but Connie's mother had insisted on it. She'd seen it in a movie once, and felt that this was The Way Detectives Worked, and if they didn't work that way, they damned well ought to. He'd left her down in the car, her own watch gripped tightly in her left hand, while she crossed herself feverishly with her right. That and her incessant

114

praying had moved his start time up by several minutes. There had to be a limit to what he would put up with for a couple of souls and a lot of cash, and sitting in the car with that woman was several steps beyond it.

He checked his watch again—time to make his move.

Glibspet crossed the room slowly, navigating the thick marijuana haze like a plane on instruments. He stopped by Connie. "Why don't you come downstairs with me, sweetcheeks?" he suggested.

She looked up at him. Glibspet watched the rapid calculation in those sullen eyes. He obviously wasn't in the band and didn't even look like a roadie. No way was she going to let some other groupie get a piece of her.

"Drop dead, old man," she told him. "I don't do charity." The tough-girl delivery was tentative, but Glibspet gave it a B.

"Suit yourself, dearheart," he said, and backed off.

Okay, he'd told Mom he would try to get her out of there—now he had tried. Glibspet grinned. He hadn't said anything about succeeding. What came next was going to be fun.

The Fulmen's drummer, "Dreg," shambled in from the adjoining suite and sank down on an industrial-strength hotel sofa. Mostly on it anyway—rolls of fat oozed over the cushions like high water cresting a levee. Glibspet wondered if pork sought its own level. Connie and one of the pushier groupies, an overripe and sagging brunette, darted in and started trying to undress him, but he barely seemed to notice; he was too busy carrying on an intense conversation with Jack Daniels. The girl and the older woman had his belt undone and his zipper down, but there was just too much Dreg crammed into his jeans for them to be able to force his fly button open. If they did, Glibspet thought, the levee would break for sure. He'd love to see that. But some other time. This was the perfect opening for the little scenario he'd sketched out.

Glibspet walked over to Dreg. "Hey, man."

If Dreg heard him, he gave no indication. Glibspet didn't have time to waste. Mom downstairs wouldn't have a lot of patience. He reached forward, and snagged the bottle from Dreg's slack grasp. That got Dreg's attention, and a ham-sized fist seized Glibspet's arm suddenly with a grip that wasn't slack at all.

"My Jack." Dreg's voice was a low growl, almost a gargle. "Le' go 'n live," he said and squeezed.

Glibspet made no effort to extricate himself. "You don't need any more of that crap," he said. "Not while I've got hot rocks. Primo stuff, my man. Look!" He used his free hand to reach inside his jacket pocket and pull out a long, thin clamshell case. He slid the catch and it popped open. Inside were thirty-five vials of absolutely pristine crack cocaine. Demons didn't normally operate at the delivery end of the drug pipeline—it was too easy to hurt people, and the Hellraised couldn't directly cause harm. Glibspet's original scenario had been a little more indirect, but Dreg's size gave him an out— this guy had the body mass to take a major hit. "It's all yours, man," he told Dreg. "Free. My organization wants to do business with the Fulmen. You like it, you tell me later." He handed the case over to the drummer.

Now it was the mortal's responsibility.

Dreg's bloodshot eyes lit up. He let Glibspet's arm go, and groped clumsily through the scree on the floor by the couch. Paper flew and bottles clanked. Finally he came up with a pipe. As Connie and the other girl watched with interest, Dreg loaded a vial and lit up. Glibspet stepped back; it was not going to be a safe area in a minute, and porting was work.

Dreg took a deep hit from the pipe, and almost dropped it. "Damn," he said, "this is the best shit I ever had." He repeated the process but was unable to say anything coherent the second time. He just nodded enthusiastically.

"Hey! I want some of that!" the brunette groupie said.

"Me too," Connie said, giving up her attempt on Dreg's virtue.

"There's enough for everyone in the room," Glibspet suggested. According to his watch, he'd gone past the time he had promised Dora Franklin that he would be back at the car with her daughter. He told her that he and Connie would be out there three minutes ago, unless something had "gone wrong." He'd made very sure that she thought the worst; he also made sure that she got a good look at the gun in the glove compartment. He'd also fixed the elevator lockout for the penthouse. It was easy when you could reach through walls. Nothing that he had done so far broke the rules the Hellraised had to live under. Well, he couldn't break those rules, no matter how hard he tried.

All he could do was set up situations in which people could cause their own trouble. In a matter of seconds, they were going to be doing just that. Dora would be up here just in time to see her daughter take a hit on the cocaine. The kid would die of an overdose. Then there was going to be at least one murder, possibly followed by a suicide. The suicide wasn't anywhere near as sure a thing as the murder, but he had high hopes. All in all, it was going to be quite a tasty little haul for the soul pits. And of course he'd insisted on his fee up front on this one. High-risk operation, he'd called it.

Glibspet watched the door as Connie grabbed the pipe from Dreg and started to reload it. Just let Mommy hold off a few more seconds—

The hall door flew open, but it wasn't Mommy. It was— Who the hell *was* it? Glibspet had never seen the pair before. They weren't with the band, the hotel, or the police—the only three groups who might be expected to burst into the room. One of them, the man, was big, though not as big as Dreg. He had a hick look about him and a sheepish grin on his face. The other was a small woman who looked like she had just left off sucking a lemon. The pipe smoked unnoticed in Connie's hand as she watched the new arrivals. Behind them, at the end of the hall, Glibspet saw the elevator dial move from LOBBY to ONE. Mommy was on the way up.

"I know we probably shouldn't be here," the man said shyly as he closed the door, "and we had to sneak past the guards, but we're here all the way from Idaho for the Potato Cutworm Forum, and when we heard you Fulmen were going to be in the Triangle the same time we were, well . . . we just couldn't stay away. We're your biggest . . . Hey, look, sister! It's Dreg himself!"

Glibspet stared. These people were not supposed to be here. His plan was falling apart. When Mommy got off the elevator, she was going to find her daughter holding a crack pipe and in a state of undress, but very much alive. He had to get rid of these hayseeds and get Connie back on track. The pair was making a beeline for Dreg, and Glibspet moved to head them off. Somehow, though, he tripped and crashed into the female hick and they both ended up on the floor.

"And when you've mastered walking, do they start you on sharp edges?" she snapped.

Meanwhile, the male hick had stopped in front of Dreg, who was regarding the whole proceedings with a sort of manic coke-infused bonhomie. The hick grabbed Dreg's hand and pumped it. "Man, you're the greatest," he said. "I'll never forget your solo on 'Tracheotomy.'" He stared at the brunette. "And look, sister," he called, "a groupie, just like in the magazines, with her breasts out and everything."

"If I had those breasts, I wouldn't flaunt them," the short woman said sourly, and gathered her feet to rise. Her heel found a damp beery spot on the carpet and slipped from underneath her. Her shoe drove into

Glibspet's shin like a railroad spike into a tie. He cursed and gripped his shin, trying to will away the pain.

"And look," the man continued. "Drugs, just like we always heard about! Drugs! This is great!" He took the crack pipe from Connie's unresisting grasp and raised it to his lips. He inhaled, a whoosh of air that seemed to go on and on. "Man," he said finally, then suddenly his eyes rolled up in his head, and he dropped like a felled tree—right into Connie's bare lap.

She screamed and tried to bolt, but he had her pinned. His mouth was open, and drool was starting to run onto Connie's thighs. As far as Glibspet could tell, he wasn't breathing. Damn him! Glibspet finally staggered to his feet. This wouldn't do at all. The back-country bastard had gotten Connie's overdose, and with him dead in her lap, she wasn't about to take another. Probably ever.

And with the kid alive, why would ol' Mom want to kill Dreg? And where was Mom, anyway? This was the top floor, but it didn't take *that* long for the elevator to arrive.

Connie was still screaming as the short woman made it to her feet and raced for her brother's side. She dropped to her knees beside the stricken man and rolled him off Connie's lap. He flopped over with all the grace and volition of a week-old beached whale. "He's dead!" the woman wailed. "Oh, sweet Lord, my brother's dead!"

Something of the scene must have started to penetrate Dreg's crack-high sense of invulnerability because he sat up, waves of fat roiling like breakers through an oil slick. Before he could do any more, the woman started pummeling him with her fists. "Murderer!" she screamed. "He loved you and you killed him."

The accusation apparently penetrated. "Oh shit," Glibspet heard Dreg say. The drummer lurched the rest of the way onto his feet and gathered up the vials of crack, all now destined, undoubtedly, for a quick rendezvous with hotel plumbing. Dreg left the room, and there was the definite click of a bolt homing as the suite door shut behind him. The groupies and other hangers-on panicked and headed for the hall door. The brunette didn't even stop to find her skirt and blouse; doubtless *her* rendezvous would be with hotel security.

Connie sat stock still, looking at the dead man. Glibspet didn't think she'd breathed during the last three minutes. Her thin shoulders shook and tears ran down her pale cheeks. Glibspet considered: obviously, for whatever reason, Mom wasn't coming, and his initial plan was shot all to Heaven anyway. He could still port off and call in the cops, though—that ought to be good for some anguish. He started to prepare for the jump, but quit in mid-port as the corpse's sister grabbed Connie's hand.

"Come child," the meddling bitch said, and draped a jacket over Connie's shoulders. "We've got to get out of here. That fiend may come back and kill the witnesses too." Connie held on like a drowner to a life preserver, and the woman hustled her into the hall. "Elevator's broken," Glibspet heard. "We'll take the stairs." The stair door opened and shut, and suddenly Glibspet was alone in the room with the dead man. At the end of the hall, the elevator pointer twitched spastically between FOUR and FIVE, obviously stuck. Then suddenly it moved down to FOUR, and then to THREE, then TWO, and finally LOBBY. Glibspet began to smell a rat. He walked purposefully out of the room and to the stairwell where he opened the door and stepped onto the landing. Below, he could hear several sets of footsteps, but he didn't follow them. Instead, he counted thirty, then exited once more into the hallway. The Fulmen suite was just as he had left it—except that the body was gone.

Damn! Glibspet raised his hands and ported back down to the Lincoln. It was empty, of course. He could imagine the scene in the lobby when the elevator opened and

Mommy rushed out to take her sobbing baby in her arms. Never mind that Mommy had a pistol in her handbag or that baby wasn't wearing a bra or panties. There would be tearful talk of lessons learned, and promises never to do anything like this again—Connie's promises made sincere by having had a dead man in her lap. It made Glibspet's stomach churn just thinking about the sweetness of it all.

Glibspet put the Lincoln into reverse and backed out carefully. He took the opportunity to rearrange the grillwork of a Hyundai, and that made him feel a little better, but there was nothing he could do about the central problem. He should have started worrying when Mom went into her praying spasm. If it was enough to get on his nerves, maybe it was enough to get Someone Else's attention. Angels in North Carolina: Who would have guessed it?

# Chapter 26

JUDGE RULES BORDER DIVINING "UNSAFE WORK"
Raleigh—Raleigh News & Courier
    Federal Circuit Court Judge Marilyn Foster
ruled against North Carolina-based survey firm
God's Acre on Friday, finding that its use of
gargoyles and imps to settle North Carolina
border disputes constituted "unsafe work" for the
creatures, and was in violation of federal OSHA
rules.
    After two days of lurid testimony, during which
several demons described the events following
any Unchained's crossing North Carolina's
border, Judge Foster refused to lift an injunction
against the company and ruled that God's Acre's
survey methods, which involved pushing an
Unchained towards the presumed border until
it was observed to disappear, were "unacceptable
in a civilized society."
    God's Acre has vowed to appeal, but sources
in Raleigh say that the state government will not
rehire the firm, regardless of the eventual
outcome.
    God's Acre based its divining methods on the
well-known, but not often applied, fact that the
Hellraised are, by the terms of God's mandate,
which placed them in the state in the first place,

immediately and painfully disincorporated upon crossing the border and returned to Hell without benefit of appeal.

Judge Foster declined to rule on the related issue of God's Acre's claim that the borders it had surveyed prior to the injunction were "ordained by God," and not susceptible to further dispute.


The storm was over when Rhea left the Angus Barn—the young hostess would be disappointed, but Rhea wasn't sorry in the least. Thunder and lightning might be calling cards from Heaven, but they reminded her of too many other things, things she'd seen that were far from Heaven indeed. She patted her briefcase to reassure herself and took a deep breath of the clean-washed air. Ozone-fresh, it was intoxicating, or maybe that was just her mood. She felt like a bobcat in a world of wiener dogs—she was having a hard time choosing which one to tip over first. She threw the briefcase onto the passenger's seat and slid under the wheel. The office first, she decided. Get the contract in the safe, and start lining up things to move on in the morning. All the little things—and some big ones—that had been hanging fire, waiting for cash. Rhea put the top down and let the slipstream tug at her hair, and drove with Adam Ant's "Goody Twoshoes" blasting from the stereo.

When she pulled into the parking lot at Celestial, Rhea saw lights on the second floor. Jack must still be here, she thought. She put the top up and slammed the car door a little harder than necessary. He was going to have to start taking better care of himself. Or maybe *she* would . . .

Still, she reflected as she shut the lobby door behind her, she was glad to find him here. It gave her someone to share the good news with.

Rhea padded up the stairs to her office, and carefully

deposited the contract in her second safe, the hidden one. It was advertised as uncrackable, but it wouldn't keep out anyone who could reach through steel. Unfortunately, she didn't dare expend the Hellawatts to have one of the sort that other Hellraised in North Carolina used. Just the simple act of drawing a document out of a Hellish safe, if she were unshielded, might be enough to tip off Lucifer to her location.

She headed up to the second floor to tell Jack the news. Almost at his office, elated to the point that she wanted to tap-dance down the hall, Rhea rapped against a wall-mounted fire extinguisher with her knuckles. It rang out with a cheerful, brassy sound that echoed up and down the empty hallway. Rhea started to smile, but frowned as the corner of her eye picked up movement. Had something darted into the doorway of Jack's office? It didn't seem likely. Certainly there wasn't any indication that Jack had heard her. She wished she dared expend the Hellawatts to just read the area. But she didn't.

Jack was sitting at his lab bench when she walked in. He was staring fixedly at a circuit board and scowling as if he could glare the electrons into their proper paths.

"Hi, Jack," she said, very softly.

After he had picked up his lab stool, and after she had stopped laughing, Rhea gave him the news. "We did it. I've got our funding locked in; we can finish this thing."

Jack smiled, but it was a wan smile that didn't reach his eyes. He said, "I'm glad to hear that," but he didn't look glad.

Rhea put her hand on his shoulder. "What's wrong?"

Jack sighed. "I just don't think I can do it. I've tried six ways from Sunday to get this board working, and when that didn't do it, I pulled two more ways from Monday, and five from Wednesday." He waved the board in front of her. "I'm at the point where I've either got to say that your design is wrong, and I've seen too much of your oddball stuff work to think that, or that it is just not in Jack Halloran to get that design on silicon and wire. You'd better give it to someone else."

"If I thought there were anyone else better, I would." She took her hand from his shoulder and crossed her arms over her chest. "Look, Jack, I'm far from perfect. I can screw up just as well as the next guy—but I don't think I screwed up when I hired you and I don't think I screwed up when I gave you this task."

"But—"

"But nothing. Let's look over the diagram and figure out where I *did* screw up. We'll take it component by component, connection by connection, and we'll verify against the board while we go."

Rhea took the printout, got a pencil from her purse and stared making marks. "First connection," she said, "from pin one of the PAL to the pull-down resistor in grid A-twenty-seven?"

"Check!" Jack said.

An hour and a half later, they had gone through every component and trace on the board. Everything checked out, but Rhea wasn't satisfied. "Something's wrong here," she said.

"No kidding, Rhea," Jack replied.

"No," she said, "that's not what I mean. Everything we've checked is right, I *know* it is, but there's something missing." She held up the diagram. "Something's screwy here. Can you bring up the original on-screen?"

"Sure, if you want." Jack stepped over to his workstation, and brought up the CAD program. It spewed the diagram over the screen like Technicolor roadkill.

"Wow." Rhea winced. "It does get flashy, doesn't it? I see why you prefer the printout." She sat down in front of the screen, put the printout in her lap and started tracing circuits onscreen with the mouse, comparing them to the hard-copy diagram. It took her about ten minutes to hit a discrepancy. "I don't believe it." She looked up at Jack, who had been leaning over her shoulder, and said, "You've got to see this."

"What?"

"Look! This circuit. There's a lead from here to here," she pointed, "and it's not on the printout." She felt Jack press close as he looked over her shoulder.

"No," he said finally, "it's not. Print that puppy, would you?"

Rhea clicked on PRINT, and Jack's laser printer started to hum. He grabbed the warm paper as it came out and compared it to the screen. "Same thing," he said excitedly. "It's missing again! And look, the line that should be there is perfectly horizontal, and looks like it would be about one pixel high. Print something else. Some text file."

Rhea pulled up the workstation help menu and printed the first screen from the introduction. Jack grabbed the paper and held it up beside the other sheet.

"It's perfect." He pointed to a spot on the page. "This line of text is exactly level with the blank spot on the diagram printout, and there are no dropouts in it at all."

Rhea absently tapped her foot against the side of the desk. This was bizarre. "Let me try printing something else in graphics mode," she said finally. Jack nodded, and she brought up the CNN feed, freezing it on a frame of the president speaking to a group of senators.

"He looks like he's in pain," Jack said.

"Republicans give him gas," Rhea said, and hit PRINT. Jack grabbed the printout. "It's back," he announced. Rhea looked. "Right through his nose," she agreed.

"So it's not a print engine problem, or it would get the text too," Jack said. "It's got to be a firmware bug in the bitmap code. What are the odds here?" He waved the paper and the president flexed, still avoiding the issues. "Out of over three thousand rows of pixels, the one line that can screw us irretrievably is the one that goes out. What's next? Michael Bolton makes a good song? Maxwell's demons let ice boil?"

Rhea stared at him. "You know . . . it just could be." She stilled herself inside, being careful not to think about what she intended to do. "Give me your coffee cup."

The mug was clear, thick glass with a flattened world logo traced on it in white, and about half full of cold coffee. Jack handed it to her carefully; he obviously wanted to ask what she was doing, but she shook her head slowly, and he held his peace.

Rhea turned to the printer and hit the cover release.

The top popped open, and she darted a hand inside with inhuman speed. She closed her fingers over something that shouldn't have been there. Something that squirmed.

"What the hell—" Jack said.

Rhea popped her find into the coffee mug, keeping her palm over the top. "Precisely," she said. Inside the mug a small figure floated, treading coffee.

It was humanoid, about two inches high, almost as clear as the crystal itself . . . and very unhappy. As they watched, it shimmered and changed to a bile green, then a brick red before going back to clear. During the whole sequence, it was beating its fists against the walls of the mug. Its imprecations and the small, glassy pings were almost as annoying as a Chihuahua in full yap mode. "Stop that!" Rhea said, and shook the cup. It lost its balance and floundered, kicking up an oily froth of brown bubbles as it sank beneath the surface.

"What is it?" Jack asked finally.

"Gremlin," Rhea said.

Jack was silent for a moment. "That figures," he sighed. He tapped at the glass and the gremlin got its head above java level long enough to scream something obscene back at him. "Guess it doesn't like instant."

"Or much of anything else at the moment."

"So now what?"

"Well, before it goes under for the third time, it's probably going to remember that it can port out of there if it feels like it, and then it's going to be history."

As if taking a cue, the imp stopped struggling and raised an arm far enough above the surface to flip them the bird. It sank slowly and forlornly, and when the last extended finger disappeared into the murky brew, there was a muffled *pop* and the gremlin vanished in a coffee whirlpool.

It reappeared, dripping, in the open top drawer of the file cabinet near the door. It tripped over HEADSETS and fell into HEATSINKS. It clambered back out again and shook its fist. "Shitsmudge! Snotswallow! I tell! She gonna get," it shouted in a voice like a swarm of mosquitoes descending, and then it vanished again.

"Shitsmudge? Snotswallow? Never heard those before."

"That was probably its name." Rhea took her palm from the mug. The air pressure equalized with a gentle *whoosh*, and she put the cup down. "That was different."

Jack leaned over her shoulder and pressed PRINT again.

This time the diagram came out perfectly. He rolled it into a tight cylinder and whacked it against his palm. "So I've been tearing my hair out and losing us money because a gremlin decided to live in my printer and kill one lousy row of pixels."

"They're not very smart," Rhea said, taking the paper and unrolling it, "but they have an innate knack for knowing how to do the most damage. I doubt it will be back; once you get the gremlins out of a system, they move on to something else."

"But what did it mean 'I tell'? And 'she gonna get'? I don't like the sound of that. And what's this *she* business, anyway? She who? It can't mean my gargoyle, can it? I mean, what are the odds of my having two Unchained on my case? Specifically."

"I'd guess low. Exceedingly low. And I can't imagine what the little monster meant." Rhea knew a bit more about the subject than she cared to say. She'd put together plaguing teams in her time—it would take at least a demon to ride herd over a team comprised of a gargoyle and a gremlin. And in any case, for Jack to have three Hellraised working on him, he would have to have a special significance to Hell over and above his value as fodder. She knew what Hell looked for in recruitment cases, and she just didn't see it.

"Anyway, you're missing the moment, Jack." She waved the diagram. "We've got what we needed. The money. The fix for the MULE drive. We're in business."

Then she smiled. "Well," she qualified, "maybe."

# Chapter 27

Jack watched as Rhea took one of his pencils from his desk and started tracing on the printout. "It'll cross *here*, *here* and *there*," she muttered, but he wasn't really paying attention. He felt like a light had been turned on in his own personal root cellar . . . like he'd been awakened from a dream in which he'd done something so unspeakably gauche that he could never face polite society again.

He savored the feeling of relief and freedom for a minute, and watched the woman who had shaken him awake. Rhea's face was intent, and she absently brushed a stray strand of hair from her eyes. Her lips were pursed in thought, but Jack found the effect quite aesthetic. He moved to stand by her and look over her shoulder, but her closeness made it even harder to focus on the diagram.

Could Jan be right? He wanted to think so. If she were interested in him, and he didn't say something now, he'd be the worst kind of fool. He could feel the heat of Rhea's presence, and hear her breathing over the gentle *skritch* of the pencil. And if Jan were wrong?

Well . . . then he'd be the second worst kind of fool— and everyone should have a goal in life. He cleared his throat.

Rhea looked up and flashed him a high bandwidth

smile, freezing him in place. "Look," she said, "this is going to take a while. Why don't we tackle it tomorrow, fresh. There's at least twenty hours of cutting traces and patching in surface wires—"

Jack finally looked— *really* looked—at the annotations Rhea had been making. "I think I can do it in sixteen hours," he said, his thoughts of the moment before forgotten.

"Whatever. The point is we've got our money, we think we've got our drive problem. It's time to celebrate!" She stood up from his chair and looked into his eyes. "Why don't we go to my place . . . no . . . better make that *your* place. We can call out for some Szechuan and *talk*." The word seemed laden with more meaning than a single syllable could bear, and her smile was back, amused and alluring at the same time.

Sometimes the world says *put up or shut up*, and Jack didn't think he was completely deaf. "I, well, yes. I mean my place looks like hell, but—"

"I doubt that," Rhea told him. She walked to the door and turned off the light. "Besides, I'm having critter problems."

Jack followed, not running—quite. "Mice?" he asked.

"No."

"Cockroaches?"

"Angels," she said.

"Oh." Jack was nonplused. "Well, I've got gargoyles, or *gargoyle*, anyway."

"But a gargoyle," Rhea said, "isn't a problem when you want to be bad."

# Chapter 28

His lead hadn't panned out, but it would be a shame to waste the trip. "Here, doggy, doggy. Here, doggy, doggy," Glibspet called, and clapped his hands. He was stopped at the curb, with the door of the Lincoln open. He was in a residential neighborhood—fairly nice, and far enough away from the Triangle's hotspots to lack most urban paranoia. Too bad for them. He smiled.

The dog was a plump poodle, and it seemed nervous about leaving its front yard. Glibspet was taking great pains to smell like a freshly cut steak. The dog danced forward, then backwards, as though it could only hold a single imperative at a time in its one-ounce brain and kept swapping gluttony for fear. Finally, it got close enough, and Glibspet grabbed it. It let out an anguished yip, shrill enough to shatter glass; then Glibspet stuffed it in his sack and slammed the car door.

"Hey!" There was a yell from the house as Glibspet gunned the Lincoln. A fat woman stood on the porch, shrieking after him. He turned the corner and she disappeared from his rearview mirror. The heavy sack on the passenger's seat gave a whine of terror, and Glibspet grinned. Life was good on Earth.

# Chapter 29

**DENNY'S DENIES DISCRIMINATION**
Dillon, SC — Reuters

In an impromptu press conference Wednesday, Janice Richardson, manager of Denny's in Robeson County, North Carolina, hotly denied claims that her restaurant discriminated against the Unchained.

A group of devils aired the charges Tuesday, claiming that they were denied service at the restaurant during an outing Sunday evening. "We sat there for two hours without seeing our waitress," claimed the group's spokesman, who identified himself as Slimespudge. Richardson did not dispute the group's claim, but denied that any discrimination was involved. She argued that the design and staffing of the restaurant made such occurrences inevitable. Under insistent questioning from the press, she became more and more agitated, finally saying, "Look—everybody gets lousy service at Denny's. It's a fact. The pictures on the menu look a lot better than the real food too." She quickly retracted the statement, but continued to deny any discrimination.

The chain's district management would say only that, "Discrimination is completely against Denny's corporate policy, and we will be reviewing Ms. Richardson's franchise very carefully."

The area in which the incident allegedly took place lies at the southernmost stretch of Interstate 95 in North Carolina. It is a popular destination for sightseeing Unchained who stand at the state line and look across into the sprawling South of the Border roadside complex in Dillon, SC. "It's like the promised land," one demon said in a recent interview.

Rhea pulled the Triumph into the driveway behind Jack's Camry and got out. She looked around appreciatively. It was dark, but that didn't bother her much, and the yard was a riot of flowers. She breathed deeply and caught the fragrance of spring. She walked over to Jack. "Nice place," she said.

"Thanks," he said. "I can't take much credit for it, though. The people who lived here before planted all the flowers. All I do is try to keep the yard up. Better than the house, anyway." Jack didn't take praise well, she thought. She would have to do something about that.

He took the white paper buckets from the back seat, and the fragrance wafting from them was even better than the flowers. Jack's stomach growled and Rhea stifled a laugh. He definitely hadn't had supper, and may not have had breakfast or lunch. She'd had an excellent supper, but her metabolism was malleable within certain limits, and the Szechuan smelled awfully good to her, too. "Shall we go in?"

Jack closed the car door and straightened up. "Okay," he said, "but remember, I warned you about the mess."

Rhea headed for the front door, but Jack grabbed her arm as she started up the steps. "NO! Not that way!"

"Who that?" A shrill sleepy voice came down from the roof.

"It's just me," Jack called back.

Rhea watched, fascinated, as the gargoyle stuck her

head out over the gutter and looked down at them. She was a good specimen, Rhea thought, though a little thin. Suddenly she noticed Rhea.

"Not just you," the gargoyle said. "You got girl! No like. I girl, you no need she."

"Just great," Jack mumbled. "I didn't figure Hell would have any problem with polygamy."

Rhea smiled at him. "Getting a bit ahead of yourself, aren't you?" She could feel the heat of his blush.

Jack looked up at the gargoyle. "She's a friend from work," he told her.

"No like!" the gargoyle repeated.

Jack shrugged. "Well, it's not my job to keep her happy, anyway," he said. "This way," he told Rhea, and they started for the carport. The gargoyle moved with them.

"I don't think she wants me in there," Rhea said.

"We'll just have to use our superior brain power, then." Jack glanced over at her. "Um . . . I left mine at the office. How about you?"

"Me too." Rhea looked up again. The gargoyle glared down. "But how about if we offered her something to eat. She looks pretty hungry." She knew she could master the gargoyle easily enough, but even so small an expenditure of Hellawatts might get her noticed. Maybe the expenditure of some of their Szechuan would suffice.

"Okay." Jack looked over the bag full of boxes. "It's not like we don't have enough." He handed Rhea the bulk of their meal, keeping one bucket. "Hold these and I'll see what I can do."

Rhea stepped back.

"Hey," he said, holding up the bucket. "You hungry?" The gargoyle's eyes tracked the bucket intently.

"Hungry, yes," she agreed. "Bad hungry."

"Well, then," Jack hefted the bucket. "Tell you what. I'm going to throw this bucket up on the roof down there at the end. You go down there and eat it, and you can have the whole thing. If you don't, I'll pull it down and hide it and you won't get anything. Okay?" He walked back to his car and got some string from the trunk, tying a long piece to the bucket handle. "Okay?" he repeated.

The gargoyle stared from him to the bucket in his hand, then to Rhea, then back to the bucket. "Okay," she said after a long pause. "I eat."

Jack took the bucket, walked to the end of the house and threw it up on the roof. He took care not to stand directly beneath the eaves, and he held onto the string.

The gargoyle sidled across the roof towards the food, moving very quickly at the end. She grabbed the bucket. "Deal?" Jack asked, still holding the string.

"Deal," the gargoyle replied.

Jack let go of the string and walked back to join Rhea. "After you, miss," he said, ushering her onto the carport. "There's no way you could have pulled that bucket back after she grabbed it," Rhea said.

"No," Jack agreed, looking for his keys, "but maybe she didn't know that. Or maybe she's not such a bad gargoyle underneath it all." He found the key he was looking for, and inserted it in the lock, turning it slightly. Rhea heard a faint click. Then he replaced the first key with another, and turned again. There was a louder click, and Jack turned the knob, lifting slightly. The back door came open.

"What was all that?" Rhea asked. "Security lock?"

"No," Jack admitted, "my keys just don't work very well. I've been meaning to get that fixed. The door's a little warped too."

Rhea followed Jack into the kitchen. It was a cozy room with pine cabinets and red-checkered curtains. "Nice place," she commented.

Jack set the food down on the round table off to the outside edge of the room. "Thanks," he said. "I keep it clean, if not neat, but that's about it. And it has its quirks."

He opened a drawer by the sink and started fishing for silverware.

Rhea looked at the printout unrolled from the edge of the kitchen, through the dining room and all the way down the hall. "What's this?" she asked.

"Umm, carpet protector," Jack answered after a short pause.

Rhea looked closer at the code on the printout. It seemed to be from a minor project they had abandoned last year. "Well," she said, "you might want to think about that. It's got to be a fire hazard."

"I will," Jack said. He laid out the silverware, and unwound some paper towels for place mats and napkins. "Would you like some coffee or tea? I might have some Coke in the fridge. Coke doesn't spoil, does it?"

Rhea sat down at the table and slipped off her shoes.

She moved the silverware to put the two place settings adjacent to each other. "I'll have hot tea," she said. "Green if you have it."

"Just Lipton."

"Okay."

Jack filled a glass kettle with fresh water from the sink. He took it over to the stove, put it on a back burner, and lit the oven. Then he lit the burner diagonally across from the kettle's. Finally he lit the burner under the kettle and turned off the oven and the other burner.

Rhea had been watching the display in fascination. "What was all that about?" she asked.

"I'm not sure," Jack admitted, "but I know if I don't do it that way, I'll have a flame-out every time. I've been meaning to look at that." He set a plate down in front of her. "Here you go."

Rhea spooned rice and vegetables onto her plate. They were still warm. Good. She could use the chopsticks, but she wasn't going to if Jack wasn't. Jack sat down beside her and started heaping his plate.

"So, Jack," Rhea said, "tell me a little about yourself. The things that aren't on your résumé." She saw his fork freeze in midair and rushed to reassure him. "Hey, this isn't a test. I just want to know you better." She put her hand on his knee. It wasn't subtle, but it seemed effective.

"Well," Jack said, "not much to tell. I was born in Myrtle Beach, great parents, two sisters and a brother. I had a happy childhood, no hidden traumas. I went to MB High, worked summers at Painters Ice Cream, graduated, went to Clemson and got my double-E Masters. Worked for a few loser companies, then found Celestial."

"That certainly is a thumbnail sketch, I know there's more than that," Rhea said.

"Maybe," Jack said, "but it's not any more interesting in detail. It's like Columbia: It's a great place to live, but you wouldn't want to visit there." They ate for a few minutes in silence. Rhea didn't move her hand, and Jack didn't ask her to.

The teapot began to whistle, and Jack got up. "How do you like it?" he asked.

Rhea batted her eyelashes at him theatrically. "Strong and hot," she said. Jack nearly spilled the water.

They took their tea into the living room. There were two couches, several bookcases, a small TV and a large rack of CDs and audio ROMs, mostly jazz and old R&B. Jack hesitantly put his arm around her shoulder as she studied them. She leaned into the embrace, and selected an Oscar Peterson disk from the rack.

"How about this?" she asked.

"Perfect," he said, though she was pretty sure he would have answered the same way if she had selected *Great Artillery Battles of World War II*. She put the disk in the player and hit PLAY. Nothing happened.

"Tap it on the right side, about two thirds of the way towards the back," Jack instructed. Rhea did, and the warm tones of Peterson's piano filled the room.

They retired to the couch, and Rhea put her arm around Jack, too. His manner was warm and relaxed, but she could feel his pulse racing. They sat for a while, sipping tea and listening to the smoky beat, then Rhea put her cup down and turned to Jack. "Kiss me, you fool," she whispered.

"Not a problem," he replied slowly. He put his arms around her and drew her to him, gently, but with an urgency she hadn't expected. He surprised her again, kissing the hollow of her throat before settling on her lips. She relaxed and lured his tongue in, giving as good as she got, then following its retreat back into his mouth. He was a spectacular kisser. *This is going to be great*, she thought.

There was a rap on the window. They ignored it, but it came again. Jack pulled away. "Jesus, what is it now?" he muttered. There was an arm dangling across the top of the front window—an ugly arm. Jack opened the front door and yelled out, "Well!?"

"Sauce soy, please?" The high tones floated down from overhead. "Just little bit?"

Jack strode into the kitchen and picked out several packets, opened the screen door and hurled them onto the roof. "Okay?" he demanded.

"Okay."

He slammed the door and looked at Rhea, breathing hard. She looked back steadily for a moment—then her control broke and she dissolved in laughter. Jack looked hurt for a second, then sheepish. Then he broke down too.

# Chapter 30

When he was done laughing, Jack joined Rhea back on the couch. The gargoyle might have done him a favor, he decided, or given him one final chance to be a fool— or maybe to be smart. "Rhea," he said, "is this a good idea?" He sat straight, with his hands on his knees. "Remember, tomorrow morning I work for you."

Rhea put her hands over his, and he felt his resolve waver. "Jack," she said seriously, "if you don't want this, tell me now. I'll go, and tomorrow we'll get back to work. That'll be the end of it."

He didn't think he could stand a *might have been* like that, but he had to go the distance. "And if you don't go?" he said. "What will we do tomorrow then?"

Rhea brought his hands to her lips and kissed them gently. She raised her eyes and held his while she traced her tongue down his lifeline. "You're sweet," she whispered, her breath drying the slight moisture, "but we're grownups. We'll deal with it. Still want me to go?"

Like he wanted a date with Jesse Helms. "No," he said, "not in this lifetime." He pulled her hands to him for his own caress, then slowly drew each finger into his mouth for individual attention, paying homage to each ridge and cuticle. The stray thought, *Mama never told me not to suck someone else's thumbs*, drifted through the transom of his mind.

When he was done, Rhea closed her arms around him and laid her head against his. "That was wonderful," she breathed into his ear, "but don't forget . . . I've got toes, too!" She nibbled at his earlobe, and Jack felt his breath catch.

"I think I'll take the scenic route," he said and turned to cover her mouth with his. Rhea pushed him back into the couch and swung her leg over his to straddle him, sitting in his lap facing him. He was suddenly and wonderfully aware that at most four thin layers of cloth kept them from an NC17 rating, and from her vantage point, Rhea had to know it too.

She broke their kiss and grinned down at him. "That peak's not in my atlas."

"Then I'll have to make a new entry." He took the opportunity to unfasten the first few buttons of her blouse; she leaned back and wriggled her atlas distractingly, but he would not be diverted, and slowly the lush curves of her breasts came into view. He licked the hollow between them; it was already salty with her sweat. Rhea shivered, though he was sure she wasn't cold.

She started undoing his shirt, working the buttons much more effectively than he had hers, yanking the shirttails from his trousers after she freed the last one. She ran her fingers through the sparse hair on his chest, then dropped her mouth to his nipples.

"Hey," he said after a moment, "turnabout is fair play, you know." He pushed her back and undid her final button. He slid the blouse down her shoulders and stared, transfixed for the moment, at a fire-engine red microbra holding breasts that obviously didn't need the support. "My God," he said, "you wear that all day at work?"

Rhea cupped her breasts. "Or less," she confirmed.

"That's going to drive me crazy, knowing that," he said.

"Good."

He edged his hands under hers, holding the firm, lush

curves of her, feeling the thrust of a nipple in each palm. Awkwardly, he freed the center clasp of the bra and drew the cups away.

"Well?" Rhea said when he was silent for a second.

"They say anything more than a mouthful is a waste," Jack said finally. "Here's to wretched excess!"

He pulled her forward and traced an areola with his tongue. The nipple rose even higher and he took it into his mouth. He could feel the pulse of her blood racing through it, and he savored the beat of life.

Rhea moaned softly into his ear, and started working his belt and zipper. She worked her hand inside his pants; then it was his turn to moan. Jack was trying to unfasten her skirt—a simple engineering problem normally—but his attention was distracted and he wasn't making any headway.

"Let me," Rhea whispered. She leaned back, and Jack let go reluctantly. She worked magic with the clasp and zipper, and her skirt fell open across his lap. The panties she was almost wearing were fire-engine red too, except where they were darker with moisture. She raised up, and Jack eased them off. He was suddenly aware of what he *hadn't* noticed before on her arms and legs — Rhea had no body hair.

He used the waistband elastic as a rubber band and shot the panties across the room; they landed on the television. "Best thing that's been on TV this year," he murmured.

Rhea stood, and tossed the unfolded skirt aside. He drank her in from head to toe—every inch a wonder— and the old Mose Allison song came to him: "Your molecular structure—it really suits you fine!"

Rhea grinned. "Thanks," she said. "Now it's your turn." She tugged on his trousers and Jack raised his hips obligingly. She took down the pants, and worked them over his feet. Getting his underwear off was more complicated than hers had been—a problem she solved finally by grabbing the source of the obstruction and moving it bodily above the waistband. She looked him up and down critically. Jack couldn't pretend to himself that she saw anything other than a pale, slightly overweight desk worker's body, but she winked, squeezed where she was still holding him and said, "You pass! Now how about that scenic route you promised me . . ."

Jack set out to see the sights. First there was a bit of leisurely mountaineering in New England, and he was sorry to see the peaks fade from view, but going on maneuvers at the Norfolk Naval Station was almost as fun, and the flatlands of Mexico had their own charm. He flew over Central America, making a brief stop in Panama, and after some hard slogging, finally found himself off the coast of Tierra Del Fuego.

Jack looked up at Rhea. She raised her head and grinned. It wasn't the kind of grin you brought home to mother. "Do that again," she said.

He looked at her feet. He'd never really noticed them before. All the toes were straight and true, even the littlest ones. That was unusual. He nipped at one lightly, and earned an encouraging moan. He worked for a few more minutes, then decided it was time to head north to Panama again.

As he started serious excavation work at the canal, Rhea murmured, "You said turnabout was fair play— so . . . turn about."

It took a bit of seismic activity and plate slippage, but in the end he was able to stay in the Canal Zone while Rhea headed for the North Pole—it had been a while since there was any volcanic activity there, but the magma was building.

"A liggle hiter, yeth, yeth! Right there!" Rhea said.

"Don' tak wif your mout full," Jack remonstrated. He didn't take his own advice too seriously, but shifted his attentions obligingly to the low promontory above the canal.

The disaster, when it came, was nearly total. The pole erupted in volcanic fury, and earthquakes rocked Central America. In the end, the two survivors could only hold on to each other and ride it out.

"Wow," Jack said, when he could speak again.

Rhea rolled off of him, and landed catlike on the floor. "That was a good start," she said.

# Chapter 31

Jack lay on his back with his hands clasped behind his head. They had made it to his bedroom, and done some more exploring, but right now he didn't think he would be able to move a muscle. Ever again. So he concentrated on studying the ceiling and grinning.

He heard the shower stop in the bathroom, and moments later Rhea came through the bedroom door, fresh-scrubbed and towelless. The ceiling could wait, he decided. It was a rare moment, at least he hoped it was rare, when he could admire her without any tinge of lust, and appreciate fully life's ten-billion-year journey from the first protocell to evolution's ultimate culmination: the naked human female. Or at least *this* naked human female; he could overlook some of the journey's little detours like Bella Abzug and Rosanne Arnold.

Rhea poked him in the ribs. "Scoot over," she said. He did, and she eased down into his outstretched arms.

She was still damp and smelled faintly of sunshine and roses. Jack pulled her close, and savored a long, uncomplicated moment of silence. It ended with a suddenly-vivid memory of the last hour's activity. "Where *did* you get those feathers?" he asked.

Rhea laughed softly. "Remember the scout motto," she said. " 'Be Prepared.' "

"That's the *Boy* Scout motto," Jack said, "and I think

we've just established that you would flunk the physical."

"Well, maybe *I* gave the physicals to all the little Boy Scouts." She smiled and ran a finger across his chest. "It would sure beat selling cookies." She grew serious for a second, "Jack, I'm not going to pretend you're the first man I've slept with. Nor am I going to apologize. I am what I am."

He nodded. "Likewise," he said. Then, thinking of something he hadn't really considered in a long time, he laughed.

"What?" Rhea asked.

"This is a lot drier than my first time, anyway," he explained, remembering.

After a minute, Rhea pinched him. "Are you going to elaborate on that or just lie there wearing nothing but a big grin?" she asked.

"Well, they say a gentleman never tells."

Rhea made a face at him.

"But I'm no gentleman," he continued. "Besides, I know Natsu wouldn't mind. You remember I grew up in Myrtle Beach?"

Rhea nodded.

"Well, at the time, there was an Air Force base in town, and they got in lots of new families regularly—the Air Force likes to keep moving the troops around. Most of the kids went to school on post, but some of them ended up in public school. I met Natsu Forrester in sixth grade."

"Natsu? That's a Japanese name?" Rhea asked.

"It's an American name," Jack said. "As American as Kate or Shamika. But, yes, her ancestors did come from Japan. Anyway," he continued, "she was the only girl in school who would talk to me about science fiction and astronomy. When we moved up to middle school, we were the only two kids in the model rocketry club and we put together the first computer network at school with old IBM-PC Jrs. and doorbell wire."

"So you saw a lot of each other," Rhea prompted.

"Yeah, just buddies, you know? Then one day I noticed her shirt didn't hang straight down anymore—when you're a fourteen-year-old guy, something like that can suddenly become the most important thing in the world."

"It works both ways," Rhea said. "Or so I hear."

"Biology is a strange and wonderful thing," Jack agreed. "So it was springtime, and we sure didn't want to stay inside any more than we had to. So we cooked up this scheme and sold it to our science teacher. We'd take a model rocket with a little 8mm movie camera in it out onto Murrel's Inlet and take aerial pictures of the marsh. I think we were going to look for the effects of boat wakes on the Spartina or something—it didn't matter, just anything to get out of the classroom. So there was some kind of scheduling fiasco, and the teacher wasn't there, but we had the boat rented anyway so we took it out."

"And made another kind of launch," Rhea hazarded.

"Well, yes. I mean, we *did* make our launch. It wasn't according to the model rocketry association safety standards, but we had a big piece of sheet tin we raised at the stern of the boat, and huddled behind for the firing. We weren't real sure of the balance with that camera on it, but the rocket went up like a charm, and while we were celebrating, we suddenly noticed we were squinched close together, and not wearing a heck of a lot."

"And so you attacked her virtue," Rhea accused.

"Madame, you wound me," Jack said. " 'Twas the lady that ravished my tender virtue; though as I recall, by that point it wasn't all that tender, and perhaps not very virtuous either. At any rate, things escalated quickly from there, and somehow our flat-bottomed, ultra-stable john boat ended up upside down with us underneath it. We lost the tin sheet, the rocket launcher, Natsu's bikini top, the reserve gas can and half the seat cushions. Luckily the outboard was bolted on, and still ran when we finally managed to turn the thing back over. We even managed to recover the rocket.

"I gave Natsu my shirt and we thought up a cover story for everything else."

"And the teacher bought it?"

"Well, until he developed the film."

Rhea laughed out loud. When she stopped, she tilted her head back at him, and asked, "So what happened?"

"Well, we didn't get any class credit on that project, I'm afraid—but the teacher was a nice guy, just out of college himself. We got a lecture on responsibility and birth control, but I think he really wanted to say 'Go for it, kids.' Anyway, he didn't tell our folks. Not that it would have been the end of the world for either of us, but there are things you want to protect your folks from having to be understanding about, you know?"

Rhea nodded. "But obviously you're not still together."

"Yeah, well, we were joined at the hip for about a year, then her father got transferred. We kept in touch regularly for a while. She went into AFROTC and pilot training, then took fighters when they opened that up to women. Last I heard, she was a captain stationed in Korea. Even saw some action in the Hong Kong fiasco."

"Sounds like quite a woman," Rhea said quietly. "We're lucky to have people like that looking out for us."

Jack stretched and put his arms behind his head. "Yeah," he said after a moment, "that's our blessing, I think. America's blessing. No matter how hard the system works against it, we have enough good ones to pull us through." He was silent for a second. "Rhea?"

"Yes?"

"I want *us* to be the good ones. NASA's got cataracts and the rest of the world is blind. If we don't make this work, I don't think there'll be another chance. It may not matter in our lifetimes, or our kids'. But if we don't get off Earth, that's it for America. That's it for humanity."

Rhea took his hand and squeezed. "It'll work," she said fiercely. "We *are* the good guys, and we are going to make it work."

# Chapter 32

Glibspet considered the collar carefully and thought. Most of those with names on the tags he hung on the top row, but he already had several Fifis in his collection, and the plaid fabric would look better in the middle. He already had a collar on the peg he wanted, but that one would balance nicely against the plaid from over in the corner once the new collar was in place—he moved it and hung Fifi on its peg: Perfect.

He stepped back to admire the effect. The pegboard covered most of the study wall, and there were only a few empty pegs left. The empty ones *were* scattered a bit too evenly, Glibspet decided after a moment's study—a bit of asymmetry would add a hint of tension. He took Snookums down from the top row and hung him on the bottom left. He looked again and nodded in satisfaction. He had it.

The collar's smell lingered on his fingertips, and his stomach rumbled. Snookums. Now *there* was a poodle!

Glibspet closed the study door behind him and headed for the kitchen.

He'd been halfway hoping Mindenhall would call, and he sulked as he rummaged through the freezer. The man was coming to be invaluable for agency legwork, and Glibspet had been able to get him to lunch a few times, had even held his hands earnestly once or twice, but sweet Craig continued to turn down Glibspet's invitations for dinner and night life. It was infuriating.

Glibspet's hand closed on a popsicle mold. That would do. He carried it over to the sink and ran tepid water on it, then turned the handle carefully. The frozen clam-juice cylinder eased free, and he popped it into his mouth. Not bad. Could be a little saltier. He walked into the living room and sat down in front of the TV. He watched QVC for a while, and almost got another cubic zirconia, but decided finally that you could have too much of even a bad thing. Instead, he surfed over to CNN.

That cheered him up for a while, until they ran the Balkan headlines. So much human suffering and agony— and here he was stuck in North Carolina, away from it all. He bit down on the last piece of popsicle and tossed the plastic stick aside. Well, he'd just have to make the best of the hand he was dealt. He turned off the TV and closed his eyes in thought.

Okay, Averial was in North Carolina. She had to be. That was a given. The Fallen couldn't find her. Even he hadn't found her—not yet anyway . . .

She was good, no doubt about it, but was she so good that three of the Fallen and one very clever devil couldn't trace a single spent Hellawatt? Couldn't find the smallest flaw in an assumed identity? Was anybody really that good? Glibspet opened his eyes and narrowed them. There were angels in North Carolina now, too—he was sure of it. God had finally decided to make their presence active. They weren't doing much that he could tell—he hadn't heard complaints from other Hellraised, and he hadn't gotten any memos from Home Office warning that they were getting directly involved. But that business in the hotel had been a sure sign.

Coincidence? Maybe not. And angels were that good— by definition. In politics, follow the money. With angels, follow the good news. Glibspet reached for the paper.

# Chapter 33

COURIER STOCKHOLDER MEETING
DISRUPTED BY DISAPPEARANCE
Charlotte, NC — UPI

A group of dissatisfied customers picketed the annual stockholder's meeting of North Carolina-based courier Hellbent for Leather Wednesday, at one point forcing their way to the speaker's podium with a list of demands.

The company, incorporated and staffed by devils, provides instantaneous transport service across the state. Board chairman Asmodeous Smith accepted the list and promised to give it due consideration. Shortly thereafter, several company security staff approached the protesters, who were seen to suddenly vanish. The meeting continued without further incident.

Later reports placed the missing group in the center of the Great Dismal Swamp. Chairman Smith, confronted on the issue, would say only, "They must have gotten lost." Asked about his complaint against Hellbent, picketer Robert Mann said, "I proposed via Hellbent—I thought it would be special." He indicated his blackened and swollen right eye. "I don't think they're delivering the same messages we're sending."

❖    ❖    ❖

Rhea turned her head slowly and looked over at Jack. He was sleeping on his back with the sheet pulled up to his nose. His hair was a mess, and she could see the sleep in his eyes and abrasive stubble on the part of his face that wasn't covered. Jack, she decided, was a morning-challenged person. It made the hours he'd been keeping even more amazing. She sat up very, very slowly and looked down at him. The sheet over his lips traced what appeared to be a grin of epic proportions.

Rhea grinned back, and blew him a silent kiss. It flew on a wave of emotion that left her suddenly teary-eyed and brought a lump to her throat. Get hold of yourself, Rhea, she told herself. Remember the way things are. She inched her legs from underneath the cover, raised them to her chest, swiveled a degree at a time and eased them to the floor beside the bed. The pine boards were cool against her skin. She glanced at Jack again—no change. She rocked forward onto her feet, letting the bed rise micrometer by micrometer. She was tempted to play some games with gravity, but that was the sort of thing that got you noticed.

Finally, she was standing by the bed with Jack still sleeping, oblivious to the world, grin unnarrowed. The alarm clock would be a problem; she padded over to it, and ran the alarm up two hours. She looked back at Jack one last time, then took her clothes down the hall and dressed hurriedly. She surveyed herself in the small mirror in the living room. Perfect, of course; she didn't even need to brush her teeth.

Outside, dawn was under construction. The sun had almost topped the trees, and was inching into a sky of immaculate blue, totally innocent of last night's storm clouds. Somewhere, a bird was chirping. Rhea breathed the morning scent deep into her lungs. Even here, she thought, deep in suburbia, it's all so wonderful. And they just don't realize. She eased the kitchen door shut behind her, and walked to the edge of the carport.

The coast looked clear, and she made it to her car without incident. The gargoyle on the roof was just beginning to stir, and Rhea waved as she released the parking brake and pressed the clutch. The gargoyle shook her fist sluggishly. She looked awfully thin.

The car began to drift down the gentle slope towards the road. Rhea turned the key as the little Triumph rolled out into the street. The engine purred to life instantly, and she eased the clutch out slowly, heading for the main road. Behind her, when Jack's place was nearly out of sight, she saw a garbage truck come around the corner. The sound reached her a second later. On a scale of Enya to AC/DC, she gave it about a Sex Pistols. Well, she had tried. Rhea put the accelerator down and headed for Celestial. She had a lot to do.

# Chapter 34

Jan looked up from her console as Rhea came in. An R-rated grin spread across her face. "Thought so," she said. "Can I call 'em?" She reached around and patted herself on the back.

"What?" Rhea asked defensively. There was no way Jan could tell anything by looking at her. There wasn't a hair out of place.

"*One* of us didn't change clothes this morning," Jan said, "and it wasn't me. I notice also," she continued, "that one of our engineers hasn't checked in yet. The one who's been early the past month even though he loves to sleep . . ."

"Sherlock, you got me." Rhea chuckled. "We made a breakthrough last night, and the celebration kind of . . . escalated."

"Good for him! I've been giving him pep talks the last couple of weeks."

"You have? To come on to *me?*" Rhea looked at Jan sharply. "Jan, I haven't exactly been a nun, that you need to throw men at me."

Jan's grin faded. "Casual sex is great, Rhea, but I've seen your eyes sometimes when you think no one is watching." She looked down for a second, then locked her gaze with Rhea's. "You're carrying some kind of load, and it's going to break you unless you find someone to share it with." She forced the grin back. "And he can whistle. I do like a man who knows how to use his tongue."

"You're a nasty woman, Jan," Rhea said, retreating towards her office.

"Hey, I'm the one wearing clean underwear," Jan retorted

"You mean you're the one *wearing* underwear," Rhea said, and shut the door behind her before Jan could one-up *that*.

"Hello, Av—Rhea," Miramuel said.

# Chapter 35

Jack woke with a start as the alarm shrieked accusingly. The sheet was over his head, and he flailed wildly at it for a moment, trying to get his bearings. It was like clawing through molasses, but he finally managed to get his head and arms free. He reached for the clock and fumbled for the switch. Too complicated. He yanked hard, pulling the cord from the wall. The racket stopped, and Jack sank back in relief, holding the clock face to his eyes as the second hand ground to a halt. Two hours late! Damn, how did that happen? He flung the covers off and jumped to his feet.

Hitting the floor jarred his brain back into gear. Rhea. Last night. Wow. It *did* really happen. *She* must have set the clock back. He sat down again for a minute, and replayed the memories. It wasn't a complication he had planned on, and he had no idea where it was going, if anywhere. But, God, was he willing to find out.

And I didn't even have to sleep on the wet spot. Actually, there was no wet spot. That was odd.

Hell, the whole world was odd, wonderfully odd—he could feel the axis wobble if he stood still enough. He started to whistle Bruce Channel's "Hey Baby" as he showered and dressed. The pipes in the shower didn't rattle, the first two socks he grabbed for matched and he still had two clean shirts left. He was definitely on a roll.

Jack found his shoes in the living room, spared a grin
for the red panties still draped over the TV, and was
out the back door and to his car before he even thought
of the gargoyle. He waved at her as he turned the key.
No ignition. He shrugged. He could get out the hammer
and go under the hood, or he could try a rolling start.
He thought about the gremlin from the night before.
Today was his day for things to work right. He pushed
in the clutch, shifted into reverse, and released the hand
brake. At the bottom of the drive he popped the clutch
and hit the gas. The motor purred into life. Perfect: There
was no way that board was going to fail today.

At work, things were hopping. He could tell immediately
when he came in the front doors that the old atmosphere
was back. Radios were on in offices again, and the people
he met in the hall were striding instead of ambling. Not
that many people *were* in the hall—almost every office
he passed was occupied by someone working hard but
enthusiastically. It was like the early days, when he had
just signed on.

"Way to go, Jack!" an engineer on her way to the ladies'
room told him.

"Thanks, Becky," Jack said. He *hoped* she was talking
about the drive . . . Rhea must have said something that
morning. He wished he knew what, exactly. It always
made him nervous when people thanked him before he
had really done anything. But if he couldn't make things
work today, he might as well turn in his certificate and
go raise hogs in Sampson County. Or run for Congress.

Jack flipped on the lights in his office, and unlocked
his workstation screen. He had an e-mail message:

```
To: jhalloran
From: rsamuels
Subject: Sleep well?

Hope you had a good night's sleep, Jack . . .
```

```
Because I plan to keep you up late tonight!
X X X X
Rhea
```

Jack whistled appreciatively, and tapped out a reply.

```
To: rsamuels
From: jhalloran
Subject: Re: Sleep well?

Rhea,
Up late is great by me, but let's not forget to
throw in a little downtime too!
X X X X right back at you
 Jack
```

Satisfied, he hit SEND. Now to work. He really ought to be able to get those traces right with a good day's effort. Jack brought up the circuit diagram again, and made a new printout. The printer hummed and he smelled the faint scent of fusing toner. He took the warm sheet and carefully compared it to the screen. Okay. No, wait a second, it was the same damn thing, the same pixel row missing!

Jack slammed the printout down on his desk and grabbed an old-fashioned letter opener. He popped the printer latch, and lifted the lid. There was the gremlin, transparent and almost invisible, balanced on the corona wires. Jack stabbed at it and missed. Using the tight thin wire like a trampoline, the gremlin hopped over to the printer drum and thumbed its nose at Jack.

"Don't get cocky," Jack told it. He put down the letter opener. That had been a dumb idea. He couldn't hurt the Hellraised little monster any more than it could hurt him. Well, he could squash it and end up with a hellish bill from Hell for the replacement body—he'd heard stories about that. Even the tiny ones were frightfully expensive. And squashing it wouldn't even get rid of it.

He was more likely to wreck the printer. Well, he knew the gremlin didn't like coffee, but he couldn't very well pour a cup into the printer, and his reflexes weren't as fast as Rhea's. He didn't think he had a chance of catching it by hand. In fact, when he thought about it, he'd never seen anybody move as quickly as she had.

He thought for a second, then picked up the phone. "Hello?" he said. "Is this Bat Conservation International? . . . Yes . . . I'd like to make a donation. It's deductible, right?" It wasn't much as far as good deeds went, he thought as he hung up. But was it enough? He looked in the printer. The gremlin looked a little disgusted, but it was still there.

Jack sighed and closed the printer on it. He called up classic film stills on the World Wide Web and navigated menus until he found George Bailey by the Christmas tree with all his family and friends gathered around. It was the most concentrated dose of goodness he could think of. *Teacher says . . .*

He hit PRINT. There was a small wail from the printer as the image coated the paper. It wasn't a sound that could be explained by any mechanical process. Jack grinned. The printout, though, still had a row of dropouts.

He opened the printer again. The gremlin looked positively ill, but it shook its fist gamely at him.

Fine, pal. Gremlins came from Hell, and Hell was supposedly hot. Jack walked over to his workbench and pulled out an aerosol can of Freez–It circuit coolant. Normally he used it when he suspected a heat-related problem with a component. As far as he was concerned, the gremlin had just made itself a printer component.

He pointed the nozzle at the smirking face and pushed the valve. Fog enveloped the inside of the printer and when it cleared, all the metal surfaces were starting to collect frost. So was the gremlin. Jack took a pair of vise grips and grabbed it. An old Firesign Theater album title popped into his mind from nowhere: *Don't Crush That Dwarf, Hand Me the Pliers*. Unfortunately, that wasn't a real option. Instead, he cracked the window slightly and held the gremlin outside. The frost was melting, but the small Hellspawn was still blue and shivering. "Bye," Jack told it. "Don't forget to write." He let go and listened for the impact—it sounded like a tennis ball being thrown at a feather bed.

Jack shook his head. There had to be a better way to delouse. The way his life was going, he'd better read up on it.

The printout was perfect this time, and Jack took it over to his workbench to start fixing the traces. It was going to be a real pain—he was going to have to solder actual wires to the board in a couple of places. Not elegant at all. But doable. Jack cracked his knuckles and turned on his soldering iron. He whistled the first few notes of "Morningtown Ride." Time to get started.

# Chapter 36

*Whoosh.*

"How's it going, Gibbet?"

Not nearly as well as it had been a second ago—that was for sure. Glibspet looked up at Kellubrae. "That's *Glibspet*," he snarled. He put his feet down and gripped his glass of Karo on the rocks tightly.

*Whoosh.* "It might as well be *Pit Fodder*," said Venifar from his left. "You're taking too long." Venifar was not looking good. Now, along with the missing nose, his left arm had gone AWOL. And he had the raw look of someone who had been partially peeled. Evidently the Evil Dude was starting to push for results.

*Whoosh.* Linufel jostled his right elbow as she appeared. The glass of Karo flew from his grip and spattered in slow motion, running down his shirtfront and pooling in his lap. "And that would be such a shame," she purred. "I was really *so* looking forward to our time together. Oh, look, you've made a mess of your pants just thinking of it!" She pulled a handkerchief from the tightly stretched breast pocket of her suit. "Let me help you clean that up."

"That's not necessary," Glibspet said quickly, and rolled his chair under the desk. Linufel had a pretty liberal notion of what working against him meant—he did *not* think her grip would be gentle. She made a moue and put the handkerchief back.

"So, where is she?" Kellubrae demanded. He leaned down across the desk and stared into Glibspet's eyes. There were bits of flesh on his teeth, and his breath reeked of the charnel house.

Glibspet felt a sudden wave of nostalgia. Emboldened, he reached up to poke Kellubrae in the chest. "Hey," he said, "don't pull that crap on me. I've got the contract, and you'd better believe I've filed it. Mess with me, and the penalty clause comes in and kicks your ass so hard you'll be picking your souls out of the Pit one atom at a time for the next billion years. The three of you combined won't be able to make anything more ferocious than a cantankerous gremlin for so long you won't remember how to bite."

Kellubrae narrowed his eyes, and Glibspet felt his hand forced down to the desktop. The thump shook the desk.

"Never forget who we are, little devil," Venifar said from his side, "and that you signed that contract too. We've heard nothing from you but outrageous demands for funds and received nothing but invoices from escort services and dog kennels." He stepped fastidiously away from a drip of Karo. "You are contracted to provide us with the location of Averial. Where is she?"

Glibspet spread his hands. "You think I wouldn't tell you if I knew?" If you wanted to control the answer, he thought, always ask the question yourself. "I'm a professional," he continued. "What do you think I've been doing here since I started?"

"Getting yourself laid and gorged at our expense," Linufel said.

"Well, sure. You signed that expense clause freely, and I can guarantee *now* that none of those girls is Averial—but I sure couldn't guarantee it before." At the murderous look in three pairs of eyes, he quickly added, "But besides them I've been eliminating hundreds . . . thousands . . . of other people."

"We're not paying you for negatives," Kellubrae said. "I can tell you lots of places she isn't."

"Ah, but in a state this size," Glibspet said, "no one person is more than three people removed from any other, and I'm not working at random. I'll find her tracks soon—it's inevitable."

"It had better be," Venifar said. "The resources we can muster on this plane come at a price. We got the first lucky break in ten thousand years when Lucifer got sidetracked by the Maxwell's Demons Local #503 strike. If it hadn't been for that, we'd probably alr—"

Kellubrae kicked him in the shin and stepped in front of him. "If you get us noticed, it had better be because of your success, and not—"

In the lobby, the outside door swung open. "Dom?" Mindenhall called as the door shut behind him. "You in there?"

"Out," Glibspet hissed. "Now! Or I'll go slower than I already am."

Linufel made to argue but he cut her off. "Look, you want to explain this to him? If I have to get new help, it'll delay everything." She gave him a this-isn't-done-yet look, then glanced at Kellubrae, who nodded. She took her handkerchief again, reached through the desk to Glibspet's lap and wiped vigorously at the Karo. Suddenly, she *grabbed* and squeezed enthusiastically, still plying the cloth. She smiled sweetly as Glibspet's eyes glazed over. He didn't see Hell's trio take off, but through his pain he heard the triple *whoosh*. When he was able to open his eyes again, all three were gone.

Glibspet doubled over and groaned.

"Dom?" Mindenhall leaned in the door and gave him a worried look.

Glibspet pushed weakly away from the desk and curled

up in his chair. Mindenhall hurried to his side and rested a hand on his back. "Are you all right? Should I call 911? What happened?"

Glibspet straightened slowly and painfully. He reached out a sticky hand and Mindenhall took it. There were Karo tracks everywhere, and his pants were bunched over his crotch. An ice cube was Karoed into his navel, and several more were dripping down his shirt. He sighed. "Just don't ask, Craig," he said. "Just. Don't. Ask."

# Chapter 37

Rhea clicked the lock on the door behind her. Then she walked over to her desk and polarized the windows. She pressed the intercom button. "Hold all my calls," she told Jan. Finally she turned and faced Miramuel.

"What's so important that you couldn't wait and tell me in my kitchen? You know what could happen to me if anyone sees an angel here."

"Relax, Rhea," Miramuel said. She walked over to the couch and sat down, beckoning Rhea to join her. "I came in the front door disguised as your sister."

"I don't have a sister."

"You do now." Miramuel gave her a cocky grin. "Besides, no one is going to recognize me as an angel."

Rhea sat. "Like no one recognized you as an angel back in 1428?"

"That doesn't count," Miramuel said. "I wasn't working at it as hard then. And I didn't know Joan was *that* pure of heart. Besides, it turned out to be part of the plan for England and France to keep competing."

"It counts, Mir," Rhea said. "I was in charge of getting the English to burn her at the stake. I didn't have any choice."

"Well, after all, she made it to Heaven."

"No one should have to get there that way."

Miramuel hung her head. They sat in silence several

minutes, looking out the window. "I *am* working at it today," Miramuel said finally, "and you didn't come home last night, Rhea. We didn't know if you were coming home tonight either."

"Probably not," Rhea admitted. "Not to sleep anyway. So what do you want?"

"We have a message for you."

"From whom?"

"Who do you think?"

Rhea sat up straight. "No," she said, "He doesn't speak to me anymore," she smiled sadly. "I'm in a different chain of command."

"Maybe you can't commune directly," Miramuel said. "Nonetheless, I *am* a herald."

Rhea stood up and walked to the window. "So what's the message?" she asked. " 'Come home, all is forgiven'? Not likely. What I said the other night still stands."

Miramuel put her hand on Rhea's shoulder and turned her around. "No," she said, looking into Rhea's eyes, "it's just this: You've set forces in motion that are heading out of control. You still have time to stop what you're doing. You can make this project not work, and things will continue the way they are. Or you can continue on this stubborn, self-directed path you've chosen, but if you do, you'll have to take the consequences."

"I've been taking the consequences for my actions for a hell of a long time," Rhea snarled. "And that's what this is really about, isn't it? He didn't send you to get me to come home. He sent you to stop me from helping them."

"We're here to help you, Rhea. We're here to keep you from making a mistake. And it's almost too late. You're almost to the point where you won't be able to turn back."

"I don't want to turn back. It's been a long time since I've done the right thing, but I'm doing the right thing now."

"Then let me tell you something else. You know you're being hunted. We've helped some with keeping you hidden, but we can't do that forever. You can play here at being human for a while, but have you considered the effect that your playing is going to have when you aren't here anymore. What about the people who are working for 'Rheabeth Samuels' right now? Hmmm?"

"What's that supposed to mean, when I'm not here anymore? Is that a threat?"

Miramuel shrugged. "That's the message," she said. "That's all I know."

Rhea studied the angel, who gave off an aura of stubbornness along with her usual faint glow of goodness. Mir was hiding something. Something about what she'd said had been wrong . . . really wrong . . . if only Rhea could figure out what it was.

The out-of-kilter something didn't have anything to do with the Hellish force that was hunting Rhea, however. That remark was as honest as Heaven.

Rhea closed her eyes for a moment, shivering. She'd felt Lucifer's hunters on her trail recently. Felt the vibrations of her name in the aether. She hadn't wanted to believe it, but she wasn't stupid. Someone was coming, and if she couldn't deal with him, she needed to have some contingency plans in place. She went back to her desk, and brought up the Bodeans on her office speakers. Then she spoke into the intercom. "Jan, get me our lawyers."

# Chapter 38

A trace of smoke curled up and around Jack's face. It carried the sweet odor of rosin flux and he breathed it in appreciatively; it was the smell of success. The last connection cooled—he had a good join. He laid the iron down, checked his grounding strap and hefted the board in his hands, turning it over and over, checking it against the diagram one last time.

Finally, he was satisfied. It had been a peak flow experience, *Zen and the Art of Circuit Prototyping*. He didn't know when he'd ever worked that fast before, or made so few mistakes, but it was finished, it was to spec, the *real* spec, and it was perfect. He looked over at the test trolley on the table. It would be so easy to take it over there and give it a try, see if it worked before possibly sharing another disappointment. But if it did work? I could never forgive myself if Rhea weren't here, he thought. There could be only one first time. He set the board down carefully on a sheet of static wrap and unhooked his grounding wire. There were solder flecks on his pants; he stood and brushed them off. He paused by the phone a second—should he call? No. If this were it, he wanted to tell Rhea in person.

He waved to Jan as he hurried through the doors into Rhea's suite.

She looked him up and down for a moment, grinned,

and gave a low wolf whistle. "Hey, stud . . . how's it hanging?"

He could feel the blush spreading down from his face in time with Jan's widening grin. When he was sure it must have reached his toes, she chuckled and looked away.

"Well, shut my mouth," she said in a thick rural accent put on for the occasion. "Looking for Rhea?"

"You tell me," he said. "You seem to know everything else."

Jan mimed an arrow to her heart. "Cut to the very quick I am." Jack smiled in spite of himself. "So I'll tell you, since you asked. Yes, you are looking for Rhea. Yes, she is in her office. No, you can't see her yet; she's in there with our new lawyer."

Jack shivered. Suits were bad enough, but suits with a law degree were an engineer's nightmare. "That rent-a-shark? What's she want with him?"

"Don't know," Jan said, "but when there's blood in the water, you want one of those fins to be on your side." She considered. "They shouldn't be in there too much longer if you want to wait."

# Chapter 39

"Good afternoon, Ms. Samuels," the lawyer said, and shook Rhea's hand. Rhea shook back with a little more strength than strictly necessary. "Ms. Stillwater sends her regards," he continued, wincing slightly. Caldwell, Markham and Stillwater were an old Raleigh firm—solid, but not to the point of ossification. After the Unchaining, when other firms were fleeing across the border, they stood fast, and eventually forged in court many of the unique features that came to distinguish North Carolina jurisprudence. They had never tried to cheat her, and while they billed their time at exorbitant rates, the accounting was full and accurate. In short, for lawyers, they weren't bad guys, and while Rhea fully expected to see most if not all of them in Hell at some point, she fancied they might take on the occasional pro bono case there.

"Thank you, Mr. Markham." She smiled her professional smile, which didn't have the warmth of either her personal or her let-me-sell-you-something smiles. "I'm glad you could make it on such short notice. Won't you have a seat?" She gestured to the chair in front of her desk.

Markham sat. "You indicated you wanted to discuss a matter of some urgency?" He opened his briefcase, took out an old-fashioned yellow legal pad, and laid it on his knee.

"Yes. I do." She leaned forward across her desk. "First, I want to make clear that the social part of your visit is over, and that everything hereafter is covered under lawyer/client confidentiality. Agreed?"

"Of course, Ms. Samuels." Markham raised an eyebrow and made a point of sounding slightly insulted. He tapped his fountain pen on his pad. "That goes without saying."

"Today, nothing goes without saying." Rhea sat back again. "You are familiar with the ownership structure of Celestial?" she asked.

"Certainly. Ms. Stillwater briefed me thoroughly before I took on her client load. I have copies of your incorporation papers right here." He patted his briefcase. "Celestial Technologies is capitalized from a variety of sources, but sole proprietorship resides with you."

"Exactly," Rhea said. "Unfortunately, I may not be around indefinitely, and I want to make very sure today that I control what happens to Celestial in that case. I don't want my company ending up split between those investors, or worse yet, trading publicly."

Markham looked at her closely. "Are you unwell?" he asked. "Are we talking a 'death of the principal' situation?"

"Never felt better," Rhea told him, realizing in surprise that it was the truth. She considered for a second. "The situation that I'm facing is . . . considerably worse than death." She studied the lawyer, trying to decide if the plaque on his coronary arteries had already hardened to the point where he would keel over dead with what she was about to do next. She decided that, like most tough bastards, he'd do just fine. "We need to discuss some matters about my . . . personal life . . . that could have an effect on shortening my future, and threatening the future of Celestial."

"Ms. Samuels, have you been withholding information from us?" He sounded slightly exasperated, but resigned. "You'd be surprised how many people do. We cannot provide you full and effective representation and advice unless we have all the facts."

"Be careful what you ask for," Rhea said softly, and dropped her human manifestation.

Markham started. His pen point snapped beneath the weight of his whitening knuckles, and ink flowed in a steady blue stream across his pad and onto his pants. He didn't seem to notice; he was unable to take his eyes off Rhea. "Good God," he whispered.

"That's a matter of opinion." Rhea stretched her wings and watched the dark illumination of her aura crackle around her. She felt odd being in her true form again. She could feel the power of Hell coursing through her veins once more, closer and stronger than her human form could ever handle. But this body didn't feel like *her* anymore. It was as though Averial had become the disguise, and Rhea the real person. She smiled ruefully. Would that it were so . . .

Markham flinched at the sight of her smile, and she remembered the terrible, malignant beauty she presented as one of the Fallen. She resumed her human form.

"Ms. Samuels, per-perhaps you need another law firm," Markham finally managed to sputter. His face was white, his lips were tinged with blue, and he looked a lot closer to that coronary than Rhea would have suspected.

Rhea leaned back in her chair and crossed her legs. "Wrong answer," she said. "We have a contract, Mr. Markham. Legally binding to both you and me, drawn up with every line checked and approved *by* me . . . and I guarantee you I have *much* more experience than you do in looking at contracts . . . and dealing with people who break them." She got up and poured him a cold glass of water from the suite refrigerator.

He stared up at her, wild-eyed. He would have made a lousy trial lawyer, she decided. He let things shake him visibly. He wasn't a good actor. He took the water with a trembling hand and drank it in one gulp. After a moment in which he tried to pull himself together, he managed to say, "You're immortal, so we're *not* talking a death of principal scenario here. What . . . what are we talking about?"

Rhea stood by the window and looked out. "There are people looking for me," she said. "When they find me, there is a small but non-zero chance that I won't be able to fight them off. I think I can deal with them . . . but perhaps not. If they get hold of me, from a legal standpoint I might as well be dead. I won't be on Earth anymore. They might be able to force me back into working for . . . well. I might end up back here as someone else's puppet, forced to attempt to work against everything I've built. I need to make sure my company can deal with that, can withstand that."

Markham wasn't getting it. She needed him to focus on her legal problem and he was still bug-eyed over her physical problem. "There are people who can push a fallen angel around?"

Rhea sighed. "Count on it," she said.

# Chapter 40

"Where do you get these?" Jack asked Jan, indicating the magazine he had been leafing through. It was an issue of *Time*.

"What do you mean?"

He held up the cover so she could read it: NIXON RESIGNS, the headline trumpeted.

Jan considered. "I think they spontaneously generate," she said finally. "Every place I've worked, the magazines in the waiting room seem to average a print date about twenty to thirty years before the building was built." She paused a second and thought. "The worst I ever saw was when I worked in a downtown bank that was founded in 1893. I'd put out the current week's issues in the waiting room, and we'd end up with Picket's Charge and Gettysburg."

Jack flipped some more. "This movie, *The Sting*, sounds like a winner. Maybe I should try and catch it."

"Well," Jan said, "it's no *Butch Cassidy and*—whoops, here they come."

The door to the inner office swung open, and Rhea and a very disheveled lawyer exited. The lawyer looked like he had been through the wringer. His tie was off and his collar was unbuttoned. He was carrying his jacket and Jack could see sweat stains under his arms. He looked back at Rhea like he expected her to bite him. What the hell had been going on in there?

"I'll be in touch," the lawyer said, and beat a quick exit, zipping past Jack and Jan without noticing them at all.

"Give my regards to Janet," Rhea called after his swiftly retreating back.

"Well, you sure put the fear of God into him," Jan commented as the lawyer's footsteps double-timed into silence.

"Hardly." Rhea laughed, though if that had been a joke, Jack didn't get it. He gave up further speculation as she turned The Smile on him. "Hi, sport," she said, and his knees weakened. His brain calmly considered how incredibly well his life was going at that particular instant. His body was looking for a flat spot big enough to fit two people who didn't intend to lie still. He heard Jan's giggle and was aware that she had nonchalantly stepped back several paces. He felt the heat rise in his face. "Um . . . hi, Rhea," he said. That sounded lame.

"Yes?" she asked, obviously enjoying his discomfiture. Suddenly he was able to enjoy it too; was able to see himself standing there like some tongue-tied teenager. He savored the feeling for a moment. After all, how many men got to be fourteen twice? Then he pulled together the trained engineer and said, "The drive is ready for testing. Would you care to attend?"

"Most definitely," Rhea said. "Give me ten minutes." He stood there while Rhea did Rhea things in her office and Jan tapped away at her keyboard. After what seemed like an eternity, Rhea came out and waved him on.

*Everyone* was in his office. So that's what Jan had been doing, typing a summons into the on-line bulletin board and e-mail system. And Rhea must have known. He looked around. If it didn't work, and this many people saw the drive fail—instead of just hearing that it hadn't worked—that was it for Celestial. He would kill morale deader than disco.

He glanced at Rhea, and she nodded at him and gave him an encouraging smile. This was what she wanted. She thought having everyone in to see the drive work would boost morale.

She believed in him.

Jack cleared his throat. "Okay, folks—" He made his way to the test table. "I think you all know what this is," he touched the trolley lightly, and it rolled soundlessly on its new rubber wheels. "And I think you know what this test means. Either this trolley moves on this table, or we've gone to a lot of trouble to build the world's largest model rocket." He paused and indicated the power switch. "Ms. Samuels, would you care to do the honors?"

Rhea shook her head. "It's your baby now," she said, "and you've got ten centimeters dilation. I think the time has come to push."

Jack nodded, his throat dry. He positioned the trolley on the starting mark of the scale etched into the table, and checked the cables carefully to make sure their drag would be at a minimum. The board was fully seated in its slot, all the new connections he had made still looked nominal, and the power supply ready light was glowing a friendly green. He could feel the tension in the room building like the static charge before a lightning strike. Jack gripped the toggle switch firmly, and caught Rhea's eye. *Caesar, we who are about to die . . .* he thought, and flipped the switch.

There was a brief *whoosh*, followed by a deafening crash that nearly knocked him off of his feet. Someone in the back of the room shrieked, but Jack hardly heard. The trolley was not on the table, in fact the trolley was not in the room. There was a trolley-sized hole in the cement wall of his office, under the window. There was no other sign of the trolley except the settling masonry dust. "Well, call me Dick Seaton," Jack breathed, somewhat awed by what he had just done.

"Drive from hell," one of the other engineers opined in the stillness of the aftermath. Jack saw Rhea wince as the office erupted in pandemonium.

# Chapter 41

"So . . . those were some of the boss's old associates?" Mindenhall asked Glibspet the next morning.

"Yeah, wanted to know where he was," Glibspet said, pouring himself a cup of strong brew from the office's Mr. Coffee. He passed a cup to his assistant.

"Thanks." Mindenhall added a spoonful of sugar and stirred. "So what did you tell them?"

Glibspet shrugged. "That he had started a puppy farm in Chatham County last I heard."

"Is that true?"

"I think so—he doesn't talk to me much anymore. It wasn't what they wanted to hear, though."

Mindenhall looked troubled. "I thought they couldn't hurt us," he said.

"Define hurt," Glibspet said. He took a sip of his coffee. *A little bland*, he thought, but he doubted Craig would take well to some of his favorite flavorings. "It didn't hurt me to be doused with Karo syrup," he continued. "And if I ram my nuts into the edge of the desk trying to get away from them, well, they didn't do that, did they?"

Mindenhall winced in involuntary sympathy. "Where in the world did they get Karo syrup?"

"I'm sure Hell has a pantry," Glibspet said darkly and took another sip. "It's probably on the shelf right next to the Puppy-on-a-Sticks." That was true, actually, though he'd gotten his bottle at Food Lion. "Anyway, I doubt they'll bother us again."

Mindenhall sighed. "I hope not. My priest is unhappy enough about me working here without my running into demons." He finished his coffee and crumpled the cup violently, throwing the wet ball of Styrofoam towards the recycle bin. "Of course, he's always been unhappy with the whole gay thing too, even though I've been celibate lately, so what's one more sin?"

"I *like* that line of thought, Craig." Glibspet looked into Mindenhall's eyes for a long moment, then winked.

Mindenhall smiled, hesitantly at first, then with more assurance. "You've got a one-track mind, Dom," he told Glibspet, "but maybe your track leads to my station."

Progress, thought Glibspet. Solid progress. "I hope the train's an express." He set his cup down. "Now, what were you bringing me last night?"

Mindenhall went over to his desk and opened his briefcase. "Just this." He extracted a large manila envelope. "I checked the papers and the police. I've got thirty-one deaths here that meet your profile. Thought they would be worth a closer look."

"Great. Burn me some copies, then start running the standard checks. Credit histories, insurance payouts, college records, the works. I want to know anything that doesn't fit."

Glibspet watched appreciatively as Mindenhall bent over the copy machine. Soon. Very soon.

Mindenhall handed him the warm sheets of paper. Glibspet took them into his office, and after a moment's consideration, closed the door.

There were things Craig couldn't check, he reflected, like whether a decedent was currently in Hell. He got out the red modem and attached all the wires. All he wanted this time was a bunch of simple yes or no queries;

it should be easy enough to program the specifics into a script so he could go on and do other things. He only had a few menus to navigate through.

Two hours, with every curse he could think of laid on the head of whoever had designed the brain-dead COBOL-like scripting language for his com program, Glibspet finally finished his "simple" query. And it had only taken him twice as long as doing it by hand would have. A programmer had once told him that she couldn't find much difference between Hell and COBOL; of course, that had been before she went into the Pit. Still, he was starting to see her point.

He hit RUN and listened to the modem dial. It dialed only seven digits—Hell is never long distance. He listened to the modems handshaking; then, satisfied that he had a connection, Glibspet turned to his map.

The map was a large-scale representation of the Triangle area and covered most of the right wall of his office. There were pushpins stuck in various spots, some green and some amber. As yet, he could find no real pattern. Glibspet took the morning's Raleigh *News & Courier* and leafed through the main and local sections.

He found two possibles. The first was a Chapel Hill kid dying of cancer. His dog had gone missing, and when it did, the boy lost the will to live. Suddenly, after three months, the dog showed up—but at the hospital, not the home—and the kid started responding to chemo. The second was an attempted robbery at a suburban Southern National branch that failed when the intended robber's bullet missed the clerk standing two feet in front of him, triggered the silent alarm, and caused a short circuit that overloaded the light fixture directly above him, cracking the globe which fell on his head and knocked him out. Incredible coincidence or Divine Providence? Inquiring minds wanted to know.

Glibspet pushed two new green pins into the map.

Interesting . . . Was there a cluster roughly centered on Research Triangle Park, or was it a statistical anomaly? Glibspet just didn't believe in coincidences. Maybe it was time to hit the road and run down some of his best prospecting leads from the same general area.

# Chapter 42

The morning sun burned mercilessly out of a cloudless sky; it threw Escher shadows in front of buildings and blinded the mass of commuters stranded, unmoving, on the long expanse of I-40.

"Salmon," Glibspet said to Mindenhall as he maneuvered the Lincoln deftly from one side street to another and the interstate passed from view.

"What?" Mindenhall asked irritably. He hadn't had his morning coffee, and Glibspet knew he resented being put in a position where he had to make some actual response to conversation.

"Salmon," Glibspet repeated. "They come to the same river year after year, fight their way upstream, spawn and die." I-40 came back into view, and he waved down at the stalled traffic. "No one knows why they do it, or *how*, for that matter."

Mindenhall raised his sunglasses and rubbed his eyes. "Tradition, I suppose," he said, "or maybe they want a better life for their kids, something safer than growing up in the deeps."

"But the species would probably survive better in the deeps," Glibspet said. "Plenty of fish do. And people would be just as happy—probably happier—living in caves and barbecuing the odd mammoth. No hour drive just to get back-stabbed by office politics; no having to

183

be nice to idiots on the phone all day. What makes them do it?" His eyes caught a morning jogger and her dog coming out of a neatly manicured yard. They both deserved more attention than he could give them with Craig in the car. He made a note of the address.

Mindenhall sucked his lower lip pensively. It was a sensuous mannerism, and enough to turn Glibspet's attention away from the heart-shaped ass dwindling in his (aptly named) rearview mirror. He had big plans for today and Craig. "I don't buy it," Mindenhall said finally, substituting conviction for caffeine. "The happy savage thing is a myth. People aren't salmon, and we have the God-given imperative to ask *Why?*—about everything. Sometimes it leads us into traffic jams, but it doesn't keep us there forever, and along the way we get the science to raise our kids without plague, and the art to make it important to us."

"You haven't watched network television lately, have you?" Glibspet asked.

Mindenhall waved the objection away. "A detour," he said, "like the traffic jams. They'll both be gone in fifty years. We'll always have dumb people—the mammoth hunters who can't see what good a bunch of seeds could do—but those 'happy savages' are in the Devil's playground, not God's. The rest of us will keep asking *Why?*" He paused for a second. "Which reminds me," he said. "Why am I here?"

Glibspet turned into the parking lot of a nondescript stripmall. Brown's Realty was sandwiched between Borchert's Day Care and Redpath Spediprint. He cut the engine. "That's a big question," he replied.

"You know what I mean," Mindenhall said. "I don't see why it takes two of us to ask a real estate agent some questions."

"Because we're going as a couple," Glibspet said patiently. "We want to know things that, strictly speaking, are none of our business. A gay couple in North Carolina is either going to make the agent so nervous that he won't think twice about what we're actually talking about, or if we actually somehow get a gay agent, so friendly that he'll tell us whatever we want to know." He opened the door and got out. "Just remember to pat my hand occasionally, and call me *honey*."

Mindenhall grinned. "You're a wicked man, Dom," he said. "Shall I swish?"

Glibspet grinned back. "Maybe," he said, "just a little."

In fact the Realtor was neither gay, nor a man. She was a short, plump woman with streaks of gray in her hair and more than a little makeup on her cheeks. On her desk, a Bible sat next to a small Elvis snow globe with blue flakes. She was staring into it now, as if the King might start making snow angels any second. Glibspet didn't think she had looked directly at them since the first time Craig had taken his hand. "Well this one just looks *darling*," Mindenhall said, pointing at a blurry photo in the agency's listing brochure. "Don't you think so, honey?" He stroked Glibspet's hand again. The agent caught the motion from the corner of her eye and shuddered. She swirled the snow globe frantically, leaving the King all shook up.

"I don't know, Craig," Glibspet responded. "I wonder what the karma there is. You know I can't sleep in a room where anything bad happened." The house had been owned by one of Glibspet's prospects, someone too obscure for even a newspaper obit. "Gayle," he asked, "can you tell us about the house? Were they nice people who lived there? What happened to them?"

Gayle looked up from the blizzard briefly. Mindenhall caught her eye, blew her an elaborate kiss and winked. Glibspet thought it was a bit over the top, but it was effective. Gayle hunched over in her chair—trying to expose the smallest surface area possible to them, perhaps—and started to babble.

"Such a nice woman," she said quickly, "and they say it was a very gentle death." Under Elvis's watchful eyes, she gave a complete nonstop rundown on three generations of the house's owners, replete with local gossip.

It was clear to Glibspet nearly from the start that he could mark this one off his list, but Gayle seemed oblivious to any of his visual cues of waning interest. She wasn't really talking to him anyway, and the King wasn't going to stop her. "Oh no, I'm afraid it's just not *us*, Craig," he said finally, rising to his feet. "It's just too, I don't know, *neo-quasi-retro*, don't you think?"

"Absolutely," Mindenhall agreed, taking his cue, "*much* too." He stood also. "Thank you, Gayle," he said, "but it just doesn't complement our modal harmony." He put his arm around Glibspet, and they walked to the door together. Behind them, Elvis was having a Blue Christmas—probably thinking about his grandchildren.

They made several more stops, none of them as much fun as the first, and none of them productive. Early morning led into lunch at The Flying Burrito, which segued into a long busy afternoon and a full supper at Angelo's. Mindenhall was laughing as they went back out into the parking lot. Glibspet was being as urbane and witty as he knew how, and he had made it a point to ply Craig with as much of the excellent Italian red as he would take. While by no means drunk, he leaned now on Glibspet's arm from time to time for guidance. Glibspet himself was playing the model designated driver, and had had nothing but coffee.

"Shit," Glibspet said as the Lincoln came into view.

The front and rear left tires were completely flat and the big car listed visibly to the side.

Mindenhall let go Glibspet's arm. "Oh, hell," he said and walked over to the car. Touching the hood for balance, he circled around to the far side. "These look fine," he reported. "What could we have hit?"

Glibspet knelt by the front tire and inspected it. "Look at this," he called. When Mindenhall came around and crouched beside him, he pointed to a single neat hole high up in the sidewall of the tire. "I'll bet the back's the same," he said. "Someone, teenagers probably, had nothing better to do with their evening."

Mindenhall got up and sat on the hood, his legs dangling over the useless wheel. "Well," he sighed, "now what?"

Glibspet considered. "I'm not going to call a tow truck for flat tires," he said. "It's not worth it. There's a Western Auto in that plaza over there." He pointed across the street. "I'll put on the spare in the morning, then roll the other one over there and let them patch it."

Mindenhall drummed his heels on the crumpled whitewall. "And what about tonight?"

"Well, we can pay outrageous taxi bills, or we can get a room over there." *There* was a small motel about a block down the street, where a flickering sign proclaimed BOB'S DR P INN.

Mindenhall looked doubtful, "Well, I don't know—" he started to say then stopped himself. "A room, you said?"

Glibspet spread his arms and shrugged expressively. "Yeah," he said quietly. "It's been a good day, hasn't it? Maybe something's trying to tell us it doesn't have to end yet."

Mindenhall drew himself up straight and sat silently for a moment. "You're right," he said finally and hopped off the car. "I think I'd like that."

"I would too," Glibspet said. "I keep a shaving kit in the trunk. Let me get that, then I'm set." As the opened trunk blocked him from Mindenhall's view, Glibspet reached into his pocket, took out his Swiss Army knife and laid it down in a corner. The black rubber stains on the awl blade would be hard to explain.

# Chapter 43

HELMS REJECTS BAPTIST CHARGES
Capitol Hill — Charlotte Observer

Senior North Carolina Senator Jesse Helms denied Thursday that his amendments to the omnibus farm bill especially benefited North Carolina's demon farmers. The North Carolina Baptist Convention had made the charges last Friday, supported by state Agriculture Department figures showing that Unchained farmers grow tobacco almost exclusively, and have largely displaced human farmers.

"I have always supported the North Carolina farmer," Helms said in a morning news conference. "I have a great respect for the Baptist Convention, and I'm a churchgoing man, but the needs of my constituents have to come first."

The senator also denied making the statement "Well, at least they're not black" at a breakfast on Monday. "I would never say such a thing in public," he replied in response to press queries.

It had been a long two weeks, Rhea thought. An incredible time. She rolled herself deeper into Jack's embrace and sighed as his sleeping arms tightened around her. The sigh tickled his nose. "Ummm," he murmured without waking. It was a friendly sound, non-threatening.

She had almost forgotten what it was like to not probe every word for concealed threats, every course of action for hidden motives.

This quiet passion had sneaked up on her—she hadn't been looking for it at all. When the Unchaining came, she had seen her chance to flee and in the melee, she had taken it. Hell was wearing her down; she would have ended up in the Pit in a couple more centuries, at most, and she didn't think she would ever have the force of character to bring herself back to the status of fallen angel, no matter how long eternity stretched. So she was determined to go out in a blaze of glory: Prometheus gifting the savages with fire and giving a big poke in the eye to both Lucifer and The Other One.

But her grand gesture had become something much more . . . well . . . real. Starting a company was expedient and practical, but it also brought together people who shared a dream and depended on her to make it happen. She had found after a while that their dream, and their joy in dreaming, had more power than her fantasies of revenge and oblivion had ever had. Especially now, when the greatest of the dreamers was the man who held her in his arms.

Jack had made her laugh from the first day she hired him, with his abstracted mannerisms and love of music. She still delighted in the astounding pockets of naiveté that she found in him from time to time, but she'd come to realize that in anything that mattered to him, he had a steel core. He would do the right thing whether it came easily or not; whether it paid off for him personally or not; whether it felt good or not. Integrity, she thought. You just didn't find a lot of integrity in Hell. How could she offer less?

It was funny, really. Centuries of Hell had worn her down to the point that she thought she had nothing left to lose and no choice but oblivion. Then a few short years of passing for human had returned to her things she'd forgotten losing and a few she'd never had: Trust replaced fear; shared pleasures replaced solitary ravaging; the thrill of accomplishment replaced the electric blood-lust charge of desecration. She buried her face in Jack's shoulder. Perhaps, she thought, it's even brought me love.

And all of these good things would bring about her destruction just as surely as if she had remained unchanged and had followed her intended path to the letter.

# Chapter 44

Jack wasn't just whistling "Dixie"—he was working flat out while he did it. "Dixie" was, he reflected, a song that could still get you in trouble, despite Lincoln's blessing, but sometimes he just felt so good he couldn't help it. He didn't know when he'd been happier. The times with Natsu were great, but that was a teenage thing. Adults had more to give each other. Certainly the best times with Carol weren't nearly as good, and the end of that relationship. . . . He shuddered.

He ran over the final specs for the drive housing. The MULE had even more kick than Rhea had predicted, and he needed to add some extra reinforcement without changing the center of thrust. He spun his chair away from his workstation and picked an envelope off of his desk. He sketched rapidly on the back with a pencil. The pencil-on-paper approach was archaic, but sometimes he needed something hands-on to think about a problem—besides, writing on napkins, envelopes and tablecloths was an engineering tradition.

He drew in some vectors and tagged them with ballpark magnitudes, then leaned back in his chair and looked at the drawing. Nothing came to mind immediately. He concentrated, and the Domino's Pizza delivery number popped into his head. It was a good thought, but not timely. Apparently whistling took too many brain cells—

he stopped, tapping the pencil against his chin instead. Finally his mind wrapped around the problem, and he drew a countervector that *felt* right. A few minutes' checking on the workstation confirmed it, and Jack entered the changes as pending in the specification database. Three other engineers would check behind him, but he knew he had the fix right. He hadn't created a bad change; the builders down in Manteo wouldn't have to tear anything out to add the new bracing and the revision would only add a few days to the schedule.

He considered printing the revised blueprint, but decided against it. The gremlin was back in his printer; no telling what it would do to his layout. It had gotten more sophisticated once it lost the element of surprise, and had come up with a little cold suit from somewhere that protected it from his freezing spray.

Just to keep it on its toes, he keyed up a couple of pages of one of C. S. Lewis's essays on Christianity and sent it down the line. The resulting noise from inside the printer sounded like a chipmunk with indigestion and gas: his gremlin was not a happy little Hellspawn at all. The pages came out almost blank—apparently the monster had felt compelled to eat most of Lewis's thesis.

Jack looked at the time and decided that stray phone number that had bounced into his mind when he'd been trying to solve the reinforcement problem had been a sign. Like a motion to adjourn, pizza was always in order. Not Domino's, though. Something authentic. He saved his work and headed for the hall. Behind him, as he closed the door, his printer burped.

# Chapter 45

"*Good* idea, Jack," Rhea told him as the waitress set their pizza down and the aroma wafted up. The fiction that their relationship was platonic had died a fast and very public death at Celestial, and they'd decided early on they might as well be open about it. So they had left for lunch together. So far their involvement hadn't caused any problems.

"I think the Greeks understand pizza even better than the Italians," Rhea said. She lifted out one of the thick slices, broke the trailing ribbon of mozzarella, and put it down on her plate.

Jack did the same. The pepperoni were cooked crisp under the light sheen of olive oil, and the crust cut with a satisfying crunch. "*I* think so," Jack agreed. "In fact, I had a friend once with the theory that the only really *American* foods were things like Greek pizza, Mexican fish and chips and Polish eggrolls."

Rhea shuddered. "I don't think I'd go that far," she said.

"Well," Jack said, "he also had the theory that the federal tax system is voluntary. So you can take that with as many grains of salt as you need to." He paused and counted. "I think he should be out in about another three years."

Rhea laughed around a mushroom. "You run with some interesting company, don't you?" she asked.

"I've known some choice ones," Jack agreed. "Sometimes the wrong choice." He sprinkled crushed red pepper on his slice and took a bite—not as good as sex, but it could give drugs and rock and roll a run for the money.

Somehow Rhea was already on her second slice. "Tell me about Carol," she said as she pushed an olive towards the exact geometrical center.

He didn't really want to. It wasn't one of the high spots of his life, but then, he was the one who had mentioned the name in the first place.

"Not much to tell," he said. "You know, Myrtle Beach used to be a whole different place before the Unchaining. It wasn't a metropolis until all those Tarheels moved south over the state line. We had lots of tourists in the summer, of course, but as far as the locals were concerned, it was a small town, with all the small town cliques and social circles." He took a sip of tea, and Rhea nodded.

A pleasant-looking young man came in the door and went to the takeout counter. There was something familiar about him, Jack thought. "You have a large, half double anchovy/pineapple/garlic, half edible?" the man asked. The countergirl nodded and handed it to him at arms' length, as though she didn't want to be associated with it. Jack caught Rhea's eye and grimaced. "I'd take the Polish eggroll first," she confirmed.

"Anyway," Jack continued, "after Natsu moved, I started going out with Carol. Well, actually, she didn't really notice me at all until I fixed her car one day when it was broken down in beach traffic on 501 during a tropical storm. Then I was kind of an honorary part of her circle, and socially, they were all top dogs. She was a cheerleader; Mother and Daddy belonged to the right country club; and she rode horses. Thoroughbred-Arabian crosses, as a matter of fact. I distinctly remember that that mattered. On top of everything else, she was smart and funny. My buddies tried to tell me she was one stuck-up girl, but that wasn't ever the way I saw her act, and I didn't want to hear it."

"Hmm. I think I sense a little foreshadowing here," Rhea said.

"Well, *I* didn't. We were both going to Clemson, so it seemed kind of natural to continue the relationship once we got there." He stopped as the slice he had just picked up folded under the weight of too many toppings and dangled limply under the outer crust.

"That's not an omen for tonight is it?" Rhea asked, pointing.

"Well, I've never dropped my toppings yet," Jack said. He put the offending slice down and attacked it with his fork. "Carol was in the best sorority, of course, and they had lots of parties. A lot of them were formal, which I really hated, but I put on the monkey suit because it made her happy. The last one was a really big deal. She had finessed being put in charge of a big Southeast-wide dinner and dance for all the different chapters of the sorority, with a couple thousand people planned to attend. Carol got to emcee the whole thing, and she and the other organizers got to sit at the head table with their dates."

"So you were up there with a couple thousand people staring at you?" Rhea looked amused. He supposed being on display was easy for her.

"Yeah, which is pretty close to my idea of Hell, anyway," he continued. "There'd been parties in hotel rooms all day before the main event, so things started off rowdy and went downhill from there. I think each table basically got as much wine as they could drink, even before the meal. It was kind of funny seeing all these girls in evening dresses sloshed half to the gills. Carol was having her share, too.

"I was ready to go home by the time Carol was supposed to introduce the head table and start making presentations, and we still had the dance to get through afterwards. Anyway, she went up to the podium and started talking. She wasn't too focused by then, and she was making dumb jokes and dragging it out forever—I was just kind of tuning it out until she got to me."

Jack took another sip of tea. He noticed his knuckles were white and he eased his grip. He could tell Rhea had seen too. "You don't have to go on," she said gently. "I didn't know it still upset you."

He shook his head. "No, that'd be like coitus interruptus. Besides it doesn't upset me—it just makes me mad." He went on while she pondered that distinction. "The way I remember it, the exact words she said were, 'And here's my date for the evening, Jack Halloran. Would you believe I had to steal him from a slant-eyed slut? And doesn't he clean up nice?'

"I felt like a ton of bricks had fallen on me. I couldn't do anything at first—I was paralyzed. Then I knew what I had to do. I stood up and said, 'Excuse me, I don't think I need to be here,' and I walked out.

"I had to go all the way across the ballroom. It was completely silent; everyone was watching me." He shuddered. "While I was walking, I realized two things: One, I'd never seen Carol talk for more than two seconds to anyone who wasn't white. *Of course* she was always nice; everyone she associated with was white and well-to-do. And two: She was always happiest when she'd talked me into doing something I didn't really want to do.

"By the time those doors had closed behind me, I'd looked at the whole history of our relationship without the rose-colored filter. I didn't like it, and I didn't like what it had done to me." He shrugged. "We never spoke after that. I understand I humiliated her in front of her peers, and she kind of dropped to the bottom of the sorority's pecking order after that, but I really can't say

I'm sorry. You think you know someone, but do we ever *really*?" He decided not to mention the semesters of slashed tires and mysteriously missing mail. After all, there was never anything he could prove.

The pizza was cold when he tried the next bite. "Sorry," he said. "I guess I talked your ear off."

Rhea looked troubled. "No," she said, "I appreciate your telling me the details. In a lot of ways, it helps me get a better look at you." She pushed her pizza aside. "But I think we could both definitely use some dessert."

"Now you're talking!"

# Chapter 46

Back at the office, Jack stared at his printer again. The situation was getting pretty ridiculous. He really did need to make printouts, and he needed them to be reliable. No one else in the building had their own personal gremlin, much less a gargoyle. Rhea had seemed so sure that the Hellspawn would leave him alone, and he'd figured if she made the comment, it must have been because she had some experience with the problem; if she ever ventured an opinion, she could always back it up with facts and experience. But she'd been wrong this time. He hadn't mentioned it, though—she had enough on her mind, and he didn't want her thinking he was trying to show her up. And *nobody* knew much about the Hellraised. He would just have to find an engineering solution. Printer Degremlinization. If he came up with something really snappy, maybe he could publish.

He sat down and pondered. He didn't really have the time to fool around with it, but on the other hand, could he afford not to?

He accessed the World Wide Web and pulled up the Unchained home page. Someone at the NC State anthro department had started it a year ago, pulling together all the net's resources concerning the denizens of Hell both in myth and reality. Jack sifted through screenful after screenful, pausing only to mark links he wanted to come back to. A lot of the information came from the Unchained themselves, and was notoriously unreliable and contradictory, but that didn't mean it wasn't helpful in its own way.

The sun was low on the horizon when he brought back all the links he had flagged and put them on screen side by side. Belief and religious symbols: That was one common element to the driving out of demons. Jack rubbed his chin and felt the rasp of five o'clock shadow. He had to meet Rhea for supper—and other things—soon, but maybe he had something here. Christianity, Judaism and Islam all had a tradition of successful confrontations with Hellspawn, as long as the confronter believed in the symbols of his faith. Doubtless there was some crossover from vampiric lore, and the indications for faiths not derived from Judaism were less clear, but the indications *were* there. The symbols alone weren't enough, though; there had been several instances of the Unchained infiltrating churches and even posing as ministers since they came to the state.

Jack sighed. He'd been reared High Church Episcopal, but these days he tended more towards a sort of agnostic deism, the Unchaining notwithstanding. He didn't think he could muster the necessary sincerity to do a successful exorcism on his printer.

He closed out the web viewer, then sat back, struck by a thought. Maybe it didn't matter who or *what* did the believing. Artificial intelligence was a lot like power from nuclear fusion: it was always twenty years in the future. There were isolated islands of success, though, like neural nets—circuit arrays that exhibited what could only be termed patterns of learning, or, perhaps, belief.

He walked over to his parts shelf. He ought to have a few net chips; they were useful in fuzzy logic controllers. He found one, hiding under the obsolete husk of a

Pentium. It was harder to find the programming interface box—that was in the popcorn maker tucked away on the top shelf. He took it and plugged it into his workstation's interface bus, thought for a minute, then keyed in a short multi-entity scenario. He created a container entity representing his lab, with two smaller entities inside, one representing the gremlin, and one representing the neural net chip. He put the chip in *learn* mode and ran a training sequence over and over, one where the arrival of the chip in the room inevitably resulted in the gremlin's leaving.

While the sequence was running, he mounted a boilerplate driver circuit board and a small battery on a cruciform T-square. When he figured the chip was as convinced as it was going to get, he popped it from the programming box and into the socket on his makeshift cross. He flipped a microswitch and the small power LED lit. Jack struck a dramatic pose holding the assembly in front of him, and began to approach his printer. He was surprised at how uncomfortable he felt. Apparently his parents had imprinted him more deeply than he had thought, or maybe it was one thing to have doubts about religion and another to use its symbols cynically. He shrugged the feeling off and touched the cross to the printer. The gremlin popped out, but it didn't run. Instead it leaped and grabbed the T-square, sprawling across it until it looked like a Catholic crucifix. It closed its eyes, and moaned. It didn't seem to be distressed, though. As far as Jack could see, it was in some kind of feeding frenzy.

He was too confounded to drop the square as the gremlin writhed there in ecstasy. After the first throes died down, it opened its eyes, put two fingers in its mouth and gave a shrill whistle. Instantly two more gremlims appeared on the printer with small *pops* of displaced air. "I keep money, yes?" the gremlin, *his* gremlin, shrilled. The other two nodded, and the original beckoned with an arm gesture. The new arrivals jumped to join the first like grade-school looters at a candy store.

Jack had had enough. He shook the T-square to dislodge the gremlins, but they were holding on too tightly. He reached gingerly through the seething mass of small limbs and plucked the battery from the driver board. The writhing stopped, and his gremlin gave him a sour look and the finger. It dropped back into the workings of the printer; the other two scurried for the corners of the office.

Jack looked at the T-square. "Great, Halloran," he said to himself, "just great. Now you've got *three* of them." There were other uses of symbols and belief in the demonic tradition, perverse uses. He might just as well have mounted the cross upside down and lit black candles. His radio came on suddenly, tuned to a station he particularly hated. He walked over and pulled the plug. He didn't think he was going to mention this little incident to Rhea or anyone else for a long, long time.

He was in the parking lot before the thought penetrated: the little gremlin had said, *I keep money*?

What on Earth did that mean?

# Chapter 47

When Mindenhall got back with the pizza, Glibspet was poring over more old insurance records. Craig set the box down on the table in the outer office. "Here," he said, "*you* open it." He stood well back while Glibspet got up and lifted the lid. The aroma rolled over him like a fog bank, and he inhaled deeply, savoring it.

"My car is going to smell like anchovy for a week. How can you eat that stuff, Dom?"

Glibspet considered answering *because I'm a fiend from Hell*, but thought better of it. He'd only been living with Craig for about a week now. The man wasn't dependent enough on him yet to make breaking cover truly worthwhile. Besides, the sex was pretty good.

"I'm doing my part for the environment," he responded readily.

Mindenhall approached the pizza warily, like a dog circling a spoofing possum. The initial odor blast had dissipated, and he was able to get close enough to snag one of the normal slices. He took a bite and chewed thoughtfully. "How's that?" he asked from around the mouthful.

Glibspet took one of his own slices and tasted it. *Not bad*, especially considering that he couldn't have the toppings he *really* wanted. Not while Craig was around. "Well," he said, "have you ever tried anchovies?"

Mindenhall nodded.

"And you found them completely disgusting, and a potential threat to the continuance of life on Earth, right?"

Mindenhall nodded again.

"Well then," Glibspet concluded, "you can hardly oppose anything that removes this many anchovies from the environment, can you now?"

"I suppose not," Mindenhall said, "but I think you should have to get an EPA permit."

"No problem," Glibspet said. "I have a set of nice of eight-by-ten glossies that let me get anything I need from the EPA. The local EPA chief and her young nephew have such a charming *close* relationship. It's always nice to see a family getting along."

Mindenhall frowned. "Don't joke about that, Dom," he said. "You know how often we get accused of that pedo crap. It's sick and it's not funny."

Glibspet shrugged. "Hey, hold your fire," he laughed. "they can't all be gems." He resolved to have another look at the pictures later in the evening. It was always fun to go through his photo files: People behind closed doors did the most *interesting* things for a teleporter's camera. . . . He rummaged through the clutter on his desk. "Here," he said, handing Mindenhall a much scribbled on printout. "These are ten names from old insurance reports. These people are dead, supposedly, and their claims have been paid, but aside from that, I can't find out anything about them anywhere."

Craig took the paper. "Meaning?" he asked.

"Don't know," Glibspet replied. "Could be just completely obscure people who never left the house, never borrowed any money, never subscribed to anything and never had an obituary, could be insurance fraud, or *maybe* they're people who never quite finished the formalities of dying by virtue of not being dead."

# Chapter 48

CONFERENCE ON HADOCENTRISM CONVENES
Chapel Hill — Raleigh News & Courier

The first annual conference on Hadocentrism convened at the University of North Carolina Chapel Hill yesterday. The scholarly movement, which holds that Hell has been unfairly maligned during centuries of Celestiocentrism, and that the most successful early societies were Hadocentric, is especially strong in North Carolina academic circles. The weekend conference is chaired by Dr. Charles Blassius, the first Unchained to gain full professorship and tenure in the UNC system. In his opening remarks, Dr. Blassius stated his gratitude to the participants, and the belief that the conference would "usher in a new age free of the hegemony of Heaven, and the oppression of Heaven-mandated forms of conduct."

The conference is not universally popular with UNC faculty, although one prominent opponent of Hadocentrism welcomed the gathering. "This is great," said Dr. William Poundstone. "Now they can get their own building, and the rest of us can get back to work bringing new currents into the mainstream, not forming separate puddles."

❖　　　❖　　　❖

204

"Dear Rhea," the note had read, "meet me at my place 6 A.M. tomorrow. It's time for a road trip!"

She thought about it as she showered. She'd seen all the Earth's wonders at one time or another, so as far as she was concerned, the best kind of trips Jack could take her on involved movement in small distances only—generally in an up and down direction. Still, he couldn't know that, and it was sweet of him to try to surprise her. Things were going well at work: The ship was nearly done, and they had two MULEs off the line already. Nobody was likely to need her presence on a Saturday.

She dried herself, savoring the big fluffy towel, another one of life's little pleasures that humans took for granted. There were so many.

She didn't know what to wear. It depended on where they ended up. Jeans and a blouse should be sufficient for anything Jack was likely to throw at her, unless they ended up at the beach, then she would want shorts. She considered a moment; she knew white shorts were a special weakness of his, and it wasn't like the cold would affect her, even if they ended up on top of a mountain— she took a pair and wriggled into them. She contemplated and rejected a bra—she didn't have to be Ms. Responsible Corporate Citizen today—and picked a red blouse which she tied at the bottom, leaving her midriff bare. If they were going sightseeing then she wanted to be the best sight Jack saw. She slipped a bathing suit into her purse and grabbed a pair of sandals. She was ready for whatever he could throw at her.

Her nose twitched as she approached the kitchen. She distinctly smelled maple syrup over hot pecan waffles. "Good morning, Remmy," she called as she stepped through the arch from the hallway.

The big angel stopped with the fork halfway to his mouth. "Oh, hi, Av-er . . . Rhea," he said. Across the table from him, Miramuel put down the morning paper and grinned sourly. A pot of grits bubbled on the stove.

"Remmy," Rhea said, "do you know how much real maple syrup costs?"

Remufel considered. "Not much, on your salary," he said.

And that was true enough, she had to admit. "And y'all have made a habit of breakfast now?" she asked.

"Well, perhaps Remmy has," Miramuel answered. "I stay abreast of the world's happenings, and work at this puzzle of word crosses."

"That's not true, Rhea," Remmy said, "she always has a glass of grapefruit juice, too."

"And if I do?" Miramuel retorted, "At least I don't stuff myself like you." She turned to Rhea. "You're here so seldom lately, Rhea. The newspaper is a poor replacement for talking with you."

Rhea raised her hands. "I know, I know," she said. "We've been over that, and I still won't be spending much time here until you can promise you won't meddle with my love life. Besides, I read the paper too, when I have time. I don't think you're spending the whole day vegetating in my kitchen; there's been too much good news."

Both angels looked positively guilty. They gave each other fascinating furtive glances. Rhea looked away, not wanting her face to tip them off to her sudden suspicion: Remufel and Miramuel weren't supposed to be parked in her kitchen. They weren't supposed to be running around doing good deeds. In fact, she wondered if they were supposed to be in contact with her at all.

Their presence didn't fit with anything The Hallowed Busybody had done since the day He turned the Hellraised loose in North Carolina, and if she'd been thinking more clearly, she would have realized that a lot earlier. Devils, demons, imps, gargoyles, gremlins, leccubi and fallen angels . . . the state was up to its armpits in them. But actual archangels from Upstairs . . . nope. As far as she had been able to tell—and she had plenty of experience with spotting the forces from the other side—not a single angel had manifested as a physical presence in the state in the entire time she'd been on Earth. Not one.

Until Remmy and Mir showed up in her kitchen.

She turned back to her guests and said, "Folks, I've got to be going. I'll see you when I see you."

"Rhea," Remmy called after her as she went out the door, "what do I do with these grits?"

"You eat them with milk and sugar," she yelled back, "just like cream of wheat."

She spent her entire trip to Jack's trying to figure out what angle Mir and Remmy were working. What in Heaven was going on? Or more to the point, what was going on in Heaven?

# Chapter 49

Gabriel would have been more than happy to ask Rhea the same question, had he known she was asking it. Not for the reasons he would have predicted when the Glorious One took off in search of the perfect wave, or whatever it was he was doing.

To Gabriel's surprise, almost all the archangels had pitched in from the start. In that first emergency meeting, they'd debated the merits of keeping God's little vacation a secret, but they hadn't been able to find any real merits—other than avoiding a general panic—and they'd decided that they'd do a lot better if everyone in all the Heavens knew what was going on and knew that Eternity was being run—temporarily, of course—by amateurs.

To Gabriel's even further surprise, there hadn't even been a general panic. Just about everyone in all the Heavens thought the Almighty was due for a bit of time off, and in that we're-all-in-this-together way common Upstairs, had divvied up chores and rallied round in a chin-up, stiff-upper lip way that was positively British.

In Valhalla, the Teutonic lesser deities had put Wagner's *Ring Cycle* on endless replay and revved up mead production in the Heroes Halls, and now everyone was getting a regular supply of some extraordinary mead; the Catholic sector of Christian Heaven was loaning out a lot of its not-so-well-known saints to the other sectors of the afterlife for emergency prayer request duty; the Buddhists and the eclectic pagans had gone together on a clever training and orientation group for newly arrived souls that also doubled as a briefing group for their folks' souls which were headed back down—an elegant and economical solution, and very popular throughout the Heavens, though a bit of a shock to those arriving souls who were destined for nonreincarnating sectors.

Mostly, everyone had been creative, supportive, and wonderful. Mostly, everyone was wondering why God hadn't taken a vacation long ago. Mostly.

And then there were the problems. The few rabble-rousers who wanted to complain; the occasional mislaid prayers; the afterlife assignments that somehow went astray . . .

And two AWOL archangels who'd disappeared twenty-four hours after God went on vacation, and who hadn't resurfaced yet.

Gabriel had been able to track their energy to North Carolina, but hadn't been able to pin them down any more definitely than that. They were shielding themselves, and somehow seemed to be linked to Hellish influences, and they seemed to be involving themselves in human affairs. He got one or two memos per day of Hellish plans foiled by "supernatural means—unmarked angel in vicinity."

He kept hoping they'd get back before the Holy of Holies returned . . . but as the weeks dragged on, he was beginning to give up hope. And what God was going to say about angels AWOL and without orders right in the midst of His big Hell experiment, when all along His Perfection had maintained a policy of absolute nonintervention . . . well, Gabriel didn't want to think about it. He'd heard the lectures on interfering with mortal free will. Over and over and over, he'd heard them. That interference was what caused the First Rift.

He hoped there wasn't going to be a second.

# Chapter 50

Jack's gargoyle looked positively gaunt to Rhea. The creature gave her a listless wave as she went under the carport.

Her key slid smoothly into the lock and the back door swung easily on its hinges—Jack had fixed it after the second time she was locked out. Apparently in consequence, his microwave had gone on the blink and would now run only for two minutes and twenty-two seconds at a time.

Jack was in the living room, apportioning miscellaneous picnic paraphernalia between different bags and whistling Roger Whitaker's "New World in the Morning." He started as he heard her come up behind him. "Oh! Hi, Rhea." He glanced at his watch. "Right on time, I see." He did a double take as her outfit registered, then he did a long, slow inspection, starting at her toes and working upwards.

"Do I pass?" she asked.

"You know you do," he said, and hugged her, holding her close enough that she could feel the hard truth behind his words. She reached down and pinched.

He pinched back, but said, "Uh, uh, time for dessert later. First help me get this stuff out in the car, and then let's hit the road."

Rhea grabbed a bag and smiled at the fresh smells of

bread and tortilla chips. "Where are we going?" she asked.

Jack fanned a pair of tickets in front of her face. "It took a bit of work to get these," he said. "It's not like Disney World. They don't let so many people in each day that it gets intolerable. We're going to Devil's Point."

The smile froze on Rhea's face. Oh, just great. The one place in North Carolina I least want to go. The place with the highest concentration of Unchained. She looked at Jack's face. He was grinning with triumph—those tickets really *were* hard to get. And certainly it would be the last place any of her pursuers would expect her to go. She tightened her shields. "That's wonderful," she said.

# Chapter 51

Jack had his reasons for going to Devil's Point, but the drive with Rhea would have been enough. The four-hour trip from the Triangle to Pender County was passing all too quickly. He had all the windows down as the faithful Camry negotiated the back roads towards the coast. It was a beautiful day, and the stereo was blaring through a special tape of traveling music he'd put together. Rhea had seemed a bit uncertain at first, but now she chatted easily as they made happy talk about nothing in particular. He told a few more stories from his childhood and she laughed appreciatively. He'd given up asking about *her* past. From the number of times she'd slid away from the subject, and the way she had never mentioned her parents in any context, he'd concluded that maybe she had been an abused child.

*I'd like a few minutes alone with anyone who laid a finger on her.* It was an ugly thought, and he pushed it aside with the story of how his father had climbed the big pine tree to string an antenna for Jack's first crystal radio, and had gotten stuck.

"So after the hook and ladder were dispatched," he said, "it got out on the police band somehow that he was going to jump. A news crew showed up then. He'd had the antenna wire fastened through his belt loop so he wouldn't have to hold it while he climbed. When the big branch broke it got caught in the wire, and he had to shuck his pants to keep from going with it. So he's up here in this tree in his underwear, on live TV with firemen scurrying around below wrecking my mother's garden, and newsmen yelling up questions about his motive. Then my grandmother shows up, hysterical, to talk him out of jumping. Then Mom and the rest of us get home from the mall and can't park closer than a block from home . . ." Jack stopped for a moment as he passed a huge Cadillac land yacht going about forty. Naturally a man with a hat was driving.

"So what happened?" Rhea prompted.

Jack shrugged. "Oh, not much," he said. "The firemen put up a ladder and Dad climbed down. Then he went over to the news crew and told them that if they weren't off his property in one minute, he would shoot them for trespassing, and that if they couldn't believe that from a suicidal man in his underwear, who could they believe it from? He took Grandma inside and got her quieted down, hugged Mom really hard, then looked at me and told me something I've never forgotten.

" 'Son,' he said, 'for two dollars I can buy you a better radio than you'll ever build. And next time you get the two bucks!' Then he hugged me too."

"He sounds like a neat man," Rhea said.

"He is," Jack agreed. "Just don't ever call him Pinetop Halloran."

Traffic picked up as they neared Devil's Point. As he'd told Rhea, the number of people allowed in each day was carefully regulated, but even the Unchained couldn't build a hundred square miles of amusement park and not have urban sprawl blight the surrounding area. Still, the roads had been carefully reworked to handle the flow, and the signs marking the way to the entrances were well laid out. Jack had no trouble getting past the inevitable religious protesters and finding a place in the vast parking lot. He grabbed the picnic bags from the trunk, hesitated a moment, then added a small Super-Soaker to one of them. This should be the perfect place to try it. If something went wrong again, at least he wouldn't have the fallout of his mistake wreaking havoc in his office. They walked over to the tramway and caught a tram to the main gate. Or almost to the main gate—there was a state police checkpoint in front of it.

"I hadn't heard about this," Jack told Rhea.

"From what I've heard, it makes sense," she said.

They got in the long line threading past the checkpoint. A bored-looking trooper sitting at a folding table looked up and handed each of them a sheet of paper. "Read and sign this," she told them.

Jack looked. The sheet read:

> Due to the unusual circumstances surrounding the area known as Devil's Point, it has proven impossible for any Federal, State or local authority to enforce its laws within the area, to provide any emergency medical services to the area, or to guarantee the safety of people within the area in any way.
>
> Although this notice does not constitute any waiver of sovereignty, and no passport is required, your entry into the Devil's Point area is essentially equivalent to entering a foreign country, and your signature absolves all State, Federal and local government and private entities from any liability that may result from your entry into the area, and forswears any legal action that you or your heirs may bring against those entities for events that transpire while you are inside.

"Boy," Jack said, "you're not pulling any punches are you?"

The trooper shrugged. "No one's making you go in," she said.

"Have you been in?"

"Yeah," she admitted. "I'm not allowed to give you my opinion while I'm on duty, though."

"Well, we know at least one person came out, then," Rhea said. She hesitated a moment, then signed her sheet with a flourish.

Actually, it was more like tens of thousands of people, Jack reflected as he signed his. Going into Devil's Point appeared to be much safer than driving a car. There were rumors on the Internet about a section called Desire's Point, but everything else was as clean and wholesome as Disney World, or as wholesome as a Disney World with fetish and sex-change shops anyway. The line moved on and he and Rhea passed through the main gate.

Jack didn't know what he had expected, exactly; he'd seen pictures, but nothing really prepared him for the impact. The people in front of him were even less prepared—he almost ran into them as they stopped dead in their tracks. The park laid out under the crystal sky was exquisite. The walkways and buildings *were* as scrupulously clean as Disney World, but there was no similar feeling of a jumble of styles—everything seemed to have been conceived as a single organic whole, and this *despite* the fact that a fourteen-story castle towered over clusters of modern buildings and a monorail circled silently beyond. He saw several artists set up off to the side, sketching and painting intently. Devil's Point was a masterwork of architecture and landscaping that put to rest the old claim about Hell's lack of creativity— perhaps it was meant to.

Apparently that first look wasn't having quite the same effect on Rhea that it had on him. She looked around quickly, almost furtively, then grabbed his arm. "Come on, Jack," she said, "it's lunchtime." She pulled one of the courtesy maps from the stand by the front gate, and guided Jack away from the crowd that was still milling about, deciding where to go first.

The monorail track rode elegantly between cleanly sculpted support pillars, some of which were also boarding stations. They took an elevator to the top of the closest station, and waited until one of the small fleet of trains glided to a silent stop. The doors on the far side slid open and a little cluster of people debarked—the train rising slightly as the load dropped.

"Is that maglev?" Jack asked, intrigued. "There are a lot of people still trying to make that work."

"All of whom have now ridden on this train several times, I'm sure," Rhea observed as the doors on their side opened and they stepped inside. "Probably with as much sensing equipment as they could carry."

He could barely feel the acceleration as the train eased away from the station. "Impressive," he admitted, "but we've got it beat."

Rhea squeezed his arm. "Believe it!" she said.

The train traveled counterclockwise, out over an impossibly wide beach strewn with sparkling white sand. The Atlantic lapped at the edge. Further back, he could see water slides, wave pools and a lagoon with miniature tall ships tacking back and forth. One ocean-side section was set off with high dunes and palmetto trees.

"What's that?" he asked, pointing. Rhea followed his glance and squinted slightly.

"Nude beach," she reported. "Maybe I can do some comparison shopping later, hmm?"

Jack felt himself flush. He'd been working out at the Y a little lately, when he could fit it in with everything else, but he didn't think he was quite ready for prime time. He sucked in his stomach and sat up straighter. "Sure," he said, "but remember—you'll never go wrong with a name brand."

"You've cornered that market," Rhea reassured him. She pointed out the other side of the train. "Oh, look at that!"

*That* was a huge structure that seemed to be three long wings connected by a single cross-corridor. "It looks like the five-speed shift diagram for my Camry," Jack observed. "What is it?"

Rhea consulted her map. "It's the Library of Lost Books," she said and showed him the schematic. "Everything from Neolithic cave paintings in *first gear* to lost classics of the 1980s in *fifth*."

"That leaves *reverse*," Jack said. "What's there?"

Rhea looked at her map. "It doesn't say. Something appropriate, I hope. Great lost texts of post-modern deconstructionism, perhaps."

The monorail glided to a stop over a verdant swath of rolling hills set with picture-postcard shade trees, brooks and ponds. "Picnic park," Rhea said. "All ashore that's going ashore."

Considering that the whole trip was his plan, Rhea seemed to be finding her way around a lot better than he was, Jack reflected as they rode the elevator down.

Lunch was perfect. They sat under an ancient live oak on the bank of a crystal brook. Spanish moss stirred lazily in the hint of breeze, and cloud shadows crisscrossed the grassy expanse of the park, accenting the sunshine like black pearls among the white. Although Jack knew they couldn't really be alone, no other picnickers were visible. Apparently in Devil's Point you only had as much company as you wanted. He spread out the heavy paper picnic cloth and set out the food.

"Are those *real* tomatoes?" Rhea asked as he started loading a sandwich bun.

"Almost," he replied. "They didn't come from anyone's back yard, but at least they came from the farmer's market, not the grocery store." She took several slices. "And this," Jack said, "*is* real Vidalia onion." He put a thick, sweet slice on top of the tomatoes, then piled on three different types of cheese and some pepperoni.

Perfect. Rhea built sandwiches to a less heroic scale, but hers looked as eminently edible as she; she leaned back against the tree trunk with her sandals kicked off and stray flashes of sun sparkling from her hair as the breeze opened momentary pathways through the leaves above, and he wished he knew just how alone they were.

Rhea divined his thoughts. She grinned widely and made a teasing erotic act out of eating, but shook her head at his raised eyebrows, "Not here," she said, "this park is all ages. I've looked on the map and found another park for . . . this evening."

Just as they finished eating, an Irish setter ran up holding a Frisbee in its mouth and looked at them expectantly.

"I think," Rhea said, "we've just been issued a dog."

It was, Jack had to admit, the perfect way to end a picnic. The dog was very friendly in that bumbling, dumb, enthusiastic Irish setter kind of way, and an expert jumper. He made catches that Jack could hardly credit, completely leaping the stream once while making an airborne grab. Finally he looked at Jack and Rhea, wagged one last time, took his Frisbee and left.

Jack and Rhea looked at each other. "Time to go," Jack said.

Jack left everything but one small bag in the recycle bins at the entrance to the park.

"What next?" Rhea asked as they left.

"Well, I'd like to see the Library of Lost Books. I hear it's got the Greek scholars in a tizzy. The complete texts of the Alexandrian Library, Homer's *Triumph*, and lots of new Aristophanes. And most of that sucks. I'm interested in smaller stuff though."

Rhea consulted her map. "Well," she said, "I think we can just walk there. We don't need the train."

There were no crowds by the library. In fact, like Picnic Park, there didn't seem to be anyone else around. It was a good trick—Jack knew the Library of Lost Books got thousands of people a day. A tall, thin devil met them as they stepped through the huge front doors. He was the first of the Unchained Jack had seen since coming through the front gate. The devil looked out over his half-frame glasses at Jack, and Jack could almost feel the appraisal and dismissal. His look at Rhea, though, was anything but dismissive. There was a speculative gleam in his eye that Jack didn't like. Rhea was *not* available. Jack put his arm around her.

The devil smirked knowingly. "Welcome," he said, "to the Library of Lost Books. I am Lucien, your guide to the stacks. I sense that you, sir, are a man of many interests, and that you, madam . . . well, hmmm, perhaps your interests are less easily discerned, but nonetheless broad, I'm sure. How may I assist you?"

Rhea looked at Jack and shrugged. Was she a bit pale? She hadn't seemed at all squeamish about the gremlins. Well, devils were considerably more unnerving than little, squeaking gremlins. He tightened his arm around her reassuringly. At any rate, their destination was up to him.

There was very little that didn't interest him at least somewhat. He could have just started with the first book on the first shelf and worked his way through the stacks a book at a time . . . but he and Rhea were on a day trip, not a camping expedition. First things first. "Science fiction," he said, "from the last two hundred years."

"Very good," Lucien said and steepled his fingers in thought for a moment. "This way, please."

They had entered through the doors in what Jack still thought of as *first gear*. The demon lead them south to the central corridor, then east towards the last wing. He didn't offer any running commentary; in fact, he didn't look back at them at all. Jack and Rhea were left to make what guesses they could about all the statuary and exhibits they passed in the spacious hallway. "Fertility goddess?"

Jack speculated about a blatantly immodest little statue perched lustily on an otherwise somber table.

"Or a prehistoric business card," Rhea responded. "Maybe the glyphs on the tummy say 'For a good time, call Basheeba, third cave on the left past the mastodon skeleton. I'll make you Homo Erectus.' "

As they left the sections of rock carvings and clay tablets, the smell of musty paper and parchment gradually became overpowering. It seemed to Jack that they had been walking much further than was possible given what he had seen of the building from the outside. "TARDIS," he murmured to Rhea.

"What?"

"Time And Relative Dimension In Space. It's bigger on the inside than the outside." He considered. "Like my mother's pocketbook."

Finally Lucien brought them to the end of the hall, and ushered them north into the *fifth gear* area. They passed countless rows of shelves arrayed with every type of book, from leather-bound Victorian volumes to CD-ROMs and chips. Their guide opened the door to a side room and waved them ahead. "We have arrived," he said.

Jack looked around. The room was divided into two parts by a center aisle. Across the aisle to the left, poorly lighted shelves stretched on almost as far as he could see, while to the right a compact group of well-lighted, dust-free shelves beckoned invitingly.

"What's the difference?" Rhea asked, pointing to the left.

Lucien took off his glasses and wiped them meditatively. He pointed into the dimness. "Those books are lost because they were unpublishable, unsubmitted or didn't find the right editor."

"My God," Jack said, "it's the grand, cumulative slush pile of SF!"

Rhea grabbed his arm. "Be afraid," she said. "Be very afraid."

"Indeed," Lucien agreed. "It's the largest such for any of our genres. Seemingly, of every two people who read science fiction, one of them has a book he hopes to contribute to the field."

Fascinated, Jack walked to the first shelf and picked up a dusty folder. Inside, the cover page was dated May 7, 1843, in precise early Victorian handwriting. He turned to the last page and read:

"Whereat the man said, 'Good lady, I call myself Adam. And how might I politely address myself to you?' Upon which words the woman responded, 'Good sir, I have no other name than Eve.' "

Jack shuddered and put the manuscript down. "Not a book that should be put aside lightly," he quoted, "but rather one which should be hurled with great force."

"And on the other side?" Rhea asked.

"Books by known authors," Lucien said, "or good ones. Lost due to fire, war, the post or what have you. Not nearly as big a set." He put his glasses back on and settled them firmly on his nose. The lenses magnified his distinctly demonic square pupils. "Now then," he said, "there is a bellpull in the wall by the door. Do pull it when you are done here, and I shall escort you out, but for now I must attend to other business."

"Thank you," Jack said automatically.

"No thanks are necessary," the demon said primly, and disappeared with a puff of imploding air.

"Well," Rhea said, looking around, "I guess we're on our own."

Jack was already rifling through the good stacks. "Yep," he agreed happily. "Hey!" he pulled a book and leafed through it rapidly, then turned back to the first page and started reading. Before long, he was chuckling, then laughing out loud.

Rhea moved to look over his shoulder. "What is it?" she asked.

"It's the sequel to *The Witches of Karres*," Jack said. "The one Schmitz lost when he moved."

Jack looked up eventually, and saw Rhea looking at him in amusement. "How long have I been reading?" he asked.

"A little over an hour," she said, "but who's counting? Was it good?"

"Great! See what the Leewit does here?" He pointed, and soon Rhea was laughing too. He put the book aside with regret: so little time. One day he, or someone, would have to come in with a scanner. "But we've got to move on."

He put the book back and yanked on the bellpull. It rang with a vast sepulchral *thrummm* that he could feel down to the soles of his feet.

Lucien popped back into view. "Yes?" he said. "You're done?"

They nodded. "Very good, follow me." He led them back into the main stacks. "I believe we shall exit through the east doors if that is satisfactory."

"What's on the east side?" Jack asked.

"The Village," the demon answered. "Fine lodging, dining and entertainment. And," he looked over his glasses at Jack again, "Lover's Point—a spot for the most discreet of assignations. And here we are." He opened a massive door for the two of them. The sound echoed through the cavernous spaces behind. "Good day."

"I wonder if he's the image they're trying to project," Jack said as they strolled out the doors and away from the library. The afternoon was beautiful and the sun bathed Devil's Point in a wash of light, lathering it occasionally with the shadow of a passing cloud. Ahead of them, the buildings of the Village gleamed like jewels, each one cut in a different style.

"He *was* awfully stuffy," Rhea said. "Maybe he was trying to project a scholar/librarian sort of air." She didn't look convinced.

Jack considered. "He wasn't like any librarian I know. They're always glad when anyone gets some use out of the library—and I didn't like the way he looked at you." Music began to fill the air as they entered the outskirts of the Village. Jack could hear snatches of show tunes from several different eras. "Look at this," he waved a hand at the scene. "This is where the Unchained put their best foot forward, show us all what great guys they are, and the first one we interact with is a pompous ass."

"They *are* fiends from Hell, Jack," Rhea reminded him.

He looked at her; she wasn't smiling.

"Well, yes, I'll grant you that. So they say, anyway. I still think there could be other explanations. But isn't the road to Hell supposed to be attractive?"

"You didn't enjoy the picnic, or our tour of the library?" Rhea asked.

"I did. There were hundreds of books in the library I'd like to read just in the SF section—and I can't even imagine all the other things I could find there." He stared off into space, thoughtful. "I was already thinking about the next time I come here. After a few trips, I might even want more . . ." He looked over at her and nodded. "Point taken."

They stopped by an electronic YOU ARE HERE board, and he studied it with interest. The "you're all alone" illusion gave way in the Village, and they were once more amidst the press of humanity. Unchained street vendors hawked their wares from quaint carts, catering to the steady stream of people filling the curving thoroughfares. "What do you think?" Jack asked.

Rhea pursed her lips. "Well," she said, "it's been a while since I saw a Ziegfeld's Folly. How about that?"

"Pretty girls, song and dance—how could I object?"

Jack pushed the button by the description. On the screen, a glowing red line traced the path to their destination. "It's not very far, either." Where in the world, Jack wondered as they set off, had Rhea seen a Ziegfeld's stage show?

They were about halfway to the Ziegfeld theater when Rhea grabbed his arm. "I think we're being followed," she whispered. He could hear a note of urgency in her voice.

Nobody had ever told Jack that before. It wasn't something people said in real life. Not in *his* life anyway. "What do you mean?" he whispered back.

"There are four people behind us—" He started to turn his head and she dug her fingers into his arm and whispered, "No! Don't look! They haven't let us out of their sight since we got to the Village."

Jack stopped walking, but Rhea tugged him back into motion. "I don't have any enemies," he said. "You don't have any enemies. Are you thinking something industrial?"

"Maybe." She glanced at a sign they were passing, pretending to point it out to Jack. Voice low, she said, "Between the two of us, we're ninety-five percent of Celestial's intellectual property."

Jack looked at her sharply—there was something unconvincing about her tone. He'd assumed she didn't have any enemies . . . but maybe he'd assumed wrong. Her unwillingness to talk about her past could be a lot more than indications of an unhappy childhood.

"Well, it doesn't matter," he said. "Let's find a cop."

"No! There aren't any real cops here. This place is policed by Hell, and we can't trust Hell's police force." She peered intently into the crowd. "Follow me," she said, and ducked into a Scandinavian tour group coming out of a production of *West Side Story*. Most of them were still humming "Tonight"—badly. Rhea cut through like a lumberjack in tall wood, pulling Jack in her wake.

"Sorry," he said as blond heads turned and the humming broke off in confusion. "Got to run. Left the dog in the dryer!"

Rhea feinted left, then pulled a hard right into and then through a coffee shop. Walking at top speed, keeping in the center of crowds, they shot along the walkway at a painfully fast clip. At last they ducked in the doorway of a small, definitely nonkosher deli, and Rhea peered out cautiously. Jack was panting and sweat rolled down his back. As he concentrated on breathing, he noticed Rhea looked as cool as ever. He knew, intimately, how well toned she was, but this was just totally unfair. It was as if running for her life were an everyday occurrence. Well, maybe it was. He wondered if he ought to be more afraid. He wondered if he'd *feel* more afraid when he could breathe again.

When Rhea turned and looked into his eyes, he got his answer. She was terrified. Her fear was completely out of proportion to anything he could imagine—and in that instant, he became afraid, too.

"I think we lost them," she said. "Jack, let's get out of here. Now."

Jack nodded. "No argument," he said and looked at his courtesy map, calculating rapidly. "I think we're on the southeast side of the Village, here," he pointed. "Our best bet is to cut down the footpath past the Mall and catch the Monorail—You're *sure* we can't call security?"

"I'm sure," Rhea said, and her tone brooked no argument.

"Then let's go!"

"Wait," Rhea stopped him. "Have you got a rubber band?"

Jack searched his pockets, bemused. He finally came up with a thin red band that looked like it had been through the wash several times. "Here," he said.

Rhea took it, looked at it doubtfully, then pulled her hair back in a ponytail and secured it.

"That's a disguise?" Jack asked incredulously.

"All I have time for."

Rhea stepped out into the street, walking rapidly. Jack sprinted to catch up with her.

"Don't run," she said. "Keep pace with me. Look happy, and try to look like you're not in a hurry."

Jack was sweating again, already. He resolved then that finding more time for the Y would have to move to the top of his list. "How do you propose . . . to do that . . . when we're walking . . . twice as fast . . . as anyone else?" he panted.

"Point out the sights," Rhea said. "Talk casually to me."

"Talk? I . . . can't even . . . breathe."

But he managed. They moved out of the Village and past the Mall in full tourist mode. Jack pointed out each little change in the scenery, and Rhea nodded in seeming rapt appreciation. Once, a group of fifty tourists gathered around a bush he pointed at. He had no idea what it was, but they were still taking pictures of it when he lost sight of them.

Rhea was keeping an eye out for people behind them, looking back as though casually every couple of minutes. Apparently she hadn't seen anyone so far, and the relief on her face made him almost mad enough to quit being scared. Anyone who made Rhea that glad not to see them deserved some major grief. Unfortunately, he was in no position to dish it out.

They made the monorail station without incident and dived through the elevator door just as it closed, plowing ahead of a group of waiting Japanese students. Jack was sure that would spawn a spate of Rude American stories. "Au revoir," he called on impulse, waving at them as the door shut. Rude French stories were just as stereotypical, but he thought he could live with that.

Rhea looked at him intently, and he shrugged. They observed standard elevator etiquette the rest of the way up in the crowded car—both stared straight ahead at the light display over the door, and neither of them said anything.

There was a train loading on the platform. Rhea pulled them out of the natural flow leading to the car across from the elevator, and guided them to the last car of the train; except for the two of them, it was empty.

The monorail left the platform smoothly before anyone else joined them and Jack breathed a sigh of relief. "Now," he said, "can you tell me what the hell is going on? And don't give me that industrial angle. I don't buy it, and I can tell you don't, either."

The monorail sped over the Streets of the Past section of Devil's Point. Below them, the thatch roofs of a Medieval village lined narrow footpaths where rats the size of Chihuahuas scurried between piles of rubbish. Jack wondered if that section of the park got many repeat visitors.

Rhea looked as though she were wrestling with something. She stared ahead vacantly for a moment, then snapped back into focus. "Okay," she said, "I don't really think this is industrial espionage or sabotage as such, although they certainly wouldn't mind that as a by-product." She waved out the window. "This is Unchained home base on planet Earth—I think we were being followed by devils."

The territory below them shifted to Classical Greece.

A knot of men was debating excitedly beside a huge right triangle sketched on the ground. There were no women in sight. Jack felt he could use something as certain as the Pythagorean theorem. Not much else was making sense. "Well, why in the world would they do that?" he said. "And if it's demons, why are we running? Devils can't hurt us any more than the gargoyle on my roof can."

"Usually," Rhea dropped the word like a bomb. "There are exceptions to everything. And that's *devils*, not demons."

"But—" he started to say when a blast of displaced air almost knocked him from his seat. Suddenly there were four *devils* in the car with them. Devils with switchblades.

Jack had never been in fear of his life before. He'd had his share of close calls on the highway, but those were usually over before he realized it. This was different. These were beings who *meant* him harm. He'd heard of being paralyzed with fear; now he experienced it. He was trembling so hard he couldn't move voluntarily at all and his gorge was rising—he was going to be sick.

One of the devils, a female, moved slowly towards them. She looked at him contemptuously and slid past him as she advanced on Rhea.

"Well, Avy," she said, "there's someone who wants to talk to you." She motioned with the knife. "But aside from your being able to talk, they don't much care what shape you're in."

Rhea's face twisted with strain—then she blanched. The devil chuckled, "That's right, we've got a standing tap into *three* fallen angels to enforce a dead zone around you, and we're drawing on it now. Not a thing you can do. Okay, guys," she motioned the other devils forward. They grabbed Rhea's arms and legs. She struggled, but couldn't shake them. The first devil took her knife and slowly, deliberately traced a line across Rhea's cheek. It crimsoned with blood. Rhea screamed.

The fear paralyzing Jack imploded into a white-hot ball of anger. He was moving almost before he realized it, throwing himself at the devil with the knife. "Leave her alone, you bitch!" he yelled. He'd never been any good in a fight and he was way out of his class here. Two of the male devils tried to catch him, but their hands slipped off of his as if he'd been greased. He slipped past them, too, unable to get hold of either one. He sprawled facedown in the aisle, and his face and the palms of his hands lit up with pain.

Rhea was screaming behind him. They were hurting her. Cutting her. His anger cooled—cooled until it was arctic, until his pounding heart pumped ice water through his veins. Suddenly, he could think and his brain raced. He crawled towards his seat. One of the male devils eyed him and dismissed him. The female began to score Rhea's other cheek. Jack grabbed the picnic bag. He fumbled, and willed his hands not to shake; he had no time for clumsiness. He grabbed the Super-Soaker inside. A child's toy. He wished he had a bazooka. He'd only hoped he and Rhea might cross paths with some gremlins so he could test his theory before he shot the Super-Soaker into the innards of his printer.

The female saw him. Her lips drew back in a smirk.

He pulled the trigger.

All Hell broke loose. The devils screamed. Rhea screamed. Fire and smoke filled the car. He felt the heat, but it didn't burn. Then suddenly there was silence. Nothing. He couldn't see anything—the smoke filled the air, dense as heavy fog. I shouldn't be able to breathe, he thought, but he was breathing just fine.

A hand grabbed his arm and dragged him to his feet, and Rhea shouted in his ear, "Come on!"

Then he was lying on asphalt. They were in the parking lot. He had no memory of getting there. His clothes smelled of smoke. Rhea braced and levered him to his feet. Blood covered her face, but the fear was less evident in her eyes.

"We've got to get out of here," she said. "The parking lot guards are coming, and we aren't going to have any explanations."

They were beside his Camry. In a daze he pulled out

his keys and opened the door. Rhea walked around behind and yanked hard on something. He heard metal give. She slid into the passenger side holding the license plate and frame.

Through the gaps in the cars parked around them, Jack could see small shapes approaching. Small shapes with pointed ears and tails: Lot demons.

"Go, go!" Rhea said. "Those are lower level. Not too bright—we can lose them." The demons were within a car's length of them now. Jack turned the key. There was a hollow *click* from underneath the hood.

"It's that goddamn starter," he yelled and threw open the door. "I've got to hit it."

"No!" Rhea grabbed him, his legs out the door. He felt her shift and something went *thunk* in the engine compartment. "Try it again." There were demons on the hood now.

He slammed the door and turned the key. This time the engine purred into life. Jack ground the gears into reverse and popped the clutch. The car leapt backwards, shedding some demons, rolling over others. "You're going to get a huge bill for those," Rhea yelled. "I'll pay it."

One stuck its hands through the door and grabbed at Rhea. She kicked it viciously.

Jack hit first and sped for the main lot gate, leaping a curb and running down the sidewalk once to bypass the line of cars leaving the park. The demons gave up pursuit at the park boundary. "Standing orders," Rhea said.

Jack didn't honor a single traffic light or speed limit sign until they were thirty miles inland. Then suddenly he was shaking so badly he couldn't drive. He managed to pull into the empty parking lot of a small church where he killed the engine. He started sobbing uncontrollably. Rhea leaned over and held him close until he stopped.

"I was so scared they were going to kill you," he said finally, when he could speak again.

Rhea stroked his hair tenderly. "Scared men have stormed a lot of beaches," she said. She paused. "What did you do to them?"

"Holy water," Jack said. "You don't have to believe in it—it just works." He laughed without humor. "I was hoping to find some gremlins to try it on."

Rhea frowned. "But holy water *hasn't* worked since—"

"Since Church Latin started diverging from Classical Latin?" He shrugged. "Retrolinguisticians have been reconstructing lots of languages lately. I found a priest liberal enough to try the result."

Rhea nodded. "You were lucky. Holy water can drive demons, but devils, even low level ones, it only hurts. You heard those." She shuddered. "They were channeling a lot of power. You hurt them; they dropped the ball and it backed up on them. They'll probably have to be completely reconstituted."

"Just add water," Jack muttered. "My heart bleeds for them." He looked at Rhea. Her hair was blackened with streaks of soot; her once white shorts were gray and grimy, and her face was cut and covered with dried blood. She was the most beautiful woman he'd ever seen. "I've got some Wet Ones in the trunk," he said.

Rhea winced as he applied the soft towelette to her face. "Do you want to go to the doctor?" he asked.

She shook her head. "I heal fast."

She wasn't kidding. When she washed off the blood, he could see that the cuts had already closed; her cheeks bore two red lines and the palms of her hands bore more, but he was willing to bet in a few days there wouldn't even be a scar.

They could hurt her, but not him. They couldn't even touch him. She knew what they were doing, she knew what they were after, she knew they'd been channeling energy—whatever the hell that was—she knew about holy water and what it would work on and what it wouldn't.

And now he knew some things he'd only wondered about before.

It didn't matter. It just didn't matter. Jack came to a decision. After they cleaned up, he said, "I wanted to give this to you this evening." He reached into his pocket. "But I think the location is more appropriate here. And, well, life's too short to wait for perfect moments." He handed Rhea the small box.

She raised the cover to reveal a perfect band of silver. It caught the late afternoon sun and gleamed like a beacon. "Oh, Jack," she breathed, "it's beautiful!" For an instant her face was radiant, angelic. Then a cloud passed across her features and the smile vanished. She said flatly, "But I can't accept it."

# Chapter 52

Miramuel shivered. "They almost got her, Remmy."

"I know. I felt it, too."

"We could have been with her," Mir whispered. "We could have stopped them."

Remufel crouched smaller in the kitchen and hugged his knees. "But we've almost been caught down here a couple of times already. If we'd saved her, we would have showed up on Heaven's monitors for sure. And then we'd get dragged back. Maybe this near-disaster will be enough to show her that she has to leave with us."

"What if it isn't? We're running out of time. The Almighty can't stay on vacation forever. When He comes back, if we haven't won her back . . . you know what's going to happen."

"We're going to end up in Hell."

"I can hear it now. Direct contravention of orders. A couple hundred counts of physical intervention on the material plane. Fraternization with the enemy." Miramuel's face was expressionless.

"We could go back now. Ask forgiveness. We'll be dropped back a bunch of ranks, and censured—probably have to do remedial work in the files or something for a while. But we wouldn't go to Hell." Remufel didn't sound enthused about this plan. He sounded more like he was playing devil's advocate. A dangerous game in Heaven.

Miramuel looked over at him and a single tear started down one cheek. "We didn't stand behind her before. We didn't speak up for her. She's the best friend I ever had, Remmy. The best, and I stood on the side of the angels and watched her sentenced to Hell . . . and none of us spoke for her. I won't let it happen again. Not again."

"I was there, too. I know. I know. I was just saying—"

"Well, don't!" Mir glared at him. "Don't! This is the only chance we're ever going to get to rescue her. The only time when the Omnipotent One isn't watching, when we can follow our hearts and maybe bring her home. If Lucifer gets hold of her again, after what she's done this time, he'll destroy her. It will be a billion years before she pulls enough of her atoms together to even regain some awareness of what she once was . . . and she'll never be Averial as we know her again. Never. We have to make this work."

Remufel thought for a moment. Then he said, "We could tell her why we're here."

"When we didn't stand behind her before? You think she'll believe we're risking Eternity just to get her back home after all this time?"

"No." Remmy sighed. "But she's learning to love again. Surely He won't let her go back to Hell."

"She hasn't truly learned love, yet . . . and, worse, she's duplicated Lucifer's sin. She's handed them knowledge they didn't earn."

"Not because she wanted things to be easy for them!"

"You think that will matter?" Miramuel glared at him.

"I don't know."

"It *won't*!"

"Then we're already doomed."

"Probably. But I'm not giving up until we're in the Pit."

# Chapter 53

Glibspet chuckled as he turned off his terminal and unhooked the red modem. It was hotter than usual, and sizzled softly as he grabbed it with a damp rag. He could read between the lines as well as anyone—better than most. The official report had been terse, but between that, the freshly posted infernal environmental hazard warning, and the news of four devils being repitted, he could tell what was what.

His employers had screwed up big-time. They must have had Averial right in their grasp, at Devil's Point of all places. Well, actually, he supposed, it was the last place anyone would look for her. *He* certainly hadn't been looking there. She'd just had the bad luck to run into the only devil there who was dull enough to read *all* the official traffic from down under, and sensitive enough to realize that she was shielded and not just vapid. He'd have to get in touch with the library devil soon—that one might make a valuable resource.

The Three Stooges figured they had her dead to rights, and they'd gotten cocky. They didn't hurry to the scene in person, didn't even alert the park guards until their cat's-paws had run into the first true holy water reported in the last who knew how many centuries. The Idiot Trio could trace her 'port to the lot, but after that, she was back in God's territory, and the fallen angels hadn't gained a single clue. Glibspet frowned. The only downside was that they would be even more frantic now than they'd been before, and their fear was sure to have a direct effect on their dealings with him.

Luckily, he thought he had a solid lead. He'd finally come across an insurance claim that had paid out, with someone willing to say she'd seen the decedent still alive. It was in the right time period, and the complainant had nothing to gain. Now what was the name the company had paid out for? He flipped through the notes Craig had made.

There it was: Rheabeth Samuels.

# Chapter 54

## IBM LANDS DEVIL'S POINT CONTRACT
Research Triangle Park — Raleigh News & Courier

Beleaguered computer giant IBM announced Friday that it has secured the master automation contract for the massive and controversial Devil's Point amusement park in coastal Pender County.

"I think this contract confirms IBM's continued commercial viability," said Triangle Park Division Manager William Emerson. "It plays to our strengths, and I'm confidant we will be able to give North Carolina's Unchained citizens and corporations the same kind of technical expertise and service that has made our reputation."

"None of their systems talk to anything else, or to each other," said Devil's Point's chief automation officer, Fellanol, a Fallen angel. "You have to pay extra for TCP/IP and their mainframe operating systems are a disaster. Their systems belong in Hell."

In IBM's Triangle facilities, which have been subject to numerous layoffs during the past several years, spontaneous celebrations erupted at the news; at the height of the festivities, several employees were seen to loosen their ties.

❖        ❖        ❖

Jan buzzed Rhea. "Line one," she said, "I don't think you're going to like it." There had been a lot of things Rhea hadn't liked lately. Almost being captured not least among them. She hurt most because she didn't dare tell Jack the truth about why she'd turned him down. Damn it, why did he have to want to marry her? She couldn't say yes without telling him the complete truth before the ceremony. And she knew she'd really hurt him with her flat refusal and her unwillingness to give him any reasons.

Her phone beeped again. Rhea sighed and picked it up. "Rheabeth Samuels," she said.

"Ms. Samuels—" Rhea disliked the voice on the other end immediately. "This is John Dent, chief auditor with TRITEL."

Please, not another money fight, she thought. "Yes?" she said.

"You have three hundred million of our dollars."

"Your company made a three hundred million dollar investment in my company—yes," she corrected.

"No, we did not."

Rhea's gut knotted and she sat up straight. "What do you mean, you didn't?"

"No such decision ever came before the board; no such disbursement was ever authorized. Believe me, I would know."

"What are you talking about? I signed a contract with Al Roberts. The initial financial transfer went without a hitch."

"Mr. Roberts is a mid-level executive. His authority does not extend to taking on obligations of this magnitude without board approval. And, I might add, he has been missing for the last three weeks."

"He came to me with an assurance that he had full clearance, and the check was signed by whoever it is at your end that has authority to sign checks. He must have skipped your board and cleared it directly with your top people."

"Mr. Williams, our president and CEO, died unexpectedly last week," Dent said. "Heart attack. But I'm sure he would have left some kind of mention of a deal like this with his board. In his papers. *Somewhere* around here." Dent cleared his throat. "No, Ms. Samuels, you have stolen our funds."

"The hell I have!" Rhea yelled, then calmed herself forcibly. "No. I haven't stolen your funds. And I'm equally sure that this screw-up originates on your end, and that our deal with TRITEL is rock-solid. However, if for just a moment, I imagine that it isn't, and that somehow Al Roberts got access to your funds without the authorization he said he had, what do you want me to do about it?"

"It's quite simple. We want our money back."

"Impossible," snapped Rhea. "I'm not a bank. I don't keep money in a vault. I use it to make more money. TRITEL's money is in large chunks of a rocket in Manteo that is about ready for its first launch."

"I suggest you find a way to liquidate, then. We will sue if we have to, Ms. Samuels. These things can get messy."

"You have no idea how messy they can get," Rhea said softly. She hung up the phone, and all her conviction emptied out of her, as if she'd been a balloon punctured by a bullet.

She closed her eyes and put her head in her hands.

# Chapter 55

Jack was not whistling. In fact, he hadn't even felt like turning the radio on for days. He'd cleaned the gremlins out of everything and he really didn't think they'd be back again. Getting rid of the smell of fried gremlin from the office had taken the steady application of Lysol spray, and even now he thought he could still catch a faint, sulphurous whiff from time to time. Other than that, he concentrated on working. It kept him from thinking about Rhea. He'd thought he knew her, knew her well enough to know that she loved him as much as he loved her—but this was like Carol all over again.

He closed down the diagram he was working on and marked it done. It was solid if not inspired.

"Jack."

He whirled in his chair. It was Rhea. "Yes?" he said shortly.

She stood in the doorway, not coming into the office. The hall lights lit her in outline. God, she's beautiful, he thought. "We've got to bump the schedule up," she said.

Okay, if she wanted to play it all business, he was happy to play along. The schedule was already tight, though. "How much?" he asked.

"Two weeks," she said.

He leaned back in his chair. "Impossible," he said. "Can't be done."

Rhea stepped into the room. "It has to be done," she said softly. "TRITEL is pulling out, retroactively. If we can't get the bird up in two weeks, it's never going to fly."

"I used to think I could do the impossible," Jack said. "Maybe I was motivated then. But I tell you right now that the schedule I gave you is the absolute best we can do, and *it's* barely possible." He crossed his arms on his chest. "And if you don't like my pace, I can always go to Rockwell." He regretted the words as he was saying them, but he wasn't going to back down.

Rhea flinched as though he had hit her and her hands tightened into fists. "You've got a contract," she said. "With a two weeks' notice clause. You're not going anywhere."

"If you want to spend money from a bankrupt company suing me, that's fine. But the only contracts I worry about are signed in blood." She flinched again. Yeah, he'd known she would. "You're going to have a *hell* of a time enforcing my contract."

"I need it in two weeks, Halloran," Rhea said. How she stomped out barefooted he didn't know, but she managed, and slammed the door behind her.

Jack rubbed his eyes tiredly. "Halloran," he said to himself, "you have really put your foot in it now." He didn't like being angry—it burned off IQ points faster than attending tractor pulls.

He didn't want to leave Celestial. Even if Rhea were shutting him out; there was still the dream. Anywhere else, he could only make money. Here he could make history.

Screw history. Here he could touch the stars.

He took a deep breath and pulled himself together. Two weeks. He had two weeks, and a stack of gotta-haves to go through. In how many places could he replace custom rigs with two-dollar radios?

# Chapter 56

Glibspet and Mindenhall walked into the offices of Gorman & Chase, a small Chapel Hill ad agency. They both wore dark suits and shades. "Snazzy," Craig said, looking at their reflections in the firm's lobby doors.

"It's an image thing," Glibspet said. "Well-heeled, but slightly menacing. Remember, we aren't here to be anyone's friend."

"If you say so, Dom," Craig muttered. He was still uncomfortable with this part of the job, but Glibspet thought his lying was coming along nicely.

"May I help you?" the receptionist asked. She was a strawberry blonde with a good figure and dimples. Glibspet immediately thought of several ways she could help him—unfortunately, none of them were applicable.

"Dominic Glib." He handed her an impressive looking business card. Mindenhall did likewise. "My associate and I represent Federated of Omaha Insurance in claims investigation. We're currently investigating a large claim paid out on the death of one Rheabeth Samuels. I believe she worked here."

The woman frowned. "Not that I know of," she said. "When was this?"

"About three years ago," Mindenhall said.

"Hmm. Maybe you'd better talk to Helen. She's been here forever." She keyed her intercom. "Helen, there are a couple of detectives out here who need to talk to you."

There was a squawk of dismay from the other end and the receptionist lowered her voice. "No, I'm sure it's not about *that*," she said reassuringly. She looked up again. "Helen will be right out," she said. "You gentlemen have a seat right over there." She pointed to an uncomfortable-looking couch.

The two sat. "Sit straight," Glibspet hissed to Craig. "Look grim—and put the magazine down."

Craig tossed the ancient *Time* magazine back on the coffee table. "I just wanted to see how the Ford/Carter race was coming," he whispered back.

Helen was a plump brunette in her early fifties. "Hello," she said nervously. "I'm Helen Goforth?" She didn't seem very sure of it.

Glibspet stood, and Mindenhall followed suit. "Dominic Glib, Federated Omaha," Glibspet said crisply. "I understand you may have known Rheabeth Samuels."

"I—well, the name sounds a little familiar. I've been here ten years, you know—there have been so many names?"

"Just the facts, ma'am," Mindenhall said. Glibspet glared at him. "She would have worked here about three years ago," Craig continued, somewhat chastened.

"I—I'm afraid I don't remember her," Helen admitted. "She can't have worked here very long?"

Either their information was wrong, or this Rheabeth Samuels had been a complete nonentity. Glibspet said, "She moved here from out of state only a few weeks before her reported death."

"Perhaps you'll have to talk to Mr. Gorman, then? He does all the hiring?"

"Yes, that sounds like a very good idea, Ms. Goforth," Mindenhall said. "Thanks for your help?"

"It's been a pleasure?" Goforth hurried off.

"That rising intonation would drive me over the line in about ten minutes," Glibspet said. "I don't know how these people stand it."

"They're used to it?" Craig said.

"Cut that out!"

Glibspet approached the receptionist again. "I'm afraid Ms. Goforth couldn't help us," he said. "Could we talk to Mr. Gorman, please?"

She frowned. "I'll see," she said. "He's pretty busy." She negotiated on the intercom with another secretary for several minutes, then, "I think he's coming down," she said. She paused. "Don't piss him off."

Gorman was a short dark-haired man with an unlit cigar in his mouth. Full of nervous energy, he didn't wait for Mindenhall and Glibspet to introduce themselves. "Jeez," he said, "I got people tied up in Germany, got a crew trying to talk some sense into the phone company, nobody on deck here and you want to ask me questions. What do you think I do here, run a research institute?"

"We just need a minute of your time, Mr. Gorman," Glibspet said and handed him a card.

"Federated of Omaha? Never heard of it. You need an ad campaign. I can get people all over the country lining up to buy policies."

"I'm sure you could, but we just need to ask you a few questions," Mindenhall said.

Gorman looked at his watch. "You've got five minutes," he said. "Then I start billing at on-site rates." Glibspet saw a man come through the back door holding a broom. He had several empty plastic bags threaded through his belt. He went over to the receptionist's desk, lifted the liner out of her trash can and replaced it with one of his empty bags. He and the receptionist talked for a minute. She pointed, and he turned to watch the tableau in the center of the lobby.

"You hired a woman named Rheabeth Samuels about three years ago," Glibspet said.

"No I didn't—" Gorman started, then shook his head. "Yes, I did. What about it?"

"Our company paid out a large claim on her life—"

"Damn straight you should have," Gorman said. "I remember now. Promising kid. Copywriter out of Alabama. Been here two days when a semi merged into her Honda. Killed instantly. Hadn't even moved out of the hotel yet."

"And you never heard anything about her being alive?" Mindenhall prompted.

Gorman snorted. "The police showed me the picture. No live people in that many pieces." He looked at his watch. "Time's up, or five hundred dollars a question," he said.

"Thank you very much," Glibspet said hurriedly.

"Been real. Pam," he called, "I want Frankfurt on the phone by the time I get back to the office."

"Can do," the receptionist said, and started dialing.

"Hey," the man with the broom said, and walked towards Glibspet and Mindenhall.

"Hello," Craig said.

"I've been super here five years," the man said. "I remember that girl. Not many people who come through here stick in my mind, but she did. Nice girl. Short, plump little thing, really friendly. I liked her an awful lot—thought maybe . . . well. Then she died. It was a real shame what happened to her."

Mindenhall nodded.

"But you said something about looking for her alive."

"Possibly," Glibspet said.

"Well, I heard the name again. Caught my attention—was a funny name the first time, and then to hear it again, you know? It was on the local news—right at the end of the show. About a woman heading some kind of hi-tech place, something in the Triangle. But if that's who you're looking for, your records are really screwed up. She's older than the Rheabeth who started here—pretty."

Glibspet pulled the photo he'd had made from the likeness of Averial and handed it to the man.

"This looks kind of like the woman I saw. I didn't get a very good look . . . but this could be her. Darker hair now, I think. Maybe. Maybe prettier."

Really. Glibspet smiled. "That's very interesting."

# Chapter 57

"You've been spending nights here again lately, Rhea," Remufel said to her when she came in from work. He was sitting at the kitchen table, as usual.

"Yeah," she said.

"Want to talk about it?"

"No, not really."

"Want some chocolate cheesecake then?"

"N—" She paused. She'd been making bad decisions all day. "Yes, Remmy, please."

He cut her a slice. "I made it myself," he said.

The floor by the counter was covered with chocolate. "So I see." She took a bite. "It's good," she said.

Remmy nodded, and watched her intently as she finished the piece. She put down the fork and he continued to watch her.

"He wants to marry me," she said finally.

"That's commendable of him," Remmy said. "Very honorable."

"You know the rules, Remmy. If I say yes, I have to tell him everything."

"Yes," Remmy said.

"He'll know I'm a fiend from Hell."

"Right." Remmy nodded.

"He won't love me anymore! He won't want to marry me!"

Remufel cocked his head. "You won't tell him you'll marry him because then he won't marry you."

"Yes!" Rhea sobbed as tears welled up.

"So then, exactly what are you gaining?" Remmy asked quietly.

Rhea wiped her eyes and thought. After a few minutes, she grinned tentatively. It felt good. Very good. "Where's Mir?" she asked. "She would have said I was doing the right thing."

"Then," Remufel said slowly, "you're lucky you got me, aren't you? More cheesecake?"

When Rheabeth left the kitchen, Miramuel reappeared. "Do you think that will work?"

Remufel shrugged. "When he finds out what she is, he might decide he doesn't want to be with her anymore. She has to show him her true self. Maybe when he rejects her, she'll give up what she's doing and leave. And if she does, the funding will fall through and the project will die, and she won't be in trouble anymore."

"Do you really think we did the right thing by removing all evidence of the TRITEL contracts and luring Roberts out of the state?"

"Do you want Avy safely out of Lucifer's reach?"

"Yes."

"I hope Jack runs screaming when he sees her. Then she won't have anything left here to hold her."

"I hope so, too. I just wish we knew we were doing this right."

# Chapter 58

Jack was on the roof, talking to his gargoyle. "You've got to go," he told her. He had his Super-Soaker, but he hadn't had the heart to use it on her yet.

The gargoyle was looking a lot better—almost plump, in fact. It made sense, he thought wryly. He'd looked up gargoyles in the Hell database, and found out that gargoyles fed as much off of negative emotions as they did off of real food. The pickings must have been pretty slim here while he and Rhea were a going concern. So why *had* the gargoyle stayed?

"Where pretty lady?" she asked. "You, she, no clothes, make bounce-bounce. Why no more?"

"I wish I knew," Jack said. "I really do."

"I no clothes, I pretty, I bounce real good," the gargoyle announced.

Jack shuddered. He wasn't that far gone. Yet.

The gargoyle reached out and grabbed him lewdly.

"Hey stop that!" He slapped her hand back. "You've got to go," he repeated, and picked up the Super-Soaker. She looked at him in puzzlement. He sighed—he couldn't pull the trigger. Devils, yes; demons, yes; gremlins, yes—but he felt like he knew this gargoyle.

"Look," he said, "you can stay awhile. But try to do your business over the back side of the house, where it'll help the flowers. And—say, what's your name, anyway?"

"Name not Anyway," the gargoyle said sadly. "Got no name."

Jack had a wicked thought. "Really?" He grinned. "You do now. I'll call you Carol."

"Oh!" the gargoyle said. "Good name! She pay good."

A chill ran down Jack's spine, and he had the feeling an entire gaggle of geese had walked across his grave. "What," he whispered, "are you talking about?"

"You know. Carol-lady pay devil, he pay us keep you company. Me, gremlins. Good job. See?" She opened a marsupiallike pouch and pulled out a grimy twenty-dollar bill. "Been hard work, sometimes, but good worker I."

Jack stared incredulously at the pouch and at the money. Carol. She was paying a devil to plague him. No wonder his life had gotten so weird.

"Well, I'll be damned," he said finally.

"No, you nice man," the gargoyle said. And then, hopefully, "Bounce-bounce?"

# Chapter 59

"Dom?" Mindenhall yawned and stretched. The two of them sat in Craig's living room. Glibspet had one end of the couch, while Craig stretched out on his back with his head cradled in Glibspet's lap. On the television, Andy was taking Opie fishing while the famous theme song whistled its way along.

Glibspet stirred. He didn't really need sleep, but there was something almost hypnotic about the whole scene. "Yeah?" he said finally, and tousled Mindenhall's hair.

"Why are we looking for this woman?" Craig stretched lazily and rolled over on his side. "The other cases come and go, but this one goes on and on."

"I don't know," Glibspet admitted. "This one is the boss's; the last one he stuck me with before taking up poodle ranching." He wished he were poodle ranching—it would be a great job, but the market was saturated. "It was one of the conditions for his agreeing to let me buy him out." He shrugged. "I don't know why he, or whoever he was working for, cares, or even knew she was out there."

Mindenhall raised himself up on an elbow. "Well, I checked the phone books, and the city directory," he said. "If she's living around here, she's unlisted. And there are lots of hi-tech companies in the Triangle to wade through."

"But we have a name now," Glibspet said, "and we know she's a fairly public persona." He grabbed Mindenhall's arm and pulled him up into his lap. "This thing is all but over." Glibspet kissed him. "Trust me," he said. Mindenhall's breathing quickened. He kissed back, and wrapped his arms around Glibspet.

"Always, Dom," he murmured. "Always." The couch creaked as they sank down together.

"Nip it?" Andy asked from the screen. "In the bud," Barney confirmed. Glibspet hit the mute.

# Chapter 60

REGIONAL PHONE COMPANY PIONEERS NEW
SERVICE
Lumberton — The Robesonian Weekly

At a news conference Monday, local long
distance company HELLo America announced
their new Enemies and Inlaws dialing plan. The
plan, which gives rock-bottom rates to tele-
marketers, will be available nationally at the start
of the month.

When asked how the company could possibly
undercut all competition for the telemarketing
market and still make a profit, Chairman Baal
Turgos, a Devil Third Class, admitted, "It's a
gamble, but we plan to clean up on the other side."
He went on to explain that members of the new
plan are unable to call each other, so HELLo
America expects tens of thousands of households
to sign up at regular rates. "The commercial rates
will get all the boiler-room operations and the
protection will get the households." Turgos
continued, "We expect exponential growth until
the number of nonmember households drops
below the telemarketing threshold. By then, we
will have thought of something else."

When asked if it wouldn't be inconvenient for
plan households to be unable to call each other,

Turgos replied, "Thirty-seven percent of all households have teenagers. Parents will love us."

Rhea looked at the TOO HARD box on her desk. It was full, but the bills now outweighed the useless government forms—she wouldn't have believed it possible. Normally, everything went through Accounts Payable, but these weren't normal times. She took the notices and dealt them out on her desk.

It was as sorry a tarot reading as she'd ever seen. Valentine's Electronic Supply House, that would be the Lovers, and E. Thomas Dooley Hydraulic, Inc., that would be the Hanged Man. Not a good sign for those to land together. That wasn't the point, though. She swept them back up again, and started considering each in turn. The point was finding those that could possibly be put off for a little while longer. It had reached the stage where that meant anything less than a third notice. Rhea finally put two in an envelope for Accounting; the rest she put back in the TOO HARD box. She considered starting a TOO BROKE box, but who would pay for it?

Was this going to be it, then? The end of all the work and hiding, of all her hopes for finally doing something really right? Bankruptcy? If all she had built were going to come crashing down, she could almost believe that getting caught would come as a relief. Almost.

Her phone beeped. She picked it up. "Rhea," Jan said, "Jack's back. Just thought you'd like to know."

"Thanks, Jan," Rhea said automatically. Jack hadn't quit. In fact, he had flown to Manteo to oversee some work at the shipyard. She really hadn't expected him back so soon. Butterflies stretched their wings in her stomach—it tickled, but felt good somehow. She put the phone down, took a deep breath and headed for the door.

Jan had the grace to be very busy with something on

her screen as Rhea walked past. In the empty stairwell, she took the steps two at a time, slowing to a sedate pace only when she stepped out into the hallway. Jack's door was open, as always. He was sitting there with his back to her, looking out the window as he talked on the phone. She stepped inside quietly.

"I appreciate it, Thel," he said. "I know Rockwell's a great place, and I owe you for putting a word in for me, but I think I'm going to stick it out." Rhea saw that he was doodling with his free hand. She looked closely. It was a rocket ship heading nose first for the ground. "Yeah, I know," he said, and his shoulders sagged. "It would be better for my career if I came out while this is still a going concern but—yeah, I know what I said, but I've got personal reasons." He sketched a tombstone with his initials on it. "Uh huh, that's right, but I'm going to risk it. Okay, thanks again, and remember . . . not a word about this to anyone. Say hello to Angie. See you!"

Rhea backed out silently, waited a second and came back in again, noisily. Jack jumped and turned as she closed the door.

"Hello, Rhea," he said warily. "More bad news?"

"I owe you an apology, Jack," Rhea said.

# Chapter 61

Jack considered. Had she come to tread, barefooted, over his throbbing heart again? Had she heard him talking to Thel?

It didn't matter. Having her here, talking, not saying something stupid like last time—that was what mattered. Please, whoever's up there, don't let me screw this up! "No," he said, choosing the words carefully. "You've given me too much to owe me anything, Rhea." He paused. "I'd *like* an explanation, but you don't owe it to me."

Rhea pulled a chair behind his desk and sat down by him. She reached out and took his hand in a steely grip. "Jack," she said intensely, "there are *things* in my past. Things you don't know about me. Things that make marriage very difficult."

Jack's throat tightened as all his worst speculations came back. "You don't have to tell me." He looked into Rhea's eyes, pools of emerald fire—a man could drown in there, or boil. "It doesn't matter what happened before," he said. "I don't care who you were, or what you were. You just have to believe that *I* will never hurt you."

"I know that, Jack," she said, her voice husky. Her eyes clouded with tears; she blinked them away. "I wasn't finished." She took a deep ragged breath and he smelled the sweetness as she exhaled. "It's very difficult, but I want to do it."

Jack sighed. "That's okay, I un—what? You want to do what?"

Rhea smiled suddenly, sunshine peeking through clouds. "I want to marry you."

Shadows vanished from the corners of the room; the cobwebs cleared from his mind. Jack's entire world narrowed down to her face in front of him. He was laughing as he threw his arms around her. They kissed, and for a minute, he knew again the simple joy of childhood—pure sensation with no thought of the future. Then it hit him: the ring! What had he done with it?

"Don't move," he whispered. He turned and began searching through drawers, frantically tossing aside the rubber bands, paper clips and dead ballpoints that seemed to breed in their natural habitat. There! Between the metric ruler and last summer's company picnic map. He grabbed the small box.

When he turned, though, the smile was gone from her face. "Not yet," she said, holding up a hand. "I want to marry you. That doesn't mean that you're going to want to marry me."

He stopped and waited.

"I *do* have to tell you, you see," she continued. "It's part of the agreement . . . and I have to tell you before we can have any sort of formal understanding between the two of us."

"Formal understanding?"

"Before I can say, 'Yes, I'll marry you,' you have to see me. Really see me, Jack. You have to know."

He nodded. Waited. Best to let her get around to it in her own way.

She swallowed hard. "I'm one of the Hellraised."

"I already knew that. What else?"

She looked shaken. "What else? What do you mean, what else? And what do you mean, you already knew?"

He shrugged. "I had my suspicions before—little things

about you that just didn't quite add up. I knew for sure in Devil's Point, when the devils hurt you. They couldn't even touch me, but they cut you with knives." He smiled gently. "They couldn't have touched you, either, unless you were one of them."

She looked stunned. "You *knew*? You knew when you asked me to marry you?"

"Yeah."

"Oh, my God."

"I figured you had to realize I knew after our trip— when you turned me down I thought it was for some other reason. Like you didn't love me."

"But I . . . do. Love you. I just didn't see how you could love me."

"Well, I do."

"You love what you've seen so far." She closed her eyes, and the pain on her face was clear. "You haven't seen the real me."

She showed him. She shielded the room first, so that the Hellawatts it took for her to translate her human seeming back into her angelic form wouldn't show up on Hell's monitors, and then she shifted.

He caught his breath. She was both beautiful and terrible, a creature who bore the scars of unmeasurable pain and grief. Fear raced along his nerves like a jolt of lightning; from darkly glowing wingtips to fiery eyes and Hell-shaped body, she was the beautiful stuff of nightmare, seductive and terrible and overwhelming as a Giger painting. Logically, he knew he should be wanting to run for his life . . . but he could see her Hellish form and still love her—because she was this creature, but she was Rheabeth Samuels, too.

"Seen enough?" she asked.

"Yes," he said. "Unless you have more you need to show me."

She changed back to her human seeming.

He nodded. He felt a bit shaky, but only in the knees—and that was just gut reaction. He looked at her, and smiled. "Fine," he said at last. "You've shown me what you were before I met you. I understand what I'm getting myself into. *Now* will you marry me?"

She reached behind her and he heard a metallic *click*. The door lock.

Rhea walked towards him, and began, innocently, to shed her clothes. Her skirt went first, falling soundlessly to the floor; then her blouse. Somehow she managed to step out of her panties without breaking stride. His overtaxed knees gave way at last, and he dropped into his chair. She slid onto his lap, wearing only a bra and a smile.

"I—I've got something for you," he managed to say.

"I can tell," Rhea said.

"I mean—"

"I know," she said quietly, and took the open box from him. She slipped the ring on her finger. "It's beautiful, Jack." She put the box down carefully. "Now, want to give me a hand?"

Jack reached behind her and opened the bra clasp. He had gotten pretty good at it. He pulled the flimsy red annoyance away from her and took in the sight of her the way nature intended. Well, maybe nature didn't have so much to do with it, but he didn't care. They kissed again, frantically this time. His hands roamed over the wonder of her and she returned the compliment. After what seemed like an eternity, but wasn't nearly long enough, she broke away.

Rhea stood and took the phone off the hook. "You're a little overdressed, don't you think?" She bent over and began working his shirt buttons.

It was a great angle to appreciate her from and he made the most of it, but at some point he had to get rid of his pants. He stood reluctantly and worked to get them down, past the natural obstruction that had developed. Rhea knelt in front of him and helped. After his jeans and jockeys slid to his feet, she kept on helping.

She looked up with a gleam in her eyes. "Okay, mister," she said, "on your back!" She pointed to the metal trolley table.

Jack touched it dubiously. "It's awfully cold," he said.

"We'll warm it up," she said. "In the meantime, better your buns than mine."

She was right, he thought later, when thought was possible again. He *was* warm now. He opened his eyes and looked up at Rhea, still astride him. She was staring dreamily into the distance, sweat beaded on her perfect skin. Her gaze focused suddenly. She looked startled, then giggled and waved. She rose up slowly, letting Jack slide free, then walked to the office window.

What? Jack sat up and looked out. Jan was in the parking lot making a frantic cranking pantomime with her hands. As Jack's head came above the sill, she waved at him, and gave him a big thumbs-up sign, then resumed her signaling. He could feel himself flush crimson as Rhea quickly cranked the blinds shut.

"How long was she out there?"

"Long enough to know the blinds needed shutting," Rhea laughed.

"But she saw—"

"Nothing she hasn't seen before. Besides, *you're* the one who's been on film. Anyway, I'll wager she would have kept everyone else away. And if not—"

Jack got off the table. "And if not, what?" he said.

She shrugged. "And if not, let's really give them something to talk about. C'mere you!"

"You're an evil woman, Rhea," Jack said.

"I'm trying to give up being evil," she said. "But I'll always be wicked."

# Chapter 62

"Give me a pigfoot and a bottle of beer," Glibspet told the clerk at the RediMart.

"I don't know," the clerk said. He looked doubtfully at the large glass jar Glibspet was pointing to. "No one's ever bought one of those things since I was here. I don't even know what I'm supposed to fish 'em out with." He paused. "Hell, I don't even like looking at 'em."

"And I don't like looking at you," Glibspet snapped. "Use the hot-dog tongs and put it in a drink cup."

The clerk stiffened. "Okay, mister, if that's what you want." He moved with deliberate slowness, making a production of finding a cup and rinsing the tongs. He put his arm around the huge glass jar and wrestled the screw top off. The pressure equalized with a *pop*. Apparently *no one* had ever bought a pigfoot. Why then were the jars stuck in convenience stores all across the state? Glibspet smelled a brother Unchained in the loop somewhere.

The clerk took the tongs and fished through the mass of floating pink tissue until he got a solid catch. He raised it, let it drip for a second, then plopped it into the cup. It made an ugly sloughing sound. Glibspet's mouth started to water.

"Okay now, mister, let's see some ID," the clerk said.

"Do I look like I'm under twenty-one?" Glibspet demanded.

"Rules is rules," the clerk said. "You want your beer, you show me your ID."

Glibspet had lots of ID. If pressed, he could prove that he was any of thirteen different people, all of them old enough to drink. He produced a driver's license from his pocket.

The clerk scrutinized it and him. "Yeah, I guess that's you," he said. "Here you go."

Glibspet paid and hurried out the door. He was on a mission. Craig had struck pay dirt after a day in the newspaper morgue. It wasn't hard to confirm that one Rheabeth Samuels was the owner and CEO of Celestial Technologies, and that her picture looked almost too good to be human. Glibspet gunned the Lincoln and peeled out of the parking lot. He put the cold beer between his legs, raised the cup with the pigfoot and drank down the liquid that had run off of it. Not bad. A little too fresh, perhaps.

A little work at the courthouse and tracking down her driver's license turned up a home address, which just happened to lie in the rough center of his cluster of green pins. Coincidence? He popped the top off the beer bottle with his teeth and took a long swig from it. Glibspet knew all about quantum uncertainty, but he didn't believe in coincidence. He looked at the address again. For some reason, it was a hard one to remember, but he should be almost there.

A police car passed, going the other way. The patrolman glanced at Glibspet suspiciously. Glibspet raised the hand with the bottle and waved at him. Looking surprised, the cop screeched to a halt, then fired up the lights and siren as he swung the patrol car around.

Glibspet grinned. This was always fun. He swung the Lincoln in front of a school bus and jammed on the brakes. The driver swung the wheel frantically to avoid rear-ending him, and the bus careened across the road, children screaming, horn honking. Blocked, the patrol car came to a stop again while Glibspet turned down a side street. He would be blocks away before it was all sorted out, and the cop would find out later that he'd never gotten a clear glance at the license plate. Glibspet hoped they went looking anyway. People who drove Lincoln Town Cars tended to be older, well-off men, crotchety and well-connected enough to make life hell for any officer who hassled them.

Now what was that address again?

He drove by it three times before he saw it; for some reason his mind always turned to some other problem while he was counting off the numbers. It wasn't a big house—looked like three bedrooms, nicely kept, no fence so probably no dog. Mmm. Dog. That had been a really juicy pup he'd rounded up the other night when he'd fed Craig some line and had gone back to his old digs for a few hours. Probably not a pure poodle. A cockapoo perhaps, with a little more meat on the bones than usual, and really succulent ears . . .

A horn honked impatiently behind him and brought Glibspet back to the present. He was stopped in the street about a block past his goal. He flipped the hidden toggle that dumped oil in the fuel line and hit the gas, moving on, leaving the car behind him in a cloud of noxious black smoke. This time, he didn't circle back around. The house was obviously protected, and not by Averial—he would have smelled any spent Hellawatts. Unless he greatly missed his guess, there were angels in that house, and that was out of his league. Now, if this Rheabeth Samuels really were Averial, and she had angels in her house, something completely unprecedented was going on. Something he would have to think about. Glibspet bit into the pigfoot and chewed slowly. In the meantime, he would have to try to catch up with her away from home.

# Chapter 63

COURT OKAYS SUCCUBI

Fayetteville — The Fayetteville Observer

Federal Circuit Court Judge Janice Hudson ruled Monday that Bragg Boulevard club Just South of Heaven is not in violation of federal equal employment opportunity laws. The topless entertainment club which employs only succubi, had been sued by local human dancers denied employment there.

In her ruling, Judge Hudson concluded that "since over the course of an evening a succubus may manifest as any conceivable racial or ethnic group, and since federal law recognizes no general racial group of 'human' or 'Unchained,' this court has no choice but to find for the defendant."

Speaking for the plaintiffs, Elizabeth "Bambi" Scott said, "This is a real setback for Fayetteville's dancers. All of the big tippers go to that place."

A spokesman for the Fayetteville police department confirmed that the force would continue to keep a close watch on the club to forestall any of the illicit activities commonly associated with succubi. "We'll shut them down in a heartbeat if they step over the line," said Lt. Frank Devon.

Just South of Heaven reacted by offering free

doughnuts to all law enforcement officers.
Ft. Bragg officials continue to hold the club
off-limits to all Army personnel.

Rhea's cellular phone beeped. She took it from her purse and flipped it open. "Samuels," she said.

"Got some good news, I think." It was Jan, barely audible over the drone of the Cessna's engines. "I've got someone on-line who comes on like he's swimming in money, and wants to drip some of it in our bucket. Want to talk with him?"

Jack looked at her quizzically from across the cabin. "Money," she mouthed at him, then cupped her hand around the microphone to shield it from the noise. "Definitely," she told Jan. "Right now, we'll take lunch money from kids if we can get it."

"Well, this guy's no kid, but that's all I can tell you. Here you go." There was a click as Jan switched the call over.

"Ms. Samuels?" The cultured voice on the other end had a faint trace of Cajun accent.

"Speaking," Rhea confirmed.

"Domino Glibbens at your service, Ms. Samuels. You'll not have heard of me, I'm sure."

"Well . . ."

"Oh don't flatter me, Ms. Samuels. I keep a low profile, and I've been out of the country for several years. The point is I own a small herd of oil wells down in the gulf and I consider myself relatively well off, at least compared to my poor friend Ross." He paused and Rhea took the opportunity to ease her chair back. "Now, I understand you're building a private spaceship."

"That's right," Rhea said. "All the details are in our prospectus." Jack came up behind her and started massaging her shoulders. She hadn't realized how tense they were.

"And you're desperately in need of capital," Glibbens continued.

"I wouldn't put it that way, Mr. Glibbens," Rhea said. "I would say that our development schedule is ambitious and that we always have room for additional investors." Jack stopped kneading, and she could almost feel his eyes roll.

"Well, however you want to put it, I'm very interested, Ms. Samuels. Been a space buff since I was knee-high. Can we meet face to face and talk turkey?"

"I'm afraid I'm not in the Triangle now, Mr. Glibbens. In fact, I'm about to touch down in Manteo on the Outer Banks to do a few days work here at our shipyard."

"Well now, that's nigh perfect. I'm up at Corolla myself, above the lighthouse, and I'm fed up with watching those damn wild horses chomping the plants at my beach house. It's what, three forty-five now. Shall I meet you there at eight for supper?"

"That sounds fine." Rhea said, "I'll have one of my engineering staff go with us to answer your technical questions." She paused. "You do understand, of course, Mr. Glibbens, that we'll have to verify your finances before we can do business."

"I understand completely," Glibbens said. "Wouldn't deal with anyone who didn't work that way. Eight o'clock then."

Rhea gave him directions and hung up. Jack looked at her.

"I don't know," she said. "If he's legit, he could save us a lot of grief, and take some of the pressure off. On the other hand, he could be trying to run a scam on us somehow. There's something in his voice I'm not sure I like."

Jack shrugged. "We can't get much further in the hole," he said, "and you know what they say about beggars and choices."

The pilot signaled them to buckle up, and the plane began its descent to the small airstrip below.

"So why did you include me in his dinner invite?" Jack asked. "You know I like talking business about as well as I like root canals, and you invented the key technologies. You don't need me there to explain them."

The plane bucked slightly as they descended into the clouds. Rhea pulled her seat belt tight. "You need to know how the other side works, Jack," she said. "And I want you there with me."

# Chapter 64

Jack worried as the plane touched down and taxied towards the main hangar. Rhea was in a somber mood, and he couldn't seem to shake her out of it. Dealing with the TRITEL thing was taking all her juggling skills. The last time he'd seen her really happy was when they came out of his office after that second bout of intense reconciliation, with her wearing his ring. Practically the whole staff was there in the corridor, applauding. Rhea had cried then, and so had he, a little bit. After that, she had buckled down to work twice as hard.

The little Cessna coasted to a stop, and Jack and Rhea climbed down the short ramp to the tarmac. Jack looked around, and spotted the Manteo foreman waving from the parking lot. He waved back to her, and he and Rhea walked over to her car.

Kate Tamaru was a small woman with long black hair who had come to Celestial from UC Berkeley where, Jack was convinced, things were much stranger than the most Unchained-infested parts of North Carolina. Surprisingly, she was not a vegetarian, nor did she wear Birkenstocks. She was a master of organization and headed up the small on-site Celestial operation that oversaw the numerous contractors working on the ship.

"Hello, Kate," he said. "How goes?"

"Hi, Jack! Hi, Rhea!" Kate said. "About as well as can be expected, I suppose." She popped the automatic locks. "Hop on in and I'll take you over. Oh, by the way, I heard the good news. Congratulations!"

Jack left Rhea the front seat and got in back. Kate pulled out smoothly and headed for the construction yard. "I don't know, Rhea," she said as they left the airstrip. "I'm pushing as hard as I can, but even with Jack's changes, I don't think I can meet your schedule unless I can lay on some more overtime."

Jack saw Rhea tense, an almost imperceptible straightening and tightening of her posture. He wished there were something he could do, but these days it all came down to money. "Do the best you can for now, Kate," Rhea said, "I'm working a few angles, but I can't give you any more dollars yet."

Kate down-shifted and pulled into the yard. "Okay, Rhea," she said, "I just wanted to make sure you knew where we stand. We're 'go' right now, but there's no astrogation or life support."

"Thanks, Kate," Rhea said quietly. "I appreciate everything you've done."

Kate parked the car in front of the Operations hangar. "Will you be able to join me for dinner?" she asked. "I know a place with great baby-back ribs."

"Sorry," Jack said. "We're committed to a promising investor this evening."

"Well, next time, then. And you still owe me a fishing trip, Halloran."

"I haven't forgotten." Jack grinned over at her as they all got out. "But I'll never bet against you again."

"Always a good idea." Kate sighed. "I've got a mountain of government forms to fill out in the ongoing battle to prove we're not a snake pit." She shook her head. "Rhea, I know you'll want to see things firsthand, so why don't you let Jack take you out there. When you're finished, everyone can come back to the office and we'll talk numbers."

Rhea nodded and Kate strode off, her small, quick steps giving the impression of boundless energy barely controlled. "We're lucky to have someone like her willing to work out here in the boonies," Rhea said.

"No argument," Jack agreed. He headed for the nearest access gate, Rhea close behind. "Though she probably thinks of it as closer to the best fishing spots." He keyed in the code, and they stepped through and onto the field.

He heard a small *oh!* from Rhea, and his breath caught in his chest.

*Morningstar Rising* could never be called beautiful in the conventional sense. She was no graceful fifties' SF rocket ship, nor yet an aerodynamic deep-space conglomeration of shapes. Instead, she looked like nothing more than a flat-bottomed submarine, but with more windows and no conning tower. Anyone not knowing what she was could justifiably call her ugly, but to Jack, as he watched the light of the late-afternoon sun coruscating off her sides, she was easily the most beautiful machine he'd ever seen.

"Jack, she's wonderful," Rhea breathed, "and she's out of the hangar."

Jack nodded and pointed at the bottom of the hull, which rested on a many-wheeled dolly. "She came out under her own power," he said quietly. "Lateral thrust only, and exactly to spec. I asked Kate not to tell you when I found out you were coming on site today."

"She moves," Rhea said excitedly. "She moves!" To Jack it seemed a shadow passed from her face. Nothing changed, but suddenly she was the old Rhea. She struck a pose, arms spread dramatically above her head and invoked her best *Young Frankenstein*: "Give my creature *LIFE!*"

They hugged frantically for a second. Then Jack felt he had to burst the bubble. "She rolls," he said. "That's all we can say for sure. And it's a long way to Alpha C by highway."

"I know that," Rhea said, "but who can stop us now?"

# Chapter 65

Glibspet charged out into the lobby, almost running into Mindenhall, who was coming in from a routine divorce surveillance. Something he had gotten considerably less picky about, Glibspet thought.

"Come on, Craig," he said grabbing Mindenhall's arm and spinning him back towards the door.

"Whoa! What's the deal, Dom? I've got some film to develop."

Glibspet hustled him outside, and locked the door behind them. "Never mind that," he said. "We're going driving—we've got to be on the Outer Banks by eight!"

"You're joking." Mindenhall said. When he looked over at Glibspet and realized the devil wasn't joking, he shook his head. "That's really pushing it. There're some little towns and two-lane roads between here and there, and it's an awfully long way." He looked at Glibspet's Lincoln and his Volvo. "Maybe we could take a plane?"

"Don't sweat it," Glibspet said. "A plane wouldn't get us there any faster. I'm driving." Of course, he could be there in an instant if he needed to be, but he'd decided early on that when they got to this point, he wanted to have Craig along.

"It's your license," Craig muttered as they burned rubber out of the parking lot.

They took I-40 east, and I-95 north, never averaging

less than eighty-five. Glibspet noted with amusement the point at which Craig stopped flinching, and simply closed his eyes and tightened his seat belt. They left the interstate at Rocky Mount and headed east again, hitting Roanoke Island and Manteo in record time. "You can open your eyes now, Craig," Glibspet told him as they came off the bridge from the mainland.

Mindenhall did so, cautiously, then pried his hand from the armrest. There were deep indentations in it. "Jesus, Dom," he said vehemently, "don't ever do that to me again! It can't be *that* important."

Glibspet flinched at the oath. It was heartfelt, which gave it some power. Apparently, he still had a lot of work to do on Craig. "Don't bet the store on that," he said mildly.

Glibspet followed Samuels's directions and they soon came to a collection of warehouses on the waterfront of Albemarle Sound.

"Nice view," Mindenhall observed, looking out over the water. "But do you want to fill me in now, Dom?" He touched Glibspet's hand. "We're supposed to be working together," he said and Glibspet knew that he meant on more than the case.

There was a tumbledown shack at the water's edge, set deep in an overgrown lot at the end of an almost completely overgrown driveway. Glibspet eased the Lincoln down the path until the scrub and trees blocked the view from the road. "There's going to be a certain party here at eight, Craig," he told Mindenhall, "and we wouldn't want her to get lonely."

"Who?" Mindenhall asked, looking left towards the almost obscured industrial area. "The Rheabeth person we located?"

"That's the one," Glibspet confirmed. "But she's not Rheabeth Samuels. Rheabeth Samuels was just a convenient birth certificate to start building on." He reached under the seat and pulled out a pair of binoculars.

"I tracked her down from your info. We've got undercover police on their way out here for our protection, and you wouldn't believe what all else. She wasn't involved in high-tech anything. That was all a front for a massive gun-running and dope operation. We're here to meet with her. We're going to be heroes, my love."

Mindenhall said, "I thought this was the sort of thing police did all by themselves, without help from people like us."

"I have friends on the force," Glibspet told him. That, at least, was true.

"But I still think we shouldn't be involved in trying to bust open a drug operation."

"Do you know how many people die in eighteen-wheeler accidents each year, Craig?" he asked.

Mindenhall shook his head. "No," he said. "A lot, I suppose."

Glibspet peered through the glasses. The warehouse area stuck out further into the sound than the shack. He could see fairly clearly a man and woman walk into the open hatch of what appeared to be a beached submarine. "No," he said, "I checked." (He hadn't, of course.) "It's not very many at all. Semi drivers are pros, and they watch out for cars better than cars watch out for each other. Don't you think it's a little peculiar that the victim of an accident like that would get her identity stolen? One very unlikely thing happening to someone is a coincidence. Two is a plan."

Mindenhall swallowed. "You're saying the original Rheabeth's death wasn't an accident," he stated.

Glibspet shrugged. "Occam's razor, Craig," he said. "This is one ruthless woman here." He paused. "Have you been keeping up target practice like I asked?"

"You know I hate guns, Dom," Craig said.

Glibspet wasn't about to let him off the hook. "That's not what I asked," he said pointedly.

"Yes. I have."

Nothing further was happening at the site. The woman he'd seen might have been Samuels or might not have been. He knew for sure that she'd be there at eight. He put down the glasses. "Good," he said, "I've got a little firepower in the trunk. I hope we don't need it."

"Firepower?" Craig said incredulously. "Dom, let's leave this to the cops."

"Samuels has agreed to meet with us. Just us. Nobody has been able to get past her goons, but I did. I used an old cover of mine that just paid off big-time. We break this case, it's worth millions to us." He looked at his watch and put the binoculars back in the case. "We have about half an hour before we're supposed to go in. Let's get ready."

Mindenhall glanced down at the floorboard, and suddenly froze. "My God, what *is* that?" He pointed down at a pink mass of sinew and gristle that lay next to his left foot.

Glibspet picked up the remains of the pigfoot and eyed the mess with studied disgust. "Well," he said. "That's the last time I get my car washed there!"

# Chapter 66

Miramuel and Remufel thought their hiding places inside the office with Rheabeth and Jack were perfect. But suddenly both of them were dragged up and out, through the ceilings, into the sky at a tearing pace and, with rapidly increasing acceleration, back up into Heaven.

"Wait!" Mir screamed. "Not yet! Let us go back for another hour, and then you can do what you want!"

Remufel fought and struggled against the unseen hands. "You can't pull us out of this now! They need us!"

And then the two of them were in front of Gabriel, and flanked on all sides by archangels with angry expressions on their faces.

"You already know what you've done wrong," Gabriel said. "How dare you ask to compound your iniquity?"

"But Averial's in trouble," Mir said. She clasped her hands in front of her and said, "Gabriel, you've got to let us help her. If we don't pull her out of this, she's going to end up back in Hell. And Lucifer will destroy her."

"You can only hope your fate when you arrive will not be worse."

Miramuel froze. "You're . . . sending us to Hell? What about the judgment of the All-Forgiving?"

"Do you beg forgiveness for interfering on Earth?"

"No."

"Do you admit you were wrong in associating with Averial?"

"No."

Miramuel then gave Gabriel and the angels who had snatched them to Heaven her reasons for interfering as she had. She didn't leave out anything: not her feeling that this was her single window of opportunity to rescue her friend, not her certainty that Averial could be prevented from worsening her position in God's eyes, not her love of her lost friend.

Gabriel listened without comment, then turned to Remufel. "What about you?"

"I have nothing else to add. What she said goes for me, too. We did what we thought was best."

Gabriel glanced to the other angels, then back to Miramuel and Remufel. "You'll have plenty of opportunity to think again once you're in Hell." He looked coldly from one to the other. "You knew the rules when you broke them. Your reasons don't matter. God's rules, after all, are rules . . . and I'm sure that the Glorious Almighty, when He returns, will agree."

And then Miramuel saw a flash of light, followed by unremitting, unbroken darkness, and she felt terrible pain . . . and unimaginable fear.

# Chapter 67

All the construction workers had left at five, and Kate had finally finished her paperwork at seven. So Jack and Rhea were alone in the small suite of offices, waiting for Mr. Glibbens and hoping he wouldn't mind a ride in the company van.

Jack sat on Kate's desk, drumming his heels against the side, and watched Rhea. Rhea watched the clock, shifted from position to position, stood and paced, sat and sighed.

"Nervous?"

She jumped and glanced over at him, then managed a small grin. "Yeah, I guess I am, a little," she said. "We could fly *Morningstar Rising* right now if we didn't need to navigate—or breathe—but this may be as close as we get, if someone I never heard of doesn't turn out to be a phony or a fruitcake, and if he likes us, and if he's impressed by what we've done, and if . . ." She waved a hand in the air, indicating a dozen or a hundred other things she'd left unnamed.

"It's that bad, then?"

"Probably worse," Rhea confirmed. "We can't fund another week's work here. I'll be lucky to dodge enough bills to get through two more days." She sighed. "I was hoping to have some brilliant insight here today that would wrap the whole thing up by then, but it just isn't there."

Jack stopped drumming. "Your take on that alternate cable run probably saved at least a day." He paused. "I should have seen that."

Rhea squeezed his hand. "You found a week's worth of shortcuts and streamlining yourself," she said, "It just wasn't possible to find enough."

"Well, then—" Jack sighed. "It's out of our hands." He stood up. "So put it out of your mind, too." He turned on Kate's radio. She had it tuned to a public station, and someone was playing an Artie Shaw record. The clarinet wailed over the solid brass; Jack turned and spun Rhea around in her chair. "Is this dance taken, miss?" he asked.

Rhea laughed. "I thought you said you didn't dance."

"No," he replied, "I just said I didn't know how." He pulled her into his arms and led her off into what he hoped was a foxtrot. At least that was as close as it came to anything he could manage. She tried to match his spirit, but she just wasn't in it.

Jack felt it. He turned off the music and looked into her eyes. "There's more, isn't there? Tell me."

"There's more. I never told you why I came here."

"You were sent during the . . . exchange program . . . I thought. Weren't you?"

"No." She gave him a quick, sly smile. "I managed to insert myself into God's initial transfer without actually being included in the count. For over two years, neither Heaven nor Hell knew I was here. Then, not too long ago, I realized Hell had started looking for me. I'd always planned against that eventuality, but I'd really hoped I'd have more time. The record-keeping demons have been known to misplace files for thousands of years. I was hoping . . ." She stopped and shook her head.

"Thousands of years would have been good," Jack said. "But as long as we know about the problem, we'll deal with it. I de-gremlined my printer. I got rid of those devils with holy water. There aren't many things that good engineering and applied intelligence can't fix. With both of us working together, we'll find a way to outsmart Hell."

He shivered at the hollow, hopeless looks she gave him. "I'd like to think you were right."

"Then think it. Rhea ... Celestial ... and all this," Jack waved towards *Morningstar Rising.* "That's hardly low profile. You could probably have hidden a lot longer if you hadn't done all this."

"I was homesick, Jack," she said. "I couldn't have Heaven ... I couldn't let go of everything that lay between me and God. But I could have the heavens. Later, I wanted you, all of you, to have it too." She looked out the window at the setting sun. "It's something Lucifer doesn't want you to have, Jack. He likes everybody cooped up here on Earth. There's always the chance you'll all do each other in." She paused and stared out the window, into the moonlit darkness. "I'm not so sure the Almighty wants you to have this either." He could see her frown in silhouette. "There's a grain of truth to the Prometheus legend; you could wreak a lot of havoc out there."

"But?"

"But the stars are your destiny. I've watched you for a long time. Not just you, Jack. Humanity. You're magnificent. Endlessly searching, courageous in the face of destruction, full of love and hope in spite of the certainty of death. In spite of your stupidities as a race, your brutality and backsliding and bullheadedness, you are, right now, more than I ever was as an angel in Heaven ... more than any angel could ever hope to be. And you're ready to be more—but it's going to take the rigors of space to push you to that next step."

Jack held her hands. "And you'll be right there beside us, Rhea."

She shook her head. "I have this horrible feeling that

I've run out of time. That all of a sudden, nothing is standing between me and Hell." She stared down at her hands clasped in his, and for a moment she was silent and still as death. Jack's heart felt like it was going to break. When she looked up at him again, her eyes held a resolution that, just for an instant, made him think she'd come up with an answer. But then she said, "I've worked with the lawyers to make sure there won't be any difficulty in transferring command. I signed the papers yesterday. The whole thing is set up so that you don't need anything from me to take over. At the moment that you call our lawyer and tell him that you request transfer of the company—no matter whether I'm sitting at the desk in my office or on vacation in the mountains or missing and presumed dead—Celestial becomes yours." She smiled a tiny smile. "With all the financial woes and disasters that will entail. I'm sorry. I wish the whole enterprise were in better financial shape."

Jack stared at her. She was telling him she'd just given him her company—that all he had to do to take it away from her was ask. She trusted him . . . in spite of her past, in spite of what she was. She trusted him with the project she'd gambled her eternity on.

She was still talking. He tried to focus on what she was saying. "If they get me, Jack, you have to carry on. You have the hunger. You and I share the same dream. I've given you everything I can—but it won't mean anything if you don't keep it going."

"Don't talk that way," he snapped.

She held his hands tightly. "Promise me, Jack. No matter what happens to me, promise me that you'll get humanity to the stars."

He swallowed. "I promise, Rhea."

The uneasy feeling was back suddenly, stronger. She glanced at her watch. "Time to go, Jack. It's seven fifty-eight."

She quickly straightened her clothes and patted her face dry. Then she kissed him with a passion deeper and more overwhelming than in any kiss they'd ever shared. He held her close, feeling for just an instant the panic she was trying to hide. They pulled apart; he wiped at the tear stains on his shirt, they smiled at each other.

"I love you," she said.

"I love you, too. And everything is going to be fine, Rhea."

She nodded brightly. "Yes. Of course it will."

She turned out the lights and stepped to the door in front of Jack. She looked out the window, and pointed to a Lincoln Town Car that was easing into the parking lot.

When she saw the driver, she froze. He heard her gasp. Then she gripped his arm and said, "They've found me, Jack. Glibbens is a devil."

# Chapter 68

The revelations of the past few minutes had Jack's head spinning. He felt like the kid in the *Far Side* panel who said, "Teacher, may I be excused? My brain is full." So he narrowed his focus, not letting himself think of the broader implications of what Rhea said. Instead, he let himself consider only the possibility—the necessity—of escape, and how it could be achieved. Escape as an engineering problem. "I've got the Super-Soaker in the car," he said.

"No good. That's a devil in the car, not a demon, and this time they'll know you have the holy water. Without the element of surprise, it won't do any good against something that powerful."

"Then let's run like hell." He grabbed the keys Kate had left for them and threw open the office door.

"Too late," said Rhea as the Lincoln pulled up right behind the Celestial van, blocking it. The driver jumped out and started for the door. Jack slammed it quickly. The devil was armed. A second later, a dark-haired man got out of the passenger side. He was armed too.

Jack picked up the phone and dialed 911. He left the phone off the hook—someone would get out to the site to investigate the call whether he told them what was going on or not. Whether the police would arrive in time, however, was another matter entirely, as was whether they would be able to do anything to help. "Back door," he said, and the two rushed from the office into the hangar area.

# Chapter 69

Rhea's brain kicked into high gear the instant she felt the devil in the parking lot. This time it wasn't a chance encounter—Hell's minions had her human ID, had tracked her down, knew who she was and what she was connected to. She wasn't going to walk away. She'd lost. But her next few moves would determine whether the humans lost the stars, or whether they won the infinity of space for themselves and their children.

"I can hold the devil, Jack," she shouted, "but I can't do anything about the other guy—he's human."

Their attackers came running into the hangar.

"Do it!" Jack said.

And now came the time for sacrifice. But which sacrifice would be the right one? She lit up like a beacon, shutting down the devil, wrapping him in coils of light. Jack shielded his eyes. He seemed stunned. Rhea broke the spell. "Run, Jack!" she screamed. "Everything higher than a gargoyle knows where I am now!"

Jack started to run—towards the ship. Yes. Towards the ship. The right direction.

"Eee-yaaaaaaagh!" the devil screamed. "She's—she's—killing me, Craig. And the other one is getting away! Shoot! Shoot!"

She began retreating quickly, with Jack ahead of her. She kept the devil pinned down by force of will and a serious expenditure of Hellawatts—he was tough, and he was fighting her with everything in him.

The other man was running forward, gun drawn. In the darkness, Rhea could see his pale face, the sweat beaded on his upper lip, his aura of essential goodness tainted by a Hellish touch. The devil had been working hard on him.

"I'm dying. I'm dying. And she's Hellspawn! All you can do is stop—stop the man who's getting away." The devil wailed like a dying banshee and his associate pointed the gun at Jack, and began to pull the trigger.

His finger was tightening. Rhea released the devil and flung herself towards the path of the bullet, pleading with the power greater than her that she would be in time to save his life.

The devil, already knowing what he intended to do, was a nanosecond faster. He blocked her, the gun went off, Jack screamed.

# Chapter 70

Jack felt like his right leg had been beaned by the world's fastest pitch. No, worse than that. Lots worse. He seemed to be falling in slow motion with a spray of blood suspended above him. That was impossible, wasn't it? All objects fell at the same rate.

He felt Rhea pick him up, and heard her voice shouting at the man who'd shot him— "He's Hellspawn, you fool!" She did something to the devil, and suddenly Jack could see the monster for what it really was, horns, tail and all.

"You got me," the devil said equably. "But you'll get yours."

The last thing Jack saw before the hatch closed was the man who'd shot him, standing ashen faced beneath the field lights, looking down at his gun. And he heard the stranger say, "Mother Mary, help of Christians, what have I done?"

# Chapter 71

The odd ship lifted hesitantly, then moved with greater speed and surety. Glibspet leaned back, watching it soar quietly into the darkness, a pale blue trail of fire burning at its back. He stretched gratefully. That was Averial, all right. He grinned and returned himself to his human form, and straightened his clothes. Company was coming.

His clients popped onto the field with a phalanx of devils and demons in tow.

"All right, Snippet, where is she?" Venifar snapped. His head had been removed and sewn on backwards, and he didn't look happy about life. Evidently he and the Maleficent One weren't seeing eye-to-eye on timetables. Pity. "We all felt her, and she hasn't ported."

Glibspet raised his hand. "Hold on, Ven," he said. "First things first. I found her, so the contract is now payable in full, yes?"

"Yes, yes. That is agreed," the fallen angel assented. "Now. Where. Is. She?"

"Ah," said Glibspet. "That's another matter. If you'll check, you'll see there wasn't anything in the contract about conveying the information to you. I just had to find her."

"Of course you have to tell us," Kellubrae said.

"Uh-uh," Glibspet said. "You were all so busy being outraged at my Linufel clause and bearing down on her

that you just didn't read as closely as you should have."
He grinned toothily. "You, of all people!"

"What do you want?" Linufel said tiredly.

"That's easy," Glibspet said. "The same again, but
double time with you, sweetcakes."

"We could crush you like a bug," she said dangerously,
and he felt the pressure build.

"Yes, you could," he said. "But the information you want
has a very short half-life. Less than a minute probably.
By the time you crack me, you've lost her, and you have
to go explain to the big L just how it happened—this time."
The pressure eased. "I just happen to have a contract
with me. I must warn you that you probably don't have
time to read it through." His smile stretched wide.

The fallen angels looked at each other. Glibspet brought
out the paper. "Need a pen?" he asked.

"There will be an accounting someday, little devil,"
Linufel hissed as she added her sigil to the other two.

"And maybe you'll be my love slave by then," he said,
and pinched her.

"Gobbet!" Kellubrae warned.

"Well, I suppose I must let you know, then, mustn't
I?" He sighed, drawing it out. Then he stared into the
evening sky and pointed. "See that moving dot over there?
She's inside it."

"Shit!" Venifar yelped.

The trio and their minions vanished.

Craig walked up to him. "Dom?" he said brokenly.
Glibspet laughed.

"Life's a bitch, isn't it, kid? If it's any consolation, you
were a pretty good lay, for a man."

"Freeze! Police!" A harsh voice shouted at them,
coming from the office area.

Startled, Mindenhall swung around, the gun still in
hand and clearly visible beneath the pale luminous field
lights.

The bullets that tore through him left him no time to explain.

Glibspet looked down at the dying man and chuckled. "But maybe in the end that doesn't count for much." He blew Mindenhall a little kiss—the last thing he saw before life left his body. "See you in Hell. Someday." He ported out.

# Chapter 72

The g-forces had leveled out, and *Morningstar Rising* lifted at a moderate speed. She handled like a dream. Rhea hoped the automatic controls were as good as the manual ones. Even keeping the launch as slow as she could, she didn't have much time, and Jack was bleeding heavily, bright blood pulsing out all over the cockpit with every beat of his heart. The little liquid arcs were getting shallower and shallower.

She closed her eyes and rested her hand on his leg. She could feel the damage—ripped arteries, pulverized muscle, severed nerved, shattered bone. The bullet had left a small hole on impact, but a massive one on exit; most of the front of his right thigh was simply gone. They'd be sensing for her; the Hellawatt expenditure she'd need to heal Jack would bring them to her like sharks to blood. But a lot faster.

"We made it, didn't we?" He shouldn't have been conscious, but he was. His voice was so soft she almost couldn't hear it over the low roar of the engine. "They can't track us here. We'll go underground somehow, Rhea—get new identities and ride this thing out." He shifted slightly and grimaced with pain. "We'll leave the ship to Jan and them—someone will *have* to fund it now that they can see it works . . . everything's going to be fine. We're going to be fine. Damn, that leg hurts!"

She pulled the oxygen mask over his face; he didn't need it yet, but he would soon. And she wanted to make sure he was taken care of. Safe. Then she pulled in the Hellawatts and ran them through her fingertips into his flesh, focusing on healing him. She reattached the arteries first, and replaced his blood with some of her own. Then she reconnected the nerves. She was replacing the muscle tissue and starting to piece the bone back together when suddenly the cabin was full of devils and fallen angels.

"Hello, Averial," Kellubrae said. She felt their shields bear down on her, stifling any power she could draw. She was glad she'd stopped the bleeding and healed the nerves first. The bones and flesh would take care of themselves if they had to.

Kellubrae looked around. "Pretty little toy you've made. Rather a dangerous one for the humans to have, though, don't you think? You'll have to point it at the ground before we leave."

"Can't," Rhea said. "Mortal on board."

Kellubrae looked at Jack as if seeing him for the first time. "An unfortunate complication. We can't hurt him . . . we can't be the cause of his coming to harm . . ." The dark angel smiled. " . . . But we can certainly port him back to safety. Kind of us, yes?"

Venifar said, "You've led us a long chase, bitch, but you had to know you couldn't get away. Lucifer himself wants to talk to you. It's time to come home now."

She couldn't do anything with Hellawatts, but she could still move normally. She threw herself over the seat into the cockpit and yanked on the vertical thrust.

"Rhea, no!" Jack yelled.

"What? No!" she heard Kellubrae scream, and then pain tore her atom from atom.

As plans went, she wished she'd been able to think of one that didn't entail so much pain. *Morningstar Rising* tore beyond the upper limit of North Carolina airspace, and the agony rolled over her like sheets of boiling water. The ship disappeared around her—ripped itself through her, in truth, as her body ripped itself into molecules. Aware, frightened, hurting molecules.

Her body re-formed with an audible snap. And then she was suspended in space. Not the normal space above Earth, but the space-time nexus that straddled the infinity between the separated kingdoms of Heaven and Hell. Far below, she could see the Pit, burning like a cyclopean laser-eye in the center of Hell's scarred face, and even from her point thousands of miles above the surface, she could feel the heat of the flames. Kellubrae and Venifar fell past her, screaming. She started falling then, too, and picked up speed, and the heat of the Pit increased. And increased. And increased. First her skin began to blister. Then to peel away in strips. The pain was unbelievable, worse than anything she had ever experienced, worse than the worst that Hell had done to her before. Then her body convulsed and burst into flames, and flaked away into ash, leaving her soul bared to an even more exquisite unraveling.

The pain contracted on the smaller and smaller kernel that was her, burning away thoughts of Celestial, poignant memories of Jack, the joy of once again being with Remmy and Mir. Finally the only thought left to her outside of the pain, the last kernel of her that remained her own, was a single triumphant burst:

*I GAVE THEM THE STARS!*

# Chapter 73

The ship was suddenly empty.

Maybe this is one time being in shock helps, Jack thought numbly. He could always cry later, if he lived.

He dragged himself over to the console and up into the chair. His leg flopped pathetically—no bleeding, but the flesh looked like raw hamburger and the bone hadn't even begun to set when they came for her. He blacked out once from the pain and found himself looking up at the ceiling. He nearly lost the oxygen mask that time.

There was water below—he was out somewhere past the banks. He took a guess at west from the fading sunset and hit the laterals. Bingo. Land. He headed for the first flat spot he saw, behind the dunes, over the road. Managed to slow descent—one of many things *Morningstar Rising* could do that NASA's crippled birds couldn't. Take off from anywhere. Land anywhere . . . anywhere . . . and everyone said it couldn't be done. Deep-space vehicle from Earth launch . . . well . . . screw them all—she flew like an angel. Screw the money people, NASA, the government with its petty, red-tape-wielding bureaucrats, the doubters, the hecklers. To Hell with all of them. Screw them . . .

He blacked out again as he touched down.

He came to when the hatch opened. A middle-aged

man in uniform burst in, stared at the blood everywhere, shouted, "Corpsman! Stretcher, stat!"

Everything went black again

Someone stood over the bed, looking down at him.

Jack focused with difficulty, frowned. "I know you," he said at last, though he didn't know who the man was.

"Al Roberts, from TRITEL," the man said. "Celestial's . . . well, financial angel, I guess you could call me."

"Probably not," Jack said. "I'm a bit pickier about that term than I used to be. And TRITEL pulled out on us; if I called you anything, it would be our financial devil."

"TRITEL didn't pull out. First I got called back on active duty for some mess that didn't even exist—situation totally FUBAR. I ended up spending time in Antarctica while an endless succession of bureaucrats told me they knew I wasn't supposed to be there but until they received forms that verified that fact, Antarctica was where I would have to stay. Meanwhile, Williams had a massive heart attack and keeled over dead. And to complete the disaster, every scrap of paper I had documenting the channeling of government funds through TRITEL into Celestial vanished while I was trying to straighten out the military mess. Williams could have kept your funds flowing— he knew the secret. He wasn't supposed to die on me."

"Government funds. For our spaceship? That would imply intelligent life in Washington." Jack was incredulous.

"Occasionally," Roberts said. "Just occasionally." The corpsmen got Jack on the stretcher and out the door. He saw a familiar monument, brightly lit in the deepening night. "Pournelle was lobbying pretty hard there at the end, just before the funding went through."

Jack nodded. In a funny way, it made sense. "How did she come down?"

"Perfectly. Like a sweet dream. Ended up in Kittyhawk." Roberts grinned. "You put her down just about where

Wilbur did." Roberts paused. "I think he'd like that." He sighed. "Anyway, the Antarctic mess suddenly resolved itself, and I shot back to North Carolina immediately. Just missed you at Celestial, headed for Manteo on the advice of Jan . . . whatever her last name is . . . and crested the dunes in time to see the ship fading into the darkness. I thought she would have been on the ship with you, considering the . . . circumstances. Where is she?"

"Gone," Jack said dully. "She was . . . ah . . . one of the Hellraised. Hiding from them, helping us to get into space. They found her, and they took her back."

Roberts paled. "No. Christ, I'm sorry. I'm *so* sorry." He stared out the window, and his voice dropped to a whisper. "She was a remarkable woman."

"You don't know the half of it," Jack said as the darkness claimed him again.

# Chapter 74

Hospitals had all too much practice with bullet wounds. Jack was out in three days. He fumbled with the crutches as the cab pulled up to his house, paid the driver and made his way towards the front door.

Carol stuck her head over the eaves as he slowly levered himself up the front steps. "You back!" she said.

Jack waved at her weakly. She was rail thin again.

"We'll talk later," he said. "You can stay, but I'm going to show you where the IRS building is. When you get hungry, you go there. Now move away from the edge, okay?"

"Okay." The gargoyle head bobbed up and down as if she were one of those stupid fuzzy dog statues people used to stick on the back shelf of their cars. "Glad you back."

He turned the key in the lock, and mercifully, it opened without his having to do anything strenuous to it. The short walk had left him sweating, and he couldn't believe the pain in his leg.

All the pain got worse a second later. A pair of her panties were still draped across the stereo. A faint, lingering hint of roses clung to the air in the hallway. And if he closed his eyes, he could still hear her voice, could still expect to see her coming around the corner, down the hall, smiling, shedding clothes . . . wearing his ring.

Gone. All gone.

# Chapter 75

"Deee-lightful, my little chickadee. Grovel a bit more, and kiss my feet . . . marvelous. Now bark like a dog . . . good girl. You're learning." Glibspet smiled gleefully. "Now tell me how much you love Master. Come on, sweetcheeks. Let's hear it . . . ah, perfect!"

Next, Glibspet leaned back and enjoyed watching her clean the floor of his office with her tongue. It was ironic really. Linufel had the Pit coming, and she knew it, but she'd signed the contract, and there was no way out of it. So first she had her three months of serving him. No matter how bad he made it, and he intended to make it pretty bad, that would be a vacation compared with what happened when she ended up back in Hell. He would have thought she'd have been more grateful . . .

He had enough money in his bank account to give Bill Gates wallet envy. He was only taking cases for fun at the agency, and he was *having* fun. He'd gotten a promotion to Devil First Class, Grade-B for his work in tracking down Averial . . . he'd gotten extra points for thoroughly screwing over three Fallen and for actually finishing the job off with a nice death and the horrendous guilt of the police officer who had caused it.

The only damper on his total satisfaction was Mindenhall. Craig hadn't ended up in Hell after all—that damned "love" rule. He would have been promoted to Grade A if the

little bastard hadn't been in love with him when he died—
God refused to allow anyone who truly loved to burn in
Hell.

But there was always next time.

Linufel finished cleaning the floor. Glibspet decided
he could think of a dozen other interesting things he
could have her do with her tongue. His smile grew
broader.

"Come to Master," he said.

He didn't like the way she smiled at him as she crawled
over.

# Chapter 76

Gabriel got the feeling he was being watched. Actually, he'd had that feeling for about a week, ever since he'd sent Miramuel and Remufel down to Hell for their transgressions. There had been a couple of times when he'd almost been on the verge of reconsidering his decision, but he'd always come to his senses in time. If he went soft on them, all of Heaven would go to Hell . . . in a manner of speaking.

He went over the day's prayer requests, shaking his head in annoyance at some of the stupid things people actually asked for. As if God had time for ponies and puppies and winning numbers on lottery tickets. The more he dealt with humans and their idiocy, the more he couldn't see why God bothered with any of them.

He read the last of the prayer requests he'd taken responsibility for, and with a sigh, dumped the whole lot into the disposal chute. Not a worthwhile request in the bunch.

Behind him, he heard a throat clearing.

He turned to discover God watching him. God . . . back from vacation at last, and in considerably different shape than the last time he'd seen Him . . . Her . . .

Tanned, pneumatic, wearing an incredibly small bikini and big, bleach-blond hair, carrying a surfboard of all things, God leaned against one of Heaven's pillars.

Gabriel felt a twinge of guilt. None of those prayer requests had been major . . . but in all honesty, he'd never seen God dump one down the chute, and God didn't have a bunch of saints picking up 99/100ths of the incoming load.

None of them had been major . . .

"We need to talk," God said, and suddenly He was back in his Christian form again. White robes, sandals, long beard, glowing visage.

Not a good sign. Gabriel nodded. Said nothing.

"You've had a week to reconsider your actions, and you never did."

The prayer requests weren't the big issue, evidently.

"Punishment for physical interference into the mortal realm and for fraternization with the enemy, Almighty. I sent them to be with Lucifer."

"They were trying to rescue their beloved friend."

"I didn't think that mattered, All-Glorious Magnificence. They . . . broke the rules."

"Not *my* rules." God wasn't smiling. Not even a hint of a smile. Gabriel began to feel distinctly queasy. "In all the time since the Rift, how many souls have you seen me send to Hell?"

Gabriel considered. There were a lot of souls down there. A whole lot. But when he thought about it, he couldn't think of a single instance in which God had sent *anyone* to Hell. Well, they had to get there somehow. The fact that he wasn't doing his own dirty work seemed pretty immaterial. Still . . . "None, Almighty."

"But . . . ?"

"But new souls go there all the time."

"Indeed they do. Not by my choice. I would choose to have all my children with me. Some souls choose Hell because they hunger for evil, while others choose it because they feel they cannot be good, and they insist in believing that because I am God, I must require absolute goodness."

"We haven't exactly discussed this before, Your Magnificence. Don't you?"

"Why would I create fallible creatures, then demand perfection of them? I'm no sadist. I ask of them only that they learn while they're alive, and that they love, and that they try to leave life a little better than they found it. And even if they fail at that, I am always willing to forgive. I'll give them other chances . . . as many as they need. Hell was Lucifer's choice, and Lucifer's doing. He wanted his own kingdom . . . and he's made a mess of it."

Gabriel nodded. Evidently sending Miramuel and Remufel to Hell wasn't going to be quite the hit he'd anticipated. "Then why haven't you shut Hell down?"

"Even Lucifer has free will." God glowered. "As do you. I was hoping that as you considered the fate of your colleagues, your heart would soften, and you would restore them to Heaven. I gave you as much time as I could, but in good conscience, I can't let them suffer any longer in the hopes that you will learn something."

A blinding flash of light and a clap of thunder rocked Heaven. When Gabriel could see again, he found Miramuel and Remufel huddled between him and God, still weeping and screaming. His gut knotted tighter.

"It's over," God said, and his voice was as gentle as a lover's. "You're safe. And you alone of all the angels have taken the opportunity I gave you."

It took them a bit, but they quit shuddering eventually. Wiped their eyes. Grabbed each other and shouted for joy. Gabriel felt the weight of his guilt beginning to crush him. They weren't asking about the test, though, so he did.

"I gave all of you an opportunity to stretch. Left you in charge, no rules or regulations, told you to keep the place going. Out of all of you, only they took the initiative to go down to try to rescue one of our lost angels."

Remufel and Miramuel looked up, and Remufel said, "You knew about that?"

"From the moment you acted. Even when I'm on vacation, I'm still omnipotent. You shouldn't have intervened directly in the lives of mortals, but you managed to get some good results, and you didn't give your presence away to anyone except for one particularly pernicious devil. And everything you did, you did for love."

God glanced at Gabriel for a moment, and the archangel shrank inside. "Reasons *do* matter," he said softly. "And rules are never rules. There are always exceptions, if you love."

He turned back to Mir and Remmy. "You've moved beyond anything you can accomplish as an angelic soul. You've discovered a love that stands up to fear, that risks both rejection and the possibility of annihilation. That encompasses sacrifice," he said.

He touched Miramuel first, then Remufel. "Go, now . . . back to Earth. You'll each find an infant waiting to be born, and when the time is right, you'll find each other again. You're ready to be human."

Miramuel stood, tears running down her cheeks. "I can't go," she said.

God smiled slightly, glancing over her shoulder to Gabriel. "Why not?"

"Averial is still in Hell. I can't go if she's there."

"You see, Gabriel?" God said. "Transcendent love, which embraces sacrifice." He looked back to Mir. "Averial is on her way here now. She won't see you on Earth in this lifetime . . . she'll be waiting here for the arrival of a future soulmate of hers. Jack will be getting here in about fifty years. But you'll see each other again."

He kissed each of them. "You did well, my children,"

he said. "Now go on. And remember that I love you."

When they were gone, Gabriel said, "I made mistakes, Almighty. What will happen to me now?"

God looked at him, surprised. "You'll stay the same as you were," he said, his voice full of sadness. "You'll stay the same as you are, until you learn to be more."

# Chapter 77

"Morning, Jack," Jan said as he hobbled in to the suite. Three weeks had gotten him used to the cast and crutches, but moving any distance was still a chore.

"Morning, Jan. Anything important shaking today?"

"We've got some prospects for that pilot's position lined up," she said. "And there are the usual bullshit forms in your IN box."

"Oh, the thrill of executive power," Jack said sourly.

"You're doing better than most," Jan told him.

"Yeah, right." He hopped into the private office (he still thought of it as Rhea's office), struggled over to the desk, and sat down. Rhea and the lawyers had done a perfect job on the paperwork. Jack Halloran now controlled one hundred percent of Celestial Technologies, and was responsible for keeping food on everyone's table. He was learning to play the suit game well enough to get by, and he would have to be a moron to run the company down now. Besides, bitterness and hurt and emptiness aside, he knew that what he was doing mattered.

He keyed up the Beach Boys on the stereo, and the plaintive harmonies of "In My Room" filled the air. He reached for the stack of résumés Jan had left on his desk. Celestial definitely needed pilots. He didn't ever want to do *that* again.

He was deep into a résumé remarkable only for its tedium when a faint musical *tap* sounded from one of his desk drawers. He looked up from the paper and frowned. The sound had come from the third drawer down; he didn't have anything in that one yet. Certainly nothing that went *ting*. He reached down and slid the drawer open, wondering if the cockroaches had gotten musical.

His ring was inside—Rhea's ring. It sat on a small, exquisitely folded note that smelled of roses, which sat on top of what looked like another résumé. He lifted the note first and opened it.

"I'll be waiting," it said, "and in the meantime—"

It seemed to end there. No. He could make out the shadows of writing on the other side. He turned the paper over.

"Light is not made less for shining through two windows.

Love again, my love."

He looked at it in bemusement. He picked up the résumé that had lain beneath the note. He studied it, first in disbelief, then in growing delight. It read "Captain Natsu Forrester, USAF, Ret."

Jan's voice over the intercom snapped him out of his reverie. "Jack," she said, "the first interview is here. A . . . Captain Forrester?" From the puzzlement in her voice, he could tell she didn't remember setting up the interview . . . but he was willing to bet the name was down in her appointment book.

"Send Captain Forrester in," he said. "I've been expecting her."

Then he looked up. "Not evil anymore, are you, my love?" He began to chuckle. "But you'll *always* be wicked."

# *Catch a New Rising Star of Fantasy:*
# ☆ HOLLY LISLE ☆

*"One of the hottest writers I've come across in a long time. Her entrancing characters and action-filled story will hold you spell-bound." —Mercedes Lackey*

## ARHEL NOVELS

*Fire in the Mist*                72132-1 ★ $5.99 _____
A fiery young woman struggles to master her magic. Compton Crook Award winner.

*Bones of the Past*                72160-7 ★ $5.99 _____
An expedition of mages searching for a lost city of the First Folk unleashes a deadly menace from the ancient past.

*Mind of the Magic*                87654-6 ★ $5.99 _____
Faia Rissedotte of *Fire in the Mist* returns.

## OTHER NOVELS

*Minerva Wakes*                72202-6 ★ $4.99 _____
Minerva's wedding ring is actually a magical talisman of ultimate power from another universe, and though everybody wants it, nobody else can use it—as long as she's alive....

*When the Bough Breaks*                72154-2 ★ $5.99 _____
(with Mercedes Lackey) A SERRAted Edge urban fantasy. "What would happen if Mary Higgins Clark and Stephen R. Donaldson decided to collaborate? ...a novel very much like *When the Bough Breaks*."                —*VOYA*

*The Rose Sea* (with S.M. Stirling) 87620-1 ★ $5.99 _____
Bound together by the fortunes of war, a soldier and a rancher's daughter must battle an insane demon-god, with the future of their world at stake.

- - - - - - - - - - - - - - - - - - - - - - - - - - - - - -

If not available through your local bookstore, send this coupon and a check or money order for the cover price(s) to Baen Books, Dept. BA, P.O. Box 1403, Riverdale, NY 10471. Delivery can take up to ten weeks.

NAME: _____

ADDRESS: _____

_____

I have enclosed a check or money order in the amount of $_____

*Paksenarrion, a simple sheepfarmer's daughter, yearns for a life of adventure and glory, such as the heroes in songs and story. At age seventeen she runs away from home to join a mercenary company, and begins her epic life . . .*

# ELIZABETH MOON

THE DEED OF PAKSENARRION

"This is the first work of high heroic fantasy I've seen, that has taken the work of Tolkien, assimilated it totally and deeply and absolutely, and produced something altogether new and yet incontestably based on the master. . . . This is the real thing. Worldbuilding in the grand tradition, background thought out to the last detail, by someone who knows absolutely whereof she speaks. . . . Her military knowledge is impressive, her picture of life in a mercenary company most convincing."—**Judith Tarr**

*About the author: Elizabeth Moon joined the U.S. Marine Corps in 1968 and completed both Officers Candidate School and Basic School, reaching the rank of 1st Lieutenant during active duty. Her background in military training and discipline imbue* The Deed of Paksenarrion *with a gritty realism that is all too rare in most current fantasy.*

"I thoroughly enjoyed *Deed of Paksenarrion*. A most engrossing highly readable work."
—**Anne McCaffrey**

"For once the promises are borne out. *Sheep-farmer's Daughter* is an advance in realism. . . . I can only say that I eagerly await whatever Elizabeth Moon chooses to write next."
—Taras Wolansky, *Lan's Lantern*

\*　　　　\*　　　　\*　　　　\*

**Volume One: Sheepfarmer's Daughter**—Paks is trained as a mercenary, blooded, and introduced to the life of a soldier . . . and to the followers of Gird, the soldier's god.

**Volume Two: Divided Allegiance**—Paks leaves the Duke's company to follow the path of Gird alone—and on her lonely quests encounters the other sentient races of her world.

**Volume Three: Oath of Gold**—Paks the warrior must learn to live with Paks the human. She undertakes a holy quest for a lost elven prince that brings the gods' wrath down on her and tests her very limits.

\*　　　　\*　　　　\*　　　　\*

These books are available at your local bookstore, or you can fill out the coupon and return it to Baen Books, at the address below.

# MERCEDES LACKEY

## The Hottest Fantasy Writer Today!

### URBAN FANTASY

**Knight of Ghosts and Shadows** with Ellen Guon
Elves in L.A.? It would explain a lot, wouldn't it? Eric Banyon really needed a good cause to get his life in gear—now he's got one. With an elven prince he must raise an army to fight against the evil elf lord who seeks to conquer all of California.

**Summoned to Tourney** with Ellen Guon
Elves in San Francisco? Where else would an elf go when L.A. got too hot? All is well there with our elf-lord, his human companion and the mage who brought them all together—until it turns out that San Francisco is doomed to fall off the face of the continent.

**Born to Run** with Larry Dixon
There are elves out there. And more are coming. But even elves need money to survive in the "real" world. The good elves in South Carolina, intrigued by the thrills of stock car racing, are manufacturing new, light-weight engines (with, incidentally, very little "cold" iron); the bad elves run a kiddie-porn and snuff-film ring, with occasional forays into drugs. *Children in Peril—Elves to the Rescue.* (Book I of the SERRAted Edge series.)

**Wheels of Fire** with Mark Shepherd
Book II of the SERRAted Edge series.

**When the Bough Breaks** with Holly Lisle
Book III of the SERRAted Edge series.

# HIGH FANTASY

## Bardic Voices: The Lark & The Wren

Rune could be one of the greatest bards of her world, but the daughter of a tavern wench can't get much in the way of formal training. So one night she goes up to play for the Ghost of Skull Hill. She'll either fiddle till dawn to prove her skill as a bard—or die trying....

## The Robin and the Kestrel: Bardic Voices II

After the affairs recounted in *The Lark and The Wren*, Robin, a gypsy lass and bard, and Kestrel, semi-fugitive heir to a throne he does not want, have married their fortunes together and travel the open road, seeking their happiness where they may find it. This is their story. It is also the story of the Ghost of Skull Hill. Together, the Robin, the Kestrel, and the Ghost will foil a plot to drive all music forever from the land....

## Bardic Choices: A Cast of Corbies with Josepha Sherman

## If I Pay Thee Not in Gold with Piers Anthony

A new hardcover quest fantasy, co-written by the creator of the "Xanth" series. A marvelous adult fantasy that examines the war between the sexes and the ethics of desire! Watch out for bad puns!

# BARD'S TALE

Based on the bestselling computer game, *The Bard's Tale.*℠

## Castle of Deception with Josepha Sherman

## Fortress of Frost and Fire with Ru Emerson

## Prison of Souls with Mark Shepherd

Also by Mercedes Lackey:

## Reap the Whirlwind with C.J. Cherryh

Part of the Sword of Knowledge series.

## The Ship Who Searched with Anne McCaffrey

The Ship Who Sang is not alone!

**Wing Commander: Freedom Flight** with Ellen Guon
Based on the bestselling computer game, *Wing Commander:*®

Join the Mercedes Lackey national fan club! For information send an SASE (business-size) to Queen's Own, P.O. Box 43143, Upper Montclair, NJ 07043.